D.R.E.X.
BLACKOUT

NATASHA BENNETT

D.R.E.X. BLACKOUT
2nd Edition - May 2017
1st Edition Trade Paperback, october 2016

All Rights Reserved

Dark Recesses Press
6273 132A Street, Surrey, B.C. V3X 3T2
Canada

Copyright © 2016 by Natasha Bennett

Editor: Tracy DeVore
Inset Layout and Design: Bailey Hunter
Cover Design: Bob Freeman

Library & Archives Canada ISBN
978-1-9888370-0-0

TABLE OF CONTENTS

PROLOGUE

Devon, Arizona
1999

Jake Burns squirmed uncomfortably in the leather seat. He resisted the urge to yawn as he studied a long, empty road. The heater was turned up way too high, and, as usual, nothing was happening in Devon.

"Exciting night, huh?" Sarah asked from the passenger seat. They were parked just outside of town, trying to catch speeders on the highway. Neither of them had spotted a car for hours.

"Do you think Peirre and his gang will start something?"

"It's pretty sad that a sixteen year-old gang would be the highlight of our night." Sarah chuckled.

"We should get a transfer. Somewhere that has more than thirty people." Jake sipped from his coffee, fighting another wave of fatigue. His stomach rumbled, and he glanced at his belly in misery. Maybe he should live with his brother again. He didn't use to be overweight. City life would cure that.

"*Dispatch to vehicle 841. Are you there?*" the operator asked over the radio.

Jake picked it up. Finally, some action. "841. Go."

"*We have a—*" The voice cut away to static.

"Dispatch? Are you there?"

"Jake." Sarah peered through the window. "What's that?"

Jake followed her gaze, and his breath caught in his throat. As they watched, every single streetlight on the highway died, casting them in darkness.

"Must be…some kind of electric…" Jake fumbled for the headlights and clicked them on. Nothing happened. "What the hell? Stay here."

"Wait a minute—" Sarah protested as he stepped outside.

Jake ignored her as he walked to the front of the car. To his astonishment, the beams were turned on, but some kind of black fog engulfed the lights. He tried his flashlight with similar results. Usually with fog, the light reflected back. Not in this case. He unzipped his jacket and took it off. The air felt warm, much warmer than the car.

"This isn't right," Sarah said very quietly as she poked her head out the window.

He couldn't help but agree. "Let's head back to the station."

Jake drove back into town at a painfully slow speed—only about twenty miles per hour. He peered out the windshield, without any success. They were driving blind. A couple of times they drifted into a pothole, and Sarah swore.

"Sorry. I think we're almost there," Jake said. "On the plus side, if we hit a building, I'll know when to stop."

"Maybe we should get out and walk," Sarah suggested. She twisted a curl of her red hair nervously. "They didn't forecast fog today. Even if they did, this isn't normal—"

Suddenly they heard a *thack* on the side of the car, followed by the outline of a person. A second later, it disappeared.

"Jesus!" Jake snapped, slamming on the brakes. Blood sprayed against his window as he saw a woman's face squished against the glass. He struggled to open the door and grabbed her before she could flee. "Theresa, it's me!" he shouted, recognizing the cashier who ran the liquor store.

"Help me!" she screamed. Blood trailed from her nose. "I can't see!"

"It's okay." Jake gripped her shoulders. "You're not blind. The whole city is like this. See?" He turned on the flashlight, so at least she could see the light bulb.

Theresa trembled, but nodded.

Jake turned around. He could hear more people running, but the black fog was just as thick in the town itself, and he could barely see anything beyond what was right in front of him. "Shit, where are we? Where's the station?"

Suddenly he heard an ear-piercing shriek, followed by glass breaking. Then, the ground trembled. Theresa screamed as Jake blindly dragged her toward a wall. He clamped a hand over Theresa's mouth. "Shh. Quiet." To his left Sarah nervously clasped his hand. He couldn't understand what was happening, but it terrified him.

For a moment, they heard a noise similar to flapping, and then stomping. Theresa trembled in his grip. Gradually, the stomping faded to nothing. Jake waited, but heard nothing else. He released his hand. "I think they're gone."

"You're supposed to be a cop," Theresa whispered, her voice pleading. "Do something."

"What the hell was that noise?" Sarah demanded.

Gunfire rang out, and all three of them jumped. Seconds later, it stopped.

"Maybe that was our guys," Sarah said. "We need to help them."

Jake studied the wall, which had a yellow poster of a lost cat. The cat in question had been found five months ago, and no one had bothered to remove the sign. Jake was grateful, however, because it also indicated where he was. With this and other landmarks, he could find the way back to the police station pretty easily. "Let's get out of here. Sarah, do you want to—"

Another gunshot rang out, and Sarah slid back to the ground, a bullet hole in her forehead. More bullets fired near them. Theresa shrieked and ran away. Jake ran in the opposite direction. He didn't stop running for five minutes—long enough to be completely lost again. Finally he stopped, gasping for breath. He could still hear gunfire, but it seemed to be farther away. "Oh God." That all happened too fast...*Sarah*...

He turned to the left, and stopped. He could hear someone shouting. People? He ran forward, almost tripping over a trashcan in the process. He stumbled toward the noise, using a wall to navigate. A minute later, he heard other voices. "Thank God."

The relief didn't last long. He approached several spotlights set up in a high school basketball court, which somehow managed to penetrate the darkness. Perhaps the fog was lifting? Jake didn't know, and couldn't focus beyond the horror of what he was seeing. Several military police surrounded a young boy, roughly ten years of age. Jake had seen the boy before at school, but didn't really know who he was. The boy was screaming in a language he couldn't understand, with a gun pointed at his own head. The military didn't make a move to help him—in fact, one was recording on a cell phone

"Mountains!" the boy hollered in English. "I'm sorry!" He pulled the trigger and slumped over, dead.

Jake backed away, and hid against the side of the school's building. "No..." he whispered. He peered back around, just in time to see the military personnel surround the kid. "Mountains. What did that mean?"

"I must be out of my goddam mind," Jake muttered to himself as he reached the outskirts of town an hour later. Thankfully, it had grown quiet, besides an explosion he heard five minutes ago.

That was the good news. Unfortunately, even though the fog had lifted, it was still pitch-black and he had lost his flashlight somewhere along the way. There was only one path he knew of which led up to the mountain, one that teenagers would usually go up to drink. He would find it eventually. Blindly he crawled his way forward.

"Who's there?" a voice called out.

Jake relaxed. He knew that voice. "Ian, is that you?"

"Jake?" the voice was closer. Finally, Jake recognized his flannel jacket and jeans. Ian had his own business selling barbeques and patio equipment. The redneck was also very tall and muscular, but never tangled much with the law in the past. "What are you doing here?"

"Checking out the cause of…whatever this is. What about you?"

"I just ran." Jake felt a light, reassuring touching on his shoulder. "Can't see a thing. What are the police doing? Where's your backup?"

"My backup is dead," Jake said flatly. "You should get out of here too. It isn't safe."

"And go where? The nearest town is more than a day's walk from here. Besides, have you been to Devon? The military is shooting it up! Jesus. It's too risky to go back for a car." Ian released a sob, then controlled himself. "Are you sure this is happening because of the caves?"

"Yeah, I'm pretty sure," Jake replied.

"Then I'm coming with you," Ian said. His voice indicated he would brook no argument. "I have a flashlight, and a shotgun. Do you?"

Jake didn't argue. Secretly, he welcomed the extra company. "Okay. But stay close."

"You don't need to tell me twice," Ian muttered.

The two of them eventually located a narrow path leading up to the caves. At one point, they heard someone walking, and both of them braced against the rock face. Jake released a held breath, and was astonished to see it glow red in the flashlight.

"What the fuck is going on here?" Ian whispered, scared out of his wits as he stared at his own strange breath. "Jake, what's happening to us?" The ground trembled as something walked past them. Seconds later, it disappeared.

Jake waited, but couldn't hear anything else. "Don't worry about it. Let's go."

"I see a light up there," Ian said as they climbed the next hill. Jake followed his gaze. It was true, he could see a pulsing blue light from the top. The entrance to the cave.

"We should get out of here, man. Take our chances in the desert," Ian said. "Neither of us understands what's going on here."

"True," Jake agreed, but he couldn't take his eyes away from the cave. The light was almost intoxicating. "But I need to find out. The light…it…" He couldn't finish.

"Yeah," Ian agreed. "It's beautiful."

Without waiting for a response, Ian walked up the small path. Jake swore, but followed him. The light…they needed to know what it was.

Above him, a jet flew toward the town.

CHAPTER 1

Ottawa, November 28, 2013

In the farthest recess of his mind, Matthew Burke could hear a siren in the distance and wondered if it was for him. Perhaps the police would break down the front door to the house any second. If they did, they would find him in a pretty incriminating position. Matt had to smile at the thought. It seemed incredible that he was worried about this, but then, he was covered in the blood of his wife with his daughter's head in his lap, and by this time his mind had floated far away.

Details before entering his house had gotten a little fuzzy. He worked as an account manager, selling internal lighting to several upcoming businesses. Today the printer in his office died, and he was late for several meetings. Most customers took it well, others were irritated. Matt bore it in silence. That was nothing compared to the war, where he—

"Get down!"

—heard nothing but screaming, and blood. He raised his daughter's lifeless arm, which fell to the ground with an audible thunk.

"Hands behind your head!"

The police were in his house now, pointing guns at him. Not that Matt really noticed. He could still see himself drinking coffee with his wife and kissing his daughter. He could remember it so clearly. His daughter hated kisses, but still allowed him to peck her on the cheek once in a while. Today he had gotten away with it.

Someone grabbed him and pushed him into the carpet, breaking his nose in the process. He didn't feel it, couldn't feel anything. Tears sprang to his eyes, but not because of the pain. This couldn't be happening. It just couldn't. He looked up at his wife's vacant eyes, a bullet hole in the top right of her forehead. At some point, his briefcase had snapped open, and several signed contracts were soaked in a puddle of blood. He wondered if this would upset his customers.

A paramedic entered the house and looked him over. They took him outside and threw him in the back of an ambulance. Matt shivered. He hugged his wife earlier today. For years, she had worked as a telemarketer, selling computers. It wasn't unusual for her to be late. Why did he have to be late instead?

He could recall that earlier in the day she had seemed... preoccupied. He remembered she burned her hand while cooking the eggs.

"Are you all right?" he had asked.

"Fine," she replied. *"I just had a rough night. Don't worry about it."*

But what if he had worried? What if he had insisted that he stayed home? She had been so preoccupied that she hadn't kissed him today. She kissed him every day. Why hadn't he noticed that? Tears ran down his cheeks as they handcuffed him.

The door slammed shut behind him, and he screamed.

Toronto, Jan 15, 2014

Jacobs examined his reflection in the mirror, and with a small frown adjusted his frock. His thinning brown hair was easy to comb, but he could do little about the bags under his eyes. Who was he trying to impress, anyway? His adoring fan base? With a sigh, he left his small office. The wooden staircase leading from the attic to the church was small, but he took his time.

The chapel was meant for a large audience—almost twenty benches were nailed to the floor. Near the front of the entrance was a small table with a guestbook and a vase of flowers—flowers which had dried up weeks ago. He kept forgetting to replace them from another set in his garden outside. He should also get around to hiring someone to clean the windows, he supposed. The bottom of the stained glass was covered with mud.

Only about ten people were in attendance this morning, sitting far apart from each other. All of them were probably in their late sixties or seventies. Surprisingly, this was a better turn out than last week.

Jacobs made his way up to the altar, and glanced in surprise at the sermon he had chosen for today. Why did he pick this one? For a few seconds he contemplated choosing another from memory, then shook his head. If anything, the sermon was a little amusing. "Good morning. My name is Father Jacobs, although I am sure you know that. I recognize several faces here. I will be leading the sermon today, and then we will continue with chorus." He cleared his throat. "Adultery is a sexual sin which has been forbidden by the God of Heaven on Earth. From the book of Matthew, Chapter 5, verse 28: A man is accountable for adultery when he 'as much as looketh on a woman to lust after her'…"

Later that night, Jacobs swallowed a mouthful of whiskey in his office. He wasn't too far from his home. Heck, he practically lived right down the block, but somehow he couldn't muster the energy to walk over there. The house was too big for him now… too full of bad memories. He leaned back in his chair and released a content sigh as the liquid ran through his body. If he passed out here, it wouldn't be the first time.

Jacobs opened his eyes and stared at the cross nailed to the wall at the end of his office. The entire church was quiet, except for the wood creaking as a breeze pushed against the old building. "God," he said, but it was full of scorn. He could still hear the sound of his congregation singing today, a bunch of scattered, old voices completely out of tune. He swallowed another mouthful of whiskey.

'*I should consider another job*,' Jacobs thought, surprising himself. He had been a minister for the past twenty years. He had spent an eternity preaching here. Not to mention that the church gave him a good, fat paycheck at the end of each month. If he quit now, what would he do? He shook his head as he helped himself to another mouthful. No, this would do for—

"Excuse me, Father," a voice said respectfully.

Jacobs screamed and almost fell backward out of the chair. He definitely didn't hear or see a man standing behind him. He appeared to be in his mid-thirties, but a black cowboy hat covered most of his features. Jacobs could see enough that the man had brown stubble.

"I didn't mean to disturb your drinking," he added, with no hint of amusement.

Quickly, Jacobs put a cap on his whiskey. "Yes, well...after hours," he stammered. "What may I do for you, my child?"

"I heard your sermon. It was interesting," he said. "As it says in the bible, "Behold, I will cast her into a bed, and them that commit adultery with her into great tribulation, except they repent of their deeds. And I will kill her children with death; and all the churches shall know that I am he which searcheth the reins and hearts; and I will give unto every one of you according to your works.""

Jacobs nodded. "Revelations, two twenty-two."

Even though the hat covered the man's face, Jacobs was sure the man was watching him closely. "Is that what you did with your children, Father?"

Jacobs glanced up, outraged. "Who—"

The man had disappeared. Suddenly, he heard a scraping noise below, in the chapel. Maybe he was so drunk he was starting to hallucinate? It wasn't in the realm of impossibilities. He took the bottle of whiskey and walked down the stairwell.

Jacobs opened the door, but didn't see anyone. Just an empty room. He shivered as he realized he had left one of the windows propped open, a last-ditch attempt to cure the stuffiness in the room. It didn't prevent most people from yawning during his sermon.

"The bible was created by man. And man is flawed. Don't you agree?" the man's voice echoed around the chapel. Jacobs whirled around, and saw him standing in the shadows.

"No...no, you're not real!" Jacobs whispered, taking a quick shot of whiskey. "I'm drunk. You're just an imaginary friend." For some reason, the thought struck him as incredibly funny, and he laughed.

"Or maybe I'm CGI or a YouTube sensation, is that right?" the man asked. "Every miracle can be explained in this day and age." He turned around and walked toward the cross. "You know, I pity the time when your Lord Jesus will actually be reborn. He will be met with scorn and ridicule. Isn't that right, Father? Isn't that how you feel?"

Jacobs glared suspiciously through blurry eyes. He really wanted to see under the man's hat. "Church is closed, mister. Get out." He pointed to the door.

"Or you'll do what?" Suddenly the man stood behind him. He laughed, a booming, horrible laugh, which didn't seem quite human.

"Get out, you fucker!" Jacobs swore, and threw the bottle at him. It went straight through and landed on the tile with a loud clatter. "Who—what are you? Some kind of daemon?"

The man chuckled. "No. Not a daemon, not an angel. But where I come from, I used to be a King." He tipped his hat. "I ruled a realm quite different from this one, and my law was fair and didn't cater to adulterers. For example, one time I too caught a woman having an affair with another man. I ordered her to have sex with every male in my realm, and to not stop until she had a child. Bear in mind that not all species are the same, and some positions are... uncomfortable." He grinned. "She would marry the first man to give her a child. If she couldn't decide her mate, then destiny would."

For some reason Jacobs found that insanely funny, and giggled. He waved a hand. "Sorry, friend. I know you're full of bullshit, but I can just imagine my ex-wife going through that. The cheating bitch would deserve that."

"Yes, she would," the man agreed. "Where I come from, there are no junkies. No homeless people. My Kingdom is a paradise, Jacobs, because everyone knows better than to break the law. Out here, junkies are lined up in the street, living only for their next fix. Then you have people who sit at their computer all day, completely desensitized to the world because they think they have seen every movie imaginable, every single miracle marginalized by special effects. And the rest..." he shrugged. "...go through the motions, living from paycheck to paycheck. All of them are looking for a sign, to believe in something."

Jacobs stepped forward and saw a glimpse of the man under his hat. He screamed and tripped backward, hitting a bench in the process. The whiskey bottle broke against the concrete, spilling everywhere. The man leaned forward to touch him, and Jacobs was too terrified to crawl away. He gasped as a shot of power ran up and down his body. It left his body tingling.

"We can give them that sign, Jacobs, you and I," the man said.

His face...those eyes... Jacobs shook his head. "And what will it cost me? Huh? My immortal soul? How do I know you're not the devil instead?"

The man chuckled. "The devil. What a cliché. I simply desire to return to my Kingdom. You can even see it, if you want to. In return, I will give everyone here, including yourself, a reason to believe. I do have that power." He snapped his fingers, and the chapel trembled slightly.

With a small shriek in the back of his throat, Jacobs watched as every bench in the chapel broke free and slowly floated upwards. Above him, the cross decorating the wall shook violently and fell.

"I am not a god, Father, nor do I pretend to be. But I *can* show people indisputable proof that there is something greater out there, and they will need someone to lead them. To show them the next step. Your faith is dead. It can be reborn."

Jacobs stared at him. "Me? But—"

"Too many people in this world have lost hope. I want to show them heaven. How can that be the work of the devil?" The man lowered his hand, and the trembling stopped. The benches fell to the ground with a clatter. "You could be...a prophet. You could set your own rules, so that cheating whores will never take advantage of you again."

As he spoke, Jacobs had a sense of something powerful. And holy. He could almost hear the angels singing in the background. Jacobs lowered his head. He was right, too many had lost hope, including him. All of this...felt right. "What...what do I call you?"

The man chuckled. "Call me Ethan."

"Ethan," Jacobs whispered. Dazed, he extended his hand. "I'm Father Jacobs."

Ethan replied, still amused. "A pleasure to meet you. You understand that this doesn't come without a price, Father. I don't need your soul. But I do require that we work more intimately together."

Quick as a snake, Ethan grabbed his hand. Suddenly Jacobs saw a flash of light, and then he was gone.

Jacobs glanced at his outstretched hands. He felt normal. Gasping in shock, he tried to stand, then fell back and stared at his decimated chapel in astonishment. Did that just happen?

CHAPTER 2

They gave Matt thirty-five years to life.

For a short time, he was held in the hospital for observation. He barely said anything, and didn't eat or drink. Gradually his shock faded away to an unending abyss of grief he couldn't escape. After a while he was moved to prison.

He lost track of time in a cell. He couldn't post bail. No one came to visit except his brother, who pleaded with him to get a lawyer. Matt could barely understand him.

They gave him a court-appointed lawyer, a stuffy woman in a business suit. She gave him a list of options, and for the most part Matt ignored her. First, she pleaded with him, then screamed at him, and Matt only stared blankly at the wall. Eventually she left.

It might have been minutes, or days later that he was in the courtroom, dressed in a suit someone had given him. His face was unshaven, and his brown hair was dirty. The courthouse was packed with people, most of them photographers flashing lights in his face. People were paraded inside, people he knew. He listened as his wife's sister, Carol, proclaimed loudly how glad she was that Matthew Burke was locked away, because she knew he always had the glint of a murderer to him. He always drank a little too much at parties, after all, and he even hit on her once.

His defense lawyer stood and glared at Matt, silently blaming him for providing nothing. She provided a hasty defense. He had the option to speak, but shook his head. A smug prosecutor slammed evidence against him. Something about money.

'I love you,' Lisa had whispered in his ear. He could still remember the night when they found out they found out they were going to have a baby. That was the happiest moment of his life. Numbly he looked at the forensic photos of his daughter, shot to death.

After the trial ended, the jury found him guilty and sentenced him to thirty-five years with no possibility of parole for at least fifteen. He allowed himself to be led away from the courts. A few people were crying. Others looked satisfied.

He could remember one night years ago, when Lisa had come home. She had been preoccupied with something. "Honey, what's wrong?"

"Nothing," she replied, opening the fridge to grab an orange juice. "Forget it." Suddenly the juice slipped from her fingers and crashed to the ground. To his surprise, she started to cry.

Matt reached forward and hugged her. Most men would chalk this up to hormones, but Lisa had not been happy in her job for a long, long time. "Look, honey, you're always down. Always preoccupied with your work," he had told her. "You should quit."

"This is nothing. I'm fine, really," Lisa said.

"I'm worried about you," Matt persisted. "We can find you something else. There are plenty of jobs in Ottawa!"

Lisa rubbed her red eyes. "No," she had said. "I can't go."

"Honey—"

"I can't leave," she said, determined. "I have too much invested with that company. The medical plan is great, and so is the pension. Once we retire, we could be millionaires."

Matt sighed. "I wish you would at least tell me what's making your job so stressful."

"I screwed up today. That's all. Seeing you, and our daughter, makes it all worth it," she added with a smile.

Matt nodded, and gave her a hug. "Okay. But promise me you'll take it easy, okay?" No matter what happened, he would support her.

But he didn't. He failed her.

In the courtroom, they put him in a temporary cell until the transport was ready. Suddenly, he heard footsteps and looked up. Was it his defense lawyer, about to tell him that everything was a big mistake?

No. A priest stepped into the light. Matt noticed that he didn't dress like a traditional priest. He wore blue jeans and a black t-shirt with a cross on top of it. Matt didn't say anything at all, and stared at him.

"My son," the priest said. "Do you require any aid?"

Matt shook his head and looked down.

The priest bowed his head. "Very well. When you are in prison, please do not hesitate to call me if you need to. Perhaps I can give you a good book to read."

Matt didn't respond. He just wanted the man to go away.

After a moment, he thankfully did.

"Ottawa," Ryan muttered under his breath as he drove toward the jail. "What a cold fucking place." He tried to peer through the windscreen, but all he could see was snow, and more snow. As the light turned red, he munched on a burger and glanced at Matthew Burke's file in the passenger seat. Somehow, this man had gotten the attention of D.R.E.X. Poor bastard.

The light turned green, and he continued toward the jail—not the one where Matt was temporarily housed, but the one he would eventually be going to. He wasn't ready to meet Matt, not yet. He was here to see someone else.

When he reached the jail, he pulled up to the gate and handed the guard his identification. The guard gave him an odd look, and reached for his red phone. Ryan simply flashed him a smile and cranked up the music on his radio. After a few minutes of talking, the guard handed him his identification and directed him on where to park.

As he exited the car, a chubby police officer with a bushy mustache came out to meet him. "Sorry, sir, we weren't expecting you."

"You're Officer Morre?" Ryan said, rubbing his hands against the cold.

"Yes, sir. I'll escort you to the prisoner."

"Thanks." Ryan was escorted into the prison itself, and through several checkpoints. Every time they went through a checkpoint, the guard on the other side would look at Ryan in astonishment.

"No way," one of them said. "This is bullshit. D.R.E.X was a story, a rumor—"

"Call it in. This is real," Morre said.

As the officer did so, Ryan studied the small cells as prisoners screamed obscenities at him. There was a time, and not so long ago, when Ryan had been in one of those cells, usually for possession. Other times for theft. He always hated the police for making his life miserable before D.R.E.X. Not to mention the one time he really needed their help, they had proven to be useless. "Are we done yet?" he asked. "I've got other things to do today."

The gate opened. "Right this way." Morre led him to the basement level—death row. Ryan could smell the overpowering stench of bleach, and something else he couldn't identify. He didn't want to think about it, but it was likely the smell of human flesh cooking in the room down the hall. They stopped at the third cell to the right.

Simon Jones was exercising, pushing himself up and down on the cold concrete floor of his cell. It seemed kind of pointless to Ryan, given that he was only days away from the electric chair. He knew that Simon's lawyer was appealing his last chance today. Not that Simon deserved one. He had happily confessed to the murders, and laughed about it in court.

"Mister Jones?" Ryan asked politely behind him. Simon turned around and glared at him, probably trying to size him up.

"Who are you? You're not the fucking priest," Simon said.

"No, and you don't need to confess to me. I already know what you did," Ryan replied. "Twenty-eight murders, most of them young women. Some of them young boys too. All of them you tortured, raped, and killed. The evidence against you is pretty concrete. Either way, you pleaded guilty, probably looking for an insanity bargain. Instead you're here."

Simon snorted. "A man has needs. What are you, part of the appeal board? Are you a new lawyer?"

"No, but I am going to do you a favor," Ryan said as the guard unlocked his cell. "You get to murder another innocent woman."

Up until the ride in the police van, Matt had been content to drown in a sea of grief. He was going to prison for the rest of his life. Maybe he would die in there. The latter seemed more appealing. His whole family was murdered. Did anything else matter?

They escorted him into the back of the van. He was the only occupant besides two guards. They chained his hands to the bench, then sat down on the opposite side. The van started, and a minute later, they were on the road.

Matt studied the small, black-tinted window. That tiny, distorted view might be the last time he ever saw the city again. He lowered his head. "My family is dead," he whispered, audible only to himself. Tears fell from his eyes.

In that moment, it felt like a firecracker exploded in his body as he suddenly realized that he wanted to live. He wanted to know who did this to his family. Matt stood, somewhat shakily.

One of the guards stood, taking out a baton. "Sit your ass—"

Matt snapped his leg out in a sweeping kick, tripping the guard, who landed with a heavy thud. Matt slammed his foot against the guard's head, knocking him out. Effortlessly he bent down, grabbed the keys from his belt with his teeth, and spat them into his waiting hand. Within seconds, the cuffs were off him, just as the other guard started to rise from the bench and draw his gun.

The cops were local, and probably never did anything heavier than breaking up a fight at a liquor store. Matt, on the other hand, had served in the military. It was all too easy. Matt threw the handcuffs at the guard's head, causing an angry welt. The guard howled in pain. Within ten seconds, Matt grabbed the gun and slammed his elbow into the guard's lungs. He kicked open the van and jumped out.

The ground rushed up to meet him as he hit the pavement hard, scraping his arms and chest as he landed. He heard something crack, but nothing felt broken. Matt jumped to his feet, swearing as three police cruisers stopped in front of him. To his left were some trees. Some kind of park. If he could get there, maybe he could lose them.

The police cruiser braked, and several police officers jumped out, pointing their firearms at him. "Get down on the ground, now!"

Matt swallowed, realizing how foolish he had been. They would shoot him long before he reached the park, and this little stunt would likely add a couple of years to his sentence. He didn't want to go back, but…he couldn't shoot the cops either.

Matt closed his eyes. Maybe he should end things here. He could pretend to shoot at them, and die. It seemed like a better fate than spending thirty-five years in prison, without his family.

"You have three seconds! Three…two…"

"Yeesh. You're a bit of a troublemaker, aren't you Matt?" a clear voice rang out behind them. The cops clearly didn't expect it, and most of them turned around. A black car was parked behind the cop cars. A ghost car, perhaps? Leaning against it was a kid who was short, with black hair, and blue eyes. He wore a black jacket, a black sweater and black jeans, and was leaning casually against the hood of a black Mercedes.

Confused, several officers pointed their guns at him. "Get your hands up!"

The kid raised his hands casually. "Relax, fellas. Trust me, I outrank all of you here. Check my identification in my pocket. I'm a D.R.E.X officer."

One of the cops opened up his jacket and took it out. He flipped it open. "D.R.E.X identification."

"Bullshit. Call it in," the older police officer snapped. Matt noticed he was a sergeant. "D.R.E.X shut down fifteen years ago. And you look a little young to be a D.R.E.X operative."

The kid shrugged. "Well, you look a little old to be a police officer, but I'm not judging you. Anyway, that man over there." He gestured at Matt. "Belongs in my custody."

"That murderer just assaulted one of my officers," the sergeant snarled.

"And I'm so sorry for your loss," the kid said, with an obvious lack of sincerity. "This is an internal affair, so we will look into that for you. I'll give you a phone number where you can direct all your inquires."

The sergeant stepped up to him. "Son, you've got a lot of nerve to be talking to me that way. I've got half a mind to throw you in a cell with him."

The kid smirked. "Try it. You can't even touch me without spending thirty years in a maximum-security cell." He straightened. "Are we done here, big guy?"

"He has clearance," one of the officers behind Matt said.

The sergeant glared at him, then abruptly turned around. "I want this fucking prick's boss on the phone! Now!"

What the fuck? Matt thought, staring at the kid in astonishment as the police drove away. Did that just happen?

The kid had a small smile on his face. "Come on. I'll give you a lift out of here."

Matt hesitated.

"Me or the cops, buddy. Your choice."

Matt reluctantly went inside the black Mercedes. The kid started the car, and they drove away. "Who are you? What's going on here?"

"Of course I got there in time," the kid replied calmly, then paused. "Oh, gee, thanks for the vote of confidence. You know, if D.R.E.X had more than five guys in it, someone might have gotten on top of this a tad quicker." There was another pause. "I refuse to be blamed for your staffing issues-"

Matt studied the kid in astonishment. He was driving and not looking at him at all. That's when he noticed a Bluetooth on the kid's ear. He was talking to someone else.

"Who the fuck are you?" Matt demanded.

"Nobody."

"What's D.R.E.X?"

"Nothing. Clothing store. You did not hear that word at all," the kid replied, then frowned. "What? Sorry, I have two guys talking at once. What did you say? Okay, which one?"

"Did you have anything to do with my wife's murder? Hey!" Matt yanked the Bluetooth out of his ear, and tossed it out the window. He eyed the gun on the dashboard. He could probably grab it before the kid could do anything.

"Go ahead, try," the kid challenged, as though reading his mind. "I'm driving eighty-five on the highway. If the resulting crash doesn't kill you, the cops tailing us would love to take you back."

Matt didn't reply, eyeing the gun again.

"Just relax for a moment, dude. I did not have anything to do with your wife's murder. My orders were simply to pick you up, and drive you somewhere safe. That's all. I guess my boss figured you had a rough night already and wanted to perform a civic duty."

"What's D.R.E.X?"

"A word you're better off not knowing," the kid replied with a laugh. "Believe me."

For the next five minutes, Matt sat in the passenger seat. His head was in a whirl, and it didn't help that his forehead was bleeding from his fall. He glanced behind them. He could see a ghost car tailing them.

"Fucking cops," the kid muttered. "They only show up when you don't want them to."

"That's not true," Matt said timidly, but part of him silently agreed with the kid. They weren't particularly helpful during his trial.

"Well, they shouldn't give you any trouble. My boss will make sure of that." He put a CD in the player. "Do you like country?"

"No," Matt said flatly.

"Too bad. I do." The kid turned the music on and cranked up the volume.

For several minutes, they didn't speak to each other. Matt trembled as he realized what had just happened in the parking lot. Gradually the fear wore off, and Matt could actually use his brain. He glanced at the kid, taking in every detail. He wore a black jacket with something underneath, probably some kind of armor. If he was working for the government, there was no sign of identification or insignia. Black Ops maybe? Yet the sergeant was right—the kid seemed way too young to be involved with that. The kid seemed like a practical joker, but there was something in his eyes... When Matt had thought about grabbing the gun, he had no doubt the kid would crash the car.

Matt took in a deep breath. "I want some answers. Real answers."

"Do you have anything against three-star hotels?"

"What? I don't understand—"

"Good." The kid pulled up into the parking lot of a hotel, and got out of the car. Matt joined him a second later. "Civic duty done. The cops will leave you alone tomorrow."

"Why?" Matt said.

"Because they will see the news," the kid said impatiently. "But they still might try something tonight because they are dicks that way. Stay in your hotel room and don't open the door to anyone. And don't follow me. I've got way more important things to do tonight than babysit you any more than I already have."

Matt raised his hands. "Look, please—I'm begging you, what's your first name? I can't track you just with that."

"Ryan," the kid said reluctantly.

"Ryan. Good, okay. What do you know about my wife's murder, Ryan?"

"Like I said, absolutely nothing," Ryan replied, zipping his black jacket. "Look, Matt, I really don't mean to sound cold, but

I'm just a lackey in this. I am doing exactly what my boss is telling me. Nothing more, and nothing less."

"Oh yeah? And who's that?"

"Well his name is—come on, do you really think I'm going to tell you that?" Ryan folded his arms. "Let me give you some free advice. You had a tragic loss, and I am sorry. But once I start telling you answers, you can't go back. And you're just better off not knowing. Trust me."

Matt shrugged, his hands resting on the roof of the car. "Well, thanks. Let me give you some free advice—you're either going to tell me everything you know, or I'm going to pummel the shit out of you. It's your call."

The kid looked around the parking lot, then chuckled. "Really?" He aimed a gun at Matt and fired.

Matt grunted in pain as he felt something tear into his side. Frantically he looked down at his side. Was it a bullet? His vision swam as he sank to his knees near the passenger side door.

A second later, everything turned black.

CHAPTER 3

Matt opened his eyes to a ceiling fan slowly spinning above him.

He was lying face up on something soft. A bed. Where was he—a hotel room? He could see a television just in front of him with a brochure on top, and a spare bed to his left. To his right was a table with a list of local attractions and room service numbers. Definitely a hotel room.

Matt winced, and lifted his white shirt. There was a distinct purple bruise on his chest, but no sign of a bullet hole. Some kind of tranquilizer, maybe? He shook his head. This was some kind of crazy fucking dream.

He stood, and paused. Next to the bed was a briefcase. For a split second he hesitated, then grabbed it. His heart started to beat faster as he opened it. The entire case was stuffed with money. Five thousand dollars. He emptied the briefcase on the bed, but there was nothing else inside it.

"Fuck," Matt whispered, rubbing his face. He walked to the bathroom, and splashed cold water over his eyes. The tranquilizer was still working its way through his system. More than anything, he wanted to sleep again. He shook himself out of it, and opened the door.

In the lobby, a pretty blond receptionist was typing on a computer, and smiled at him. "Good morning, Mister Smith. Is there anything I can do to help you today?"

"Smith? My name is…never mind." Matt managed a weak smile. "Sorry, I can't remember how long I have this room for."

"Not a problem, sir." The receptionist typed in her computer. "Your checkout time is Sunday, January 25th at 9 a.m."

One week from today. "I had someone else with me. A friend," he continued. "Did he leave any messages for me?"

"No sir."

"Thanks," Matt said, and left the hotel. The parking lot had a couple of cars, but none of them were the black Mercedes. "Fuck."

Matt had free internet in his hotel room, and spent most of the day looking up the word D.R.E.X. Much to his annoyance, he found nothing. Not a single hint of a secret government agency that could release convicted murderers without any explanation. Not that he expected that to be on Wikipedia or anything. It didn't help that he wasn't the most computer literate person in the world.

"No one can be that good." Matt ran a hand over his grizzled jaw, and paused. It was true—no one good be that good! They certainly couldn't fool an entire town overnight. He walked over to the phone and, with a slight hesitation, dialed a number.

Three rings later, the phone picked up. *"Hello?"* a woman's shrill voice answered. Carol.

Matt gripped the white cord tighter. "Hi Carol."

"Matthew? Oh my god, where are you?"

"Nearby," Matt said, fighting a wave of irritation. He remembered what she said in court. "I didn't kill my wife, Carol."

"I know. I heard the police released you," Carol replied.

"How did you hear that?" Matt asked, grabbing a pen and paper.

"It was in the newspaper today. They found the real killer!"

"Real killer?" Matt asked.

"Simon Jones, the convicted serial killer? He was the one who did it! Matt, it's all over the news!" Carol was ecstatic, which to Matt sounded more than a little weird.

He gripped a chair, fighting off a sudden wave of nausea. "Carol...how do they know?"

"They—well, you don't really need to know the details—"

"Tell me!" Matt snapped, then took a deep breath. "Please. I have to know."

"The police found his car on the side of the road. Lisa's blood was in the passenger seat. The police believe that she must have escaped from the car and made it back home, before dying from her injuries."

Matt swallowed. "Where is he? Simon Jones, I mean?"

"He escaped from prison, but was killed in the shoot-out near the Oak Bay highway. Look, Matt, everyone knows that you're innocent." She paused. *"I'm sorry for not believing you. Please, come home. I really need to see you."*

"Yeah," Matt said numbly. "I'll do that."

Then he hung up the phone, with no desire to see her ever again. Matt sat on the edge of the bed. Why? Why was this happening to him? Why did someone save him, and clear his name?

He glanced at his reflection, and ran a hand through his hair. He looked like hell, with blood-shot eyes and an unshaven jaw. One thing was clear—his wife and daughter were murdered, and he was going to get some answers.

Even if it killed him.

Even though he was loathe to touch it, Matt used the money to buy himself some new clothes—a warmer jacket, pants, a black shirt and a black baseball cap. Everything he needed to hide his identity while he was in Ottawa, a city which had so cheerfully abandoned him. It didn't take him long to find a used car for five hundred bucks, and a few hours later he was back on the road.

As he drove, Matt's mind began to race faster. Who was that kid? What was D.R.E.X? Why were they interested in him?

Thankfully, Oak Bay was a park located on the very outskirts of town near the highway. He parked on the side of the road, turned on the hazard lights, and got out of the car. He zipped his black jacket against the bitter wind, and studied the crime scene in front of him.

He could see yellow tape wrapped around several trees, but there was no sign of any police officer, or anyone else for that matter. The whole area smelled of gasoline. Several patches of grass were blackened, as were a few trees. If there was a car involved, it had long since been towed away. Matt turned his head, considering. They must have brought Simon here, either alive or dead, put him in a car, and lit it on fire. He ran a hand through his hair in disbelief. In the span of one night they had gotten him released from prison and framed someone else. True, he heard of Simon Jones on the news, and he was hardly an innocent man, but he wasn't responsible for Lisa's murder. That much Matt knew for certain. It made no sense.

"Jesus Christ," Matt whispered, crouching down and touching the black grass. "You guys were busy."

The question is, why? Why did they go to so many lengths to free him?

Matt sighed. If there were any obvious clues, he couldn't find them. He wasn't a detective. What was he supposed to do next?

Eventually Matt returned to his house. Or at least, what used to be his house. As he opened the door, he released a shaky breath. It came as no surprise that the entire place had been ripped apart. Furniture was shoved aside. Scattered on the ground were clothes, paper, books, and food. Whether it was the police searching the house or some idiot who had broken in, Matt didn't know, and it didn't bother him either way. He had no plans to live here again.

Right in front of him was one of his daughter's toys, a plush red-and-green horse. Matt quickly snatched it up from the carpet, and walked up the stairs to his daughter's bedroom. His hand trembled on the doorknob. He didn't want go in there. It was too painful. Still, he opened the door a crack, placed the toy on the desk and hurried back out. He slammed the door shut.

His own bedroom had been ransacked. The covers were on the floor, and the dresser was turned over. His shoes crunched over broken glass in the carpet as he made his way to the bed. For a moment, he lay back on the mattress, wondering if it was even possible to sleep. To the right he spotted a broken picture of himself and Lisa, smiling. Their vacation on the beach. With a smile, he picked up the photo, but that smile soon turned into a frown.

The edge of the picture was curled, and there was a second piece of paper behind it. Matt shook out the remaining broken glass, and pulled it out. It was a photograph. Matt examined it for a long moment.

Six people were in the photo, wearing black clothes. His wife was standing in the middle, holding a shotgun barrel-up. To her right was another woman, with brown curly hair and a mischievous look in her eyes, and a skinny man with thinning orange hair. To her left, a dark-skinned man with glasses, another woman who was short with blond hair, and a muscular man wielding a machine gun. None of them were smiling and appeared quite serious. He had never seen these people before in his life. All of them stood in front of what appeared to be a desert. The word 'Owphiyr' was printed on the back in red pen.

Matt lowered the photo, unsure of what this even meant. As far as he knew his wife had never wielded a gun in her life. But the photo dictated otherwise.

What else didn't he know?

He spent the next hour tearing apart his house from top to bottom, even more so than whoever broke in. Matt tore apart the sofa cushions until nothing was left but white fluff, then he pried open the frames on every single picture in the house. He then searched for secret compartments in the walls and the floor. All without success.

Matt then moved on to the desk. He opened up every drawer and tore open the bottom. "Fuck," he swore, throwing them to the ground.

Next was the kitchen. He overturned the table, without finding anything. He moved the fridge and oven carefully from the wall. He gasped for breath from the exertion, and froze.

Taped to the back of the fridge was an envelope. He yanked it off, and opened it. Documents and photos slipped out. He shifted through them on the floor. More photos of the same people from the photograph earlier. Something bulky was in the envelope. He slowly took out a gun. He had used enough of them in the military. Quickly he checked it for ammo. A full clip.

He shifted through the documents themselves. The first page had names and phone numbers of people he didn't know. The second document was an old newspaper, regarding some place in Devon. Several other documents were in another language, one he couldn't quite identify.

Matt suddenly heard a click, and looked up. Someone had entered the living room! Quickly he snatched the envelope and crawled to the adjacent hallway. Footsteps moved into the kitchen. He held his breath, trying to be as silent as possible. Part of him wanted to grab the gun and fire at whoever had broken into his house. Another part of him was terrified the cops had returned. Shooting at them would do more than land him back in prison— this time he would get the electric chair.

Footsteps entered the kitchen. It was impossible for him to tell if they were female or male. He wanted so badly to peer around the corner, but there was an equal chance they could see him back. Instead, Matt waited as the intruder paced back and forth, opened a desk drawer, closed it, then left the room. A minute later, he could hear the sound of a car starting up and leaving his driveway.

Feeling unsafe, Matt stuffed the papers back into the envelope and quickly left.

The first thing he did back in the hotel was check the list of names. He Googled every single one, but came up with nothing significant. That done, he tried to call the numbers. Most of them rang without anyone picking up. A man by the name of Jeremy Hodges had an out-of-service message.

He dialed the next number on the list, Anna Bell. After two rings, it picked up.

"Hello?" a female voice said.

Matt hesitated for a moment, having no idea what to say to the woman.

"Who is this?"

"My name is Matthew Burke," Matt said. "My wife's name was Lisa. I was wondering—"

A dry click answered back.

"Hello?" Matt tried the number again. It rang, and rang, without anyone picking up.

With a sigh, he tried the last name on the list, without any luck, then went through the rest of the papers. Most of the notes were in another language, or gibberish. He unfolded the old, yellow newspaper. It was dated fifteen years ago.

'Local wildfire destroys small town!

At three a.m., a forest fire destroyed the small town of Devon, and claimed 849 lives. Firefighters had worked around the clock to contain the blaze, but were unsuccessful to prevent the quiet town from perishing.

"It's horrible, just horrible," quoted the Chief of the Fire Department, Edward Malaine. "We are still investigating the cause of the fire, but right now, the damage has already been done. Many people thought Devon would become a ghost town—very few tourists would go there nowadays, but the people that remained still wanted to try and make it something successful, and in the last few years, it was growing. Now…it's just such a senseless loss."

Closer inspection revealed that many of the buildings in the town were not up to the fire code, to which Edward Malaine has refused to comment. Many eyewitnesses from neighboring towns reported seeing military helicopters in the facility, to provide a last-ditch attempt at evacuation.

He stood. The fire had burned the town down fifteen years ago, but something was still there, something connected to Lisa. He just knew it.

It had been snowing heavily when Matt left Ottawa, but when he arrived in Devon, it was scorching hot. He had been expecting nothing but a desert with the scattered remnants of a dead town. To his astonishment, Matt found brand new buildings as he arrived at the GPS coordinates. The town itself didn't appear very big-perhaps around fifty kilometers, but it was still shocking to see. Beyond the town, Matt could see a ring of towering mountains. Even if he found the right path to go through them, the next town would take all day to reach.

As he drove into the town, he glanced to the left and right, searching for a gas station. Even though it was a relatively small town, he could see several grocery stores, which appeared closed. Bewildered, he checked the time—just after lunch on a Tuesday. He didn't see many pedestrians either—a businessman and a woman wearing a sundress were talking together on the sidewalk, but that was it. Both of them stared at him as he rolled down the window. "Excuse me. Is there a gas station somewhere?"

"Yeah." The man pointed to the left. "Two blocks down."

"Thanks," Matt said. As he turned to the left, he could see several houses that had the lights off and no one outside. Frowning, he pulled up into the gas station, which thankfully appeared open. He filled up his gas tank, then went inside.

A young woman in her twenties stood near the till, wearing a pair of very revealing shorts and a blue tank top. She was drinking a soda and watching a small television in the corner. Matt grabbed a bottle of water and some gum. He set both down in front of the till.

"Anything else?" the woman asked.

"I bought some gas, too," Matt said.

There was a pause. The woman's eyes flicked to him, then back to the till. "Twenty dollars and eighty cents. Not many people come to Devon. Are you visiting someone?"

"I—" Matt took out the money, and froze slightly. Behind the woman was a staff room. He couldn't see much past the open door, but he could see a chair in front of some computer monitors. He could just barely see a green jacket draped over the chair, and a gun sticking out of one of the pockets. Quickly he looked away as she turned back. "Yes. That's right."

"Four ninety-five is your change," the woman said cheerfully.

"Um…thanks," Matt said, and managed a smile. He snatched the gum and left. As he got back into his car, he looked at the gas station. The woman was talking on a cell phone and watching him.

Five minutes later, he drove into a strip mall, then got out of his car. The entire parking lot was empty, and every store was closed. Matt glanced up at the camera on the street light. "No," he whispered to himself. "This is crazy."

He turned around, and finally spotted a man on the other side of the street. He was also talking on the cell phone and looking at Matt.

Matt wasn't sure what was going on, but he needed to get out of here. He opened the car door, and stopped. One of the stores had the sign, 'ELENA'S FASHION BOUTIQUE' in the window.

'What's D.R.E.X?'

'Nothing. A clothing store. You did not hear that word at all.'

Quickly he got into the car and drove out of town.

CHAPTER 4

Shortly after midnight, Matt parked the car several blocks away and walked on foot to the strip mall. The only illumination came from the streetlights. Everywhere else was closed, even the gas station. For a moment, he could only marvel at how quiet everything was, and how dark.

There wasn't any sign of life as he reached the strip mall. It was possible the cameras could still be watching him, but he still had Lisa's gun with him in case he ran into any trouble. He peered through the window of the clothing store, and could only see dusty mannequins. A sign on the door said, 'Closed for Renovations.' He wasn't surprised to find the door locked. One kick took care of that.

Matt stepped cautiously into the store, gun drawn. Part of him expected an ambush at any time, but he just saw an abandoned store with three cash checkouts. The tills were open and empty. Matt strained to hear anything, but couldn't hear a whisper.

He stopped to touch the counter, and his finger ran through a line of dust. Clearly, the renovations were going to take some time. He moved from aisle to aisle, and saw nothing besides empty shelves and a few rolls of tape. He moved to the other end of the aisle and released a sigh. He was wrong. This couldn't be the right place. He turned around, and stopped as his eyes settled on a cardboard box against the wall. He focused his flashlight on the label.

D.R.E.X.

He tore the box open, and found nothing but a monitor inside. He shoved the box aside and looked at the wall carefully. There were two vertical lines on both sides. A door? He ran his hands up and down the door, and eventually found a white button at the top-right corner, almost too high for him to reach. With a click, the wall opened, revealing a dark interior. Gasping, Matt backed away, pointing his gun at an empty room. Nothing moved to attack him.

Shaking, Matt struggled to his feet, and stepped inside the room. It was a very small room, empty of furniture, with buttons near the door. He was in an elevator.

Matt pressed the button for the first level. No matter what, he was going to get some answers. The elevator closed and plunged downward for a good thirty seconds before stopping with a jerk.

Matt listened, but couldn't hear any noise at all. He looked up and spotted a security camera staring back at him. He touched the cold metal of his gun, and, reassured, moved into a pitch-black passageway. He couldn't see anything to the left or the right.

"Bang, you're dead," a male voice said behind him.

Matt spun around, just as something hard slammed against his skull, knocking all his lights out.

Pain brought him back to consciousness. His head was ringing. Matt cracked opened his eyes and found himself sitting in a metal chair. His hands were cuffed.

A chubby man stood in front of him, wearing a white t-shirt and jeans and a black baseball cap. If this was what a typical secret agent looked like, than Matt was sadly misinformed. The man was also holding a mug—coffee judging by the smell—and regarded Matt with a serious look. "Why are you here?"

Matt didn't hesitate. "To find the person who murdered my wife and child."

The man took a long sip from his coffee mug. "You know, we cleared your name of the murders. We even paid you enough money to give you a fresh start."

"Not good enough," Matt replied. "That kid who shot me—"

"Ryan?" the man supplied.

"—said that once I knew the answers, I couldn't go back."

"In a way, that's very true," the man stated. "You can't."

Matt glared at him. "I want to know why my wife died. And I'm not leaving until I get some answers."

The man nodded once. All of a sudden, Matt felt something touch the back of his skull, followed by a click.

"I cleared your name because I felt sorry for you and Lisa," the man said calmly. "She and I worked together for five years, and I know she cared about you. It would be a shame if I had to blow your brains out. Are you sure you don't want to take the elevator back up? Forget what you saw?"

"My wife never worked for you. She worked as a telemarketer," Matt growled.

The man looked up. "On the count of three, kill him. Last chance, Matt. I despise killing innocent people."

"I want to know why she died," Matt repeated. Sweat gathered on the back of his neck. "I want to know why my daughter died."

"Two. There's a stairwell right behind you as well. Easiest thing in the world."

"Fuck you," Matt said.

"Three," the man shrugged. "Okay, fire."

Matt closed his eyes, as there was a loud explosion behind him. He felt a little pain from his ear because of the noise, but that was all. He certainly didn't feel shot.

The man sighed. "Well, I gotta say you're determined. In this agency, that's the only thing that will keep you alive."

Matt released a shaky breath, then narrowed his eyes. "What are you, anyway? Government?"

"Nope. Keep on guessing, though."

Matt raised an eyebrow. "Terrorists?"

"How would you feel if I was a terrorist?" The man's brown eyes stared right into his.

That caused Matt to hesitate. Finally, he lowered his eyes and shrugged. "I don't care who you are. I just want answers."

The chubby man nodded once at the man behind him, who released Matt's handcuffs. They fell to the ground with a solid *clink*. Matt rubbed his wrists.

The chubby man took a sip of his coffee. "My name is Jeff, and this is D.R.E.X. What *we* are is a branch of authority that is beyond any government. I cleared your name of two murders with one phone call. At the same time, I can authorize the death of anyone, at any time. I can get any arrest record cleared instantly, even someone on death row. With a little bit of work I can order a nuclear strike, make you a millionaire—the list really goes on and on."

"That's a lot of fucking power," Matt stated.

"I don't take it lightly," Jeff said. "And I have my own superiors I report to, believe me."

"If you're not government, then who do you report to?"

"As to what we do," Jeff continued, ignoring him. "Our goals, essentially, are to eliminate any credible threat to world peace. The meaning behind that is that we take care of things most politicians do not want to be connected to...or can even comprehend."

"A threat from who, exactly?"

Jeff shrugged, his eyes betraying no emotion. "Anyone, really. Or anything." He looked away. "As I said, your wife worked for me for five years. She saved a lot of lives."

"You didn't know anything about my wife!" Matt snapped, but it was an automatic response. He looked down at his folded hands. Right now, he didn't know what to believe. "Why did she die?"

He was surprised when Jeff placed a hand on his shoulder. "I don't know, son. But I can tell you what I *do* know."

Several light bulbs flickered as Matt was escorted into the adjacent hallway. They were in some kind of underground bunker, but most of the rooms they walked past were empty. Other rooms only had boxes in them. The air smelled stale, and as Matt looked up, he could see exposed wiring in the ceiling.

"Something wrong?" Jeff asked as they walked past a woman carrying a duffel bag.

"This doesn't exactly strike me as a surveillance base."

Jeff shook his head. "You've arrived at a bad time. We're getting set up again."

"Again?"

"D.R.E.X has been out of commission until recently."

Matt frowned as another thought occurred to him. "Devon is a fake town, isn't it? You made a fake one and occupied it with agents."

"Partially true. There was a time, several years ago, when Devon was a real town. What happened to Devon is why we are here today." Jeff opened the door at the end of the hall. Inside the room were a dusty conference table, and a projector. He motioned Matt to take a seat.

Jeff turned on the projector. "Devon used to have a population of about 800 people. All of them were wiped out within three hours. It started with two boys." He went to the first slide, featuring the photo of two boys that looked not much older than ten. "Michael and Gavin Brook. Both of them had been exploring a network of caves inside the mountainside. That evening, both of them discovered what Gavin would eventually call 'a doorway to hell.' He wanted to run away, but Michael found a book on the ground. Gavin told him to drop the book, but instead his brother started reading it, in a language he couldn't understand."

"How do you know all this? It sounds like you have an eyewitness account," Matt remarked.

"We do," Jeff said, but did not elaborate. "After Michael finished the last verse, the entire town was instantly engulfed in a darkness that wasn't natural, and then…Armageddon."

Matt raised his eyebrow. "Armageddon," he echoed.

"What would you do, Matt, if I told you that monsters existed?"

Matt laughed. He couldn't help it. "What, vampires, werewolves, and Frankenstein? Bullshit."

Jeff shook his head. "Nothing like that, trust me. After the military arrived at Devon, they spotted twenty-eight different creatures. Most of the officers involved described things I've never even heard of before."

Matt turned around. "No, this is stupid," he said. "If this were even remotely true, I would have heard about it by now. The whole world would have heard about it."

"This *is* the real world, Matt," Jeff snapped. "How do you think the military at that point reacted? They killed whoever they could find, and then they killed whoever saw them. If that didn't work, they burned the whole town and called it a forest fire, or blew up somewhere else and called it an earthquake. Needless to say, Devon did not survive for long and became dust. But as I said, we did get an eyewitness account." Jeff took out his iPhone and slid it across the table.

Matt took it, and turned it on. He could see an entire street burning. Several people were screaming, followed by gunfire. The camera was focused on a young boy sitting in the middle of the parking lot, screaming out in a language he didn't know. Finally, the boy took out a pistol, pointed it at his own head, and pulled the trigger.

"Gavin screamed the whole story before he took his own life," Jeff supplied. "His brother is presumed dead as well."

"Wow," Matt said, and looked up. "So what happened?"

"The military buried the portal, but the damage had been done. Soon there were other eyewitness accounts around the world describing things that couldn't possibly be real. Unless somehow, some of those creatures had escaped the portal. After that, D.R.E.X was created. We were responsible for taking care of any creatures that escaped. If we heard even the slightest whisper, then trust me, we would investigate. We killed the monster, and we buried whatever proof there was."

"God," Matt whispered, looking down. "So you're like...those government agents in those horror movies. Those dicks who would show up at the last minute and kill all the good guys, and bury the evidence."

Jeff whacked the clipboard on the table, startling him. "Don't be so dramatic, Matt. It was pretty rare we had to kill anyone. We would pay people off, copy any records and destroy the originals. A lot of it is tedious work, believe me. One of our primary goals is to preserve civilian life too."

Matt shrugged. "So why did it end? Why did D.R.E.X shut down?"

He looked back at the screen. "Eventually, all of the creatures that escaped the portal were wiped out. They couldn't destroy the portal, so they buried it. D.R.E.X was then retired. That was five years ago." Jeffrey paused. "Your wife believed that someone was trying to unearth the portal again. She called me a couple of days ago. Now she's dead. I can only assume that her suspicions were correct." Jeffrey sighed. "So here we are."

Matt said nothing, absorbing all of this. He ran a hand through his hair. "This is bullshit," he whispered. "So, what? My wife says that someone might be trying to open this...portal and someone murders her? And then you come back after five years of being retired just on her word?"

Jeffrey said nothing for a moment. "Well, there is one other thing. Something we found."

Jeff led Matt deeper into the base, and down the steps. Matt couldn't help but shake his head. This was too impossible to believe. Monsters? His wife working for a secret organization? Nah, it had to be bullshit. He would humor Jeff for now, but after that, he would make his exit, then go back to his hotel room and try to make sense of this.

They entered a room in the basement, completely bare except for a metal door with a very large lock. Matt could hear a sound behind the door. It was so muffled he couldn't quite make it out. Against his better judgment, he placed his ear against it.

"There's a slot in the middle. Go ahead. Open it," Jeff encouraged.

Matt shot him a distrustful look, then did so. The metal slot stayed stubbornly closed for a moment, but on the third tug, he opened it.

A young woman with blond hair was tied to a chair and sobbing. Hearing the metal slide, she slowly looked up. Black tears were trickling from her equally black eyes. There were also pools of black liquid around her feet. "S'il vous plait aidez-moi?" she whispered, then struggled against the bonds. "Cher dieu l'aide! M'aider!"

Jeff slid the metal shut, making Matt jump. "You don't want to go near her," he said, a worried look on his face.

"Why not?" Matt demanded. "What's wrong with her?"

"She's dying. And after she dies, anything within a thirty meter radius is killed," Jeff replied. "That's what is wrong with her."

"That was French, wasn't it? What did she say?"

"She's begging for help. Right now, we are running tests on her. One of my agents found her in Paris, and she wasn't the only one. Other cases are reported. We've quarantined a thirty-block radius around the area. I need someone to investigate this. A team."

"So you believe that this is somehow connected to my wife's murder," Matt stated.

"My gut is telling me yes," Jeff said. "I think we can help each other. You know who we are, and where our location is. Those are things that my fellow agents have died to protect. This is also a very vulnerable time for us. I have very limited personnel to deal with this situation. You help me figure out what is causing this infection, and in return I'll give you everything you need to catch Lisa's murderer."

"And after that?"

"We never have to see each other again," Jeff said with a small smile.

Matt thought about it for only a few seconds. "Sounds fair. Where do I start?"

"You'll be joining three others." Jeff replied. "You've already met Ryan. He's good, especially with computers. But, he can be quite a handful. Lindsay and Stephan will meet you on the plane."

"What are they like?" Matt asked.

"Stephan's a little too gung-ho for my liking, but he's a good medic. Lindsay…well, you'll figure it out once you meet her."

Without responding, Matt stood and turned to leave.

"Oh, and consider this a friendly warning Matt—I am going to give you whatever resources you'll need while you work for D.R.E.X. Lords knows you'll need them. But if you abuse any of those privileges, then the deal between us is off. And you can be sure that I'll leave you in a very unpleasant situation."

Matt turned back. "Is that a threat?"

Jeff only smiled.

A small blond woman escorted him to a small room in the underground bunker, which was empty except for a small bed and a metal table. The bed only had one scratchy brown blanket on it. He sat down on the bed, struck by how…military this place seemed. Even though he had been up for more than twenty-four hours, he couldn't sleep. His mind was buzzing with far too many questions. Finally, he stood and left the room. He fully expected a guard to be posted outside, but to his surprise, the hallway appeared empty.

It didn't take him too long to find Ryan, who was practicing by himself at a firing range.

"You really don't quit, do you?" he asked, squeezing off two more shots from a Beretta Model 93. The kid was a decent shot, but not perfect. One bullet went into the target's paper chest, the second into the right shoulder. "No hard feelings, right?"

Matt rolled his eyes. "So what do you do around here?"

"Well, I pretty much do whatever's not in the budget—so, in other words, everything," Ryan replied. "Jeff tells me that we'll be working together."

"That's true."

"He also says that we ship out tomorrow." Ryan reloaded his gun. "I've been here for a year, rookie, and I had some pretty hard-core training. But don't get me wrong. I'm sure your ten years of selling lamps will really help the team. In other words, just stay behind me and try not to get killed."

"I'll keep that in mind," Matt said dryly, and studied the target. "So, I already know that you're Jeffrey's bitch. What else does he have over you, anyway?"

"Wouldn't you like to know." Ryan whirled around with the gun. Matt responded by twisting Ryan's wrist, disarming him. He grabbed the gun and fired three times at the target. Each bullet hit the cardboard man's forehead.

"I served two terms in the army," Matt said, shoving the gun back at him. Don't worry about protecting me. Worry about yourself."

"Dishonorable discharge, right?" Ryan said casually, and smiled when Matt glared at him. "I hacked into your file. Wasn't hard. Hm, let's see…couldn't obey a superior officer even if his life depended on it. Let's hope you don't screw up this time."

"Shouldn't be a problem. You're not my superior," Matt retorted.

CHAPTER 5

A locker. They had actually given him a damn locker with his name and everything. After a restless sleep, the same blond woman he saw earlier escorted him here to gear up. Was this the same locker that had once belonged to his wife? He touched the cold metal. Yes, he was certain this used to be hers. With a deep sigh, he opened it.

Inside was an outfit similar to other D.R.E.X operatives—a black vest, black shirt, and black jeans. No insignia on anything. The topmost shelf had a gun and small flashlight. Matt took the gun. Standard magnum, full clip inside. No sign of any markings on the gun either. Finding nothing else, he removed his dirty clothes and put on the outfit. It fit him perfectly.

Lisa wore something like this once, he thought with a sinking feeling.

He closed the locker and left. He had studied enough of the layout last night to know where Jeff's office was, but the door was closed. He could hear raised voices and strained to listen.

"I don't trust this guy, Jeff," Ryan said. "Something about him feels wrong. And you have to admit that he is here for slightly selfish reasons."

"And you're not?" Jeff replied. His voice sounded amused.

"Yeah, but I've been here way longer. I should be the leader of this little expedition. When are you going to make a decision on that? I hear there might be a better paycheck,"

"I haven't decided yet. For now, consider Matt your equal. Same with Lindsay and Stephan."

"So whoever is left standing gets to lead, right?" Ryan asked sarcastically.

"Ryan, let me make one thing clear—"

Matt strained to listen, but couldn't hear anything. Jeff was speaking far too low. Finally, getting impatient, he knocked on the wooden door.

"Come in," Jeff said. Matt entered an office which didn't look any different from any other office Matt had been to as a salesman. Jeff sat in a leather chair behind a wooden desk. The top of the desk had nothing besides a blank pad of paper and a pencil. There was even a small plant in the corner. Ryan was pacing the room. His face looked a little pale.

"Matt," Jeff greeted. "Had a good sleep?"

"Well enough," Matt replied. Meaning he had no sleep at all.

As if guessing his thoughts, Ryan snorted. Jeff shrugged. "You're going to need it around here. Please, sit down. Both of you."

Ryan and Matt did so.

"Okay, so here's the situation," Jeff said. "As you both know we found that woman in Paris, and she's not alone. A hospital reported an outbreak with similar symptoms two days ago, in the same city. We acted on this quickly and quarantined the whole area within a twenty-block radius. Fortunately, the French government is permitting us to investigate. We do have some international weight, but we can't count on it all the time." He tossed two cards to Ryan and Matt. "That being said, the local police shouldn't know too much of our involvement."

"Why not?" Matt asked, glancing at his card. A photo ID of him as a health inspector.

Jeff leaned back in his leather chair and sighed. "Just a precaution. Throughout D.R.E.X's history, the police have been more of a hindrance than a help. Officially they recognize our jurisdiction, but most of the time we don't see eye-to-eye. The less I have to involve them the better. So in this case, you both are two health inspectors. We're printing off your documents and passports right now. Lindsay and Stephan will be helping you on this one. They'll meet you at the airport in two hours."

Matt glanced at the badge. "When exactly did you have time to take my photo?'

Jeff just smiled. "Ryan, while we're waiting for their flight it'll give you a chance to show Matt."

"Sure," Ryan said.

Matt glanced at him in confusion. "Show me what?"

"The portal," Jeff said.

They entered an underground garage with ten parked black cars, Mercedes by the looks of them but nothing too flashy. Nothing that would stand out in a crowd. Ten identical black motorcycles were also at the other end of the garage.

"Yeah, we tend to go through a lot of these," Ryan said. "They're not as durable as you would expect." He opened the door to one of the cars, and tossed a bag into the backseat.

"What are those?"

"Laptops. I go through a lot of those too, surprisingly," Ryan replied. "We'll get more gear on the plane. Hop in."

Reluctantly, Matt got into the car. Ryan flipped on the radio to country western.

"Not that again," Matt groaned.

Ryan grinned. "What kind of music do you like, Matt? If it's pop you can forget it."

"Never mind." Matt rolled his eyes.

The tunnel out of the car garage led to the desert. It was a hot, cloudless day, and it didn't take long for the morning sun to bake the car. A small trickle of sweat ran down his back. "So is Jeff actually telling me the truth, or is it bullshit?" Matt asked.

"About what?"

"You know. About what happened in Devon." He raised his eyebrow. "Monsters."

"You saw that woman in the basement."

"Yeah, but that could have been something else. Maybe she had some kind of disease, or…something else. Something rational."

Ryan laughed. "Nah, what Jeff told you is not bullshit. But you're not going to believe me, so I'm not going to waste my time convincing you. But trust me, once you see them, you'll never question that again."

"And when will that be?" Matt demanded.

"With your obsession for trouble? I'm sure in the next few minutes." Abruptly, Ryan stopped the car. "Well, here we are."

Matt looked out the window. He could see nothing but a ring of mountains, and a small outpost just to the right. Strangely, the outpost wasn't protecting any buildings, and seemed out of place. "Where?"

"In the town." Ryan opened his door and stepped out. "Or at least, what used to be the town."

Matt got out and looked around. There wasn't a speck of life in the canyon at all. "I thought D.R.E.X rebuilt the town?"

"They did, but not in the same spot. The new town is about twenty-five miles to the west. This was the original site." Ryan took off his sunglasses, his face unusually serious. "I remember hearing reports about this. Keep in mind D.R.E.X was created as a result of what happened here. It was a massacre. Twenty-eight monsters ran out of the portal, and butchered everyone here. The military didn't know what they were walking into. A lot of them died. Finally, the military panicked, and fired missiles at the heart of town. By the time they were finished, not even a twig was left. Come on."

They approached the outpost.

"Morning, Ryan," a uniformed man with dark skin and glasses said. "That the new guy?"

"Yep," Ryan said, putting on his sunglasses. "Matt, this is Bates. Bates, Matt. Been in D.R.E.X way longer than I have. And he's paid considerably more than me to guard a pile of rocks."

Bates grinned and gave him the finger.

"Any sign of anything unusual?"

"You would hear about it if there was," Bates retorted. "No sign of any intruders, no unusual power readings at all."

Matt frowned. "Where is the portal?"

Bates pointed at the mountain. "In that set of caves. The military pounded it pretty hard at the time. All the entrances are collapsed, and the caverns sustained considerable damage. It'll take someone years to dig it all out."

"Well, just keep an eye open," Ryan said. "There are whisperings that someone is trying to open it again. Probably nothing, but you never know."

"My wife was killed thinking so," Matt said. He stepped closer to the mountain. Even though everything looked peaceful, he could feel something…tugging at him. He lifted his fingers, and a mild shock ran up and down his arm as he touched the air. Despite it all, he wanted to go closer, to explore it further—

"I wouldn't sir," Bates said. "This is the minimum safety distance. Nothing good is in that cave. If you step any closer, I'm afraid I would have to shoot you."

Matt paused, and glanced at Ryan.

"Yea, everyone feels the same thing here," Ryan said casually. "Not sure how you handle it, Bates."

"Like you said, having a big-ass paycheck usually helps."

Ryan snorted, then glanced at Matt. "Come on. The rest of our team is landing shortly."

"Yeah," Matt said. "Let's get out of here." As he spoke, he took one last look at the cave.

Even during the middle of a bright summer day, it looked very foreboding.

Half an hour later, they arrived at a small airfield. Two people were waiting for them by a small plane. The first, a woman with dark skin and short, red hair. She frowned as she spotted Matt. Next to her stood a man with pale skin, brown hair, and a goatee. Both of them wore D.R.E.X uniforms.

"Hey Stephan," Ryan greeted as they got out of the car. "How was the mission in Arizona?"

"Classified," Stephan replied, with a thick accent. Matt's eyes narrowed. What was it? Spanish? French? "But it was very nice of Jeff to give us another mission before we had time to return to base and relax."

"Well, he figured we could use more cannon fodder," Ryan replied.

"Fuck you," the woman said. Without waiting for a reply, she boarded the small plane.

"Lindsay. Always a pleasure to see you," Ryan called out after her.

"Don't mind her," Stephan said, noticing Matt for the first time. "She always loves teaming up with Ryan."

"Yeah, whatever. The feeling's mutual." Ryan gestured. "This is Matt. New to the team."

Matt nodded. "Nice to meet you."

"You too," Stephan said, taking his extended hand.

"Stephan's actually going to be a big help on this trip. He's the only one of us who can speak French," Ryan added, as he climbed up the ladder and entered the plane.

Stephan shrugged. "Eh, a little. It's been years since I've visited the homeland. *Comment sa va*? Ah well. I'll have time to brush up on the trip." His face turned serious. "Aside from that, it sounds like you're going to need a medic if there is actually a quarantine in effect."

Matt eyeballed the plane. "So what's the deal with those two?"

"Ryan and Lindsay?" Stephan sighed. "Honestly, I couldn't tell you. I've worked with both of them over the past year. On their own they're fine, but when you put them together...some days it feels like cats and dogs would work better together. But as to the reasons why? No clue, but I have a sense they used to know each other before D.R.E.X."

"What, like they were married?" Matt asked.

Stephan shook his head. "One time I actually asked Ryan that. He laughed his ass off for hours. So no, I don't think so. Then again, perhaps I am wrong. Perhaps they simply don't like each other." He gestured at the plane. "Shall we?"

"Sure," Matt said and they boarded the plane. The woman was already sitting in a white leather seat, listening to her IPod and sketching on a notepad.

Matt sat down across from her and extended his hand. "Hi, I'm Matt."

The woman stared at him for a moment, then reluctantly took it. "Lindsay."

"How long have you been working at D.R.E.X?"

"About a year." Lindsay replied. "I heard about your loss. Sorry."

"Thanks," Matt said curtly and leaned back in his leather chair. "So, Ryan's a hacker and Stephan's a medic. What do you bring to this team?"

"I spent the past ten years hunting deer and elk. One time I went to Africa and did the safari run. I'm pretty good with a sniper rifle."

"Yeah, the animal rights activists must really love you," Ryan said.

"Fuck you, Ryan," Lindsay said.

Matt didn't miss the look shared between the two of them. Not just disgust, but pure hatred. "Okay. Clearly there is a thing going on between you two."

Ryan laughed once, and started to play with a Nintendo DS. "I don't know, Lindsay. Is there something going on between us?"

Lindsay glared at him. "Depends. Are you going to act like less than a fucking idiot for once on this mission?"

"Wow. I dunno. You're asking a lot of me this time around. Can you act less like a fucking bitch for once?"

"Is this going to be a problem?" Matt asked.

"Hasn't been so far," Lindsay replied. "I'll protect your backs. All of them." She glared at Ryan. "Even though it might be a small mercy if some of us were to die before others."

Ryan gave her the finger. "Stay beautiful, Lindsay."

"We have a long flight," Stephan said, buckling his seat belt. "If I were you, I would watch the in-flight movie. Less drama."

A few hours into the flight, Ryan and Stephan started to play poker. Lindsay was still listening to music. Matt watched Ryan as he swore a little. He certainly seemed like a smart-ass and probably didn't know when to shut up. Once again, he thought back to Simon Jones, doused with gasoline and lit on fire. Did Ryan do that, or someone else? Could he trust him?

Could he trust D.R.E.X?

"Are you going to stare at me like that all throughout the flight?" Ryan asked, putting down his cards with a sign. "I fold."

Matt blinked. "Like what?"

"Like we're going to shoot you at any moment," Stephan answered before Ryan could. "Relax my friend, we have to work together. So says Jeff."

Matt said nothing, well aware that the other team were listening, even Lindsay. "Let's get one thing clear," he finally said, leaning forward in his seat. "I'm only here to find out what happened to my wife. If you can help, great. If I find out any of you had anything to do with it, you're dead. Got it?"

The three exchanged a quick look. Stephan finally shook his head. "I didn't even know your wife, my friend. None of us did. She quit D.R.E.X long before any of us started to work here."

Matt leaned back. "So why did any of you join?"

"Good dental plan," Ryan said, picking up a new deck of cards. Stephan laughed.

Matt doubted they were being honest.

They landed in France nine hours later, and found a black car waiting for them. From there it was only a short drive to the quarantine zone. Matt stared out the window, watching dozens of people walking in the snow.

"Something on your mind?" Stephan asked, startling him.

Matt stared at him, and shook his head. "Nothing."

"Let's get ready," Lindsay suggested, opening a bag full of weapons. She passed them to Ryan and Stephan. Ryan selected two Walter P99 pistols, Stephan a M1946 automatic rifle, and Lindsay a XM21.

Lindsay looked up at him. "Any weapon you would prefer, Matt? We've got everything here."

Matt swallowed, realizing he really hadn't picked up a weapon since his days in the war. The less he thought about that, the better. Realizing everyone was staring at him, he thought quickly. "The M1911, if you have it," he said.

Lindsay took the pistol out of the bag and handed it to him.

"Where did these come from, anyway?" Matt asked.

"Our sponsor," Ryan replied. "Although sometimes we pick up the weapons ourselves if we like them. Sound check?"

"Yeah, sure," Stephan said, grabbing a Bluetooth. "I despise using these things. They always fall out of my ear." He turned it on. "Jeff, can you hear us?"

"*Loud and clear,*" Jeff replied. "Matt? Ryan? Lindsay?"

"Present," Ryan said.

"Here," Lindsay said.

"*Matt?*"

"Yeah. I'm here," Matt said, zipping up his jacket. "Are you monitoring us?"

"*Of course. I monitor all agents when they are out in the field,*" Jeff said. "*Relax, Matt, I'm not a chatter. Most of the time you won't even notice that I'm here. I want you to back up Stephan. He's the most experienced out of the group, so he's taking point on this one. Ryan, I want you to get as much intel from the cameras as you can. The security office should be on the second floor. Lindsay, as usual cover the team.*"

Lindsay nodded, even though Jeff couldn't see her. "You got it."

As Matt gripped his pistol, he suddenly had a queer sensation, as though this was a dream. Despite what happened to Devon, he still felt like this was some kind of a practical joke. As soon as they arrived at the quarantine zone, his new coworkers would laugh and drop the charade. There was no such thing as monsters, and Lisa didn't really work for some spy organization. Best of all, she would still be alive. She would laugh at him for believing such a far-fetched story, but she would be in his arms. Matt closed his eyes. And she would be real.

But they arrived at the quarantine, and everything suddenly felt very real. Red and blue lights flashed in Matt's eyes as they pulled up to a police blockade. At least forty people dressed in army camouflage patrolled the area, and as Matt got out of the car, he could see a yellow tent set up near the blockade. A crowd was gathered near the barrier. Some of them were reporters, flashing pictures at what they could see. Others were ordinary people, looking worried. Perhaps their families were in the zone. Matt didn't know.

A brunette carrying a toddler gripped his arm. "Pouvez-vous m'aider? J'ai quitté mon argent chez moi. Je ne peux pas arriver à ti—"

Matt stared at her, not understanding a word of French. "I'm sorry. Do you speak English? Anglais?"

"S'il vous plait…" she sobbed. "Baiser!" Without waiting for a response, she walked away.

Feeling helpless, Matt noticed Ryan staring at him.

"Yeah, that can happen a lot," Ryan said. "Get used to it. Between the group, we understand maybe five languages. But we can't be expected to know every language on Earth. Not until D.R.E.X hires a linguist, anyway."

"*Not in the budget,*" Jeff said.

"Of course not."

"Tell you what, Ryan—you start producing profitable results for me, and then maybe we'll talk," Jeff said sarcastically.

"In the meantime, you have me," Stephan said with a smile. Behind them, Lindsay watched the exchange, saying nothing. Watching everything.

"Etes-vous, les inspecterus de la sante?" an army private asked, approaching them. "Est-ce elle? Quatre personnes?"

"Oui, mais nous savons ce qui se passé. Vous n'avez pas," Stephan replied.

"Um, any idea what they're saying?" Ryan asked.

"Donne-moi une pause. Quel est l'age de cet enfant?" the cop asked, with a dismissing gesture at Ryan.

"What, what did he say? That sounded like an insult. What did you call me?" Ryan demanded.

"Pouvez-vous parler anglais pour mes amis?" Stephan asked.

"Merde. Non inspecteurs de la santé, meme francais," the cop muttered, then turned to face the other three. "Welcome to Paris. I only hope you are able to help us," he said in a thick accent.

"What's the current situation?" Matt asked, glad to find someone speaking English.

The officer pitched his cigarette. "Between us and the army, we've quarantined about a twenty-block radius, and so far we have prevented anyone from breaching it. We had a few nasty situations, but managed to diffuse them before they became serious. That was six hours ago. Since then we haven't heard anything agent—sorry, what was your name again?"

Matt didn't reply.

"Well, anyway, I don't like this situation one bit. There are plenty of people holed up in there, people I know. And it scares me that we haven't heard a peep from them. I hope you know what you are doing." He turned to another officer. "Let's get these people suited up."

The officer led them into the tent, and helped him into a yellow biohazard suit. After he was done, Matt felt incredibly bulky. He doubted he would be moving quickly anytime soon.

Stephan was already done and studied a map of the quarantine zone. "There's a hospital in the quarantine, where the cases were first reported. We should try there first."

"Sounds good," Ryan said, his voice muffled to due to the mask.

"Make no mistake, my orders are clear," the officer said as they left the tent. "I am not to breach quarantine under any circumstances, so you better have these suits still on when you come back. Otherwise, all of you are on your own in there. Even if you are five feet away begging for help, it's not going to happen."

Matt nodded. "Thank you," he said. The cop opened the quarantine tape, and they slowly moved through. In front of them was an empty, dark street.

"I feel a little ridiculous in this thing," Stephan muttered.

"It could save your life," Jeff replied through the radio, startling Matt.

"This isn't good. Too quiet," Lindsay stated before Matt could reply. "If I was stuck in quarantine, the first thing I would do is try to leave it, or demand answers from the cops. Where is everyone?"

She had a point. Matt glanced around the windows with his flashlight, but couldn't see anything moving.

After half an hour of walking, they reached the hospital and approached the emergency room's glass doors. Matt waited for them to open, but they didn't.

"Power's out," Ryan muttered, pushing open the door. They entered a pitch-black lobby, which appeared empty, and spotless. There wasn't a sign of any bodies, or blood, or anything out of place.

Matt searched around the lobby with his flashlight, along with everyone else. He couldn't see anything. "Where is everybody?" he demanded. "There's always someone at a hospital."

Stephan shook his head as he searched behind the counter. "Nothing."

"Something is here," Lindsay said, making Matt whirl around with his flashlight. He still couldn't see anything.

"What do you mean?"

"I don't know," she admitted. "I just feel like there's something watching us."

Matt strained to hear anything, but didn't. "Are you sure?" he asked her.

Stephan stepped forward. "Matt, Lindsay is a very accomplished hunter, and I trust her instincts. If she says someone is watching us, then yes, someone is watching us."

"Cameras, maybe?" Ryan suggested, pointing with his flashlight. "Look, it's still working. Must be running on a different generator. According to the map, the security station is on the second floor."

"Hm, possibly. Let's keep looking," Stephan suggested.

They walked past the lobby and into the emergency ward. Instantly Matt's flashlight spotted an older man lying on a stretcher, alone and unattended. He was dressed in a hospital gown and didn't appear to be moving. Stephan reached him first.

"Is he alive?" Matt asked.

"I think so. He—" Stephan began, feeling for a pulse. He jumped back as the man's skin started to bubble, as though boiling. "Holy shit!"

"What the fuck is happening?" Ryan demanded.

"How the fuck should I know?" Stephan snapped. "I've never seen—whoa!"

The man opened his eyes, which were dripping with black liquid. He ran straight at Stephan. "Aidez-moi!" he sobbed. "Aidez-moi, s'il vous plait!"

"Monsieur, restez calme…merde! Matt, get him off me!" Stephan snapped.

"Shit, shit," Matt whispered, reaching for his gun. But with the damned suit, he was too slow, much too slow. As Matt watched in horror, one of the bubbles suddenly burst from the man, and black blood oozed from his forehead. The man opened his mouth, gave a horrifying scream, and then exploded in blood and black liquid. As Matt watched in astonishment, several orange, bright dots floated in the air, then disappeared.

"Well, that was pleasant," Stephan remarked. His bio-suit was covered in black liquid. To Matt's horror, he could see the material starting to burn away. The blood must be acidic. He looked down as he heard a hiss. Several holes were already burning in his suit. The same thing happened with Ryan and Lindsay, who had been in close proximity.

"Goddammit," Ryan said, starting to take off his suit.

"What are you doing?"

"This thing's fucking useless now and is just going to get in my way," Ryan said. After a minute, he got it off.

Matt stared at him, and realized he was right. They were all exposed. He removed his mask as Lindsay removed a glove. *Not so great for a first mission, Matty.* "We can get checked out later," he said as he took off the entire suit. "For now, let's not have that happen again. Otherwise, the next explosion will be against our flesh."

"There's another body," Stephan said, pointing at a pretty nurse with red hair lying on the floor. As Stephan stepped forward, her skin started to boil. Instantly he moved back. "Maybe close proximity is causing it?"

"*Could be,*" Jeff said.

"What's the plan, boss?" Ryan asked.

"*Ryan, I want you to find the security station and look through the camera footage. It might tell us what happened here.*"

"Got it."

Matt whirled around as he heard a sudden screeching noise, coming from below. "What was that?"

"Dunno. Something mechanical, maybe? Pipes?" Stephan's tone was doubtful. "Matt and I will check it out. Ryan, you and Lindsay go to the security office. See what you can find. Stay in radio contact."

They both nodded, and ran up the stairs.

Stephan and Matt continued down the hallway, both flashlights and guns drawn. Matt strained to listen, but he couldn't hear anything more. "What do you think that was?"

"Could have been anything," Stephan replied.

Matt shook his head. "So that...exploding man...do people in D.R.E.X see that kind of thing often?"

Stephan smiled. "Only on the good days."

"But what are you supposed to do? I mean, is there some kind of rule—"

"We're dealing with creatures that we have never seen before. There are no rules," Stephan replied.

A few minutes later, Ryan and Lindsay located the security office. Ryan scanned the room with his gun and flashlight, but couldn't see anyone. Not even a security guard. It was a small office, with a locked key cabinet, a desk, and eight active monitors showing areas of the hospital. "Area's clear." He sat at the desk and turned on the security computer. "Ugh...they have one of the old PC's from the nineties. This might take a few minutes to hack into."

"Take your time. It's not like we might be infected with a deadly virus or anything," Lindsay replied, her voice dripping with scorn.

Ryan felt a brief surge of rage. Her brown eyes were cold and revealed nothing. He shrugged and tried not to let her attitude bother him. "You know, Lindsay, you could afford to be a little nicer to me."

Lindsay laughed. "And you could have chosen not to be part of D.R.E.X. I guess we both don't get what we want."

Ryan raised his hands. "Okay, seriously? I'm really not asking for much, just for you to be a little nicer. You barely know anything about me—"

"I already know you're worse than scum, Ryan. I don't need to know anything else." Lindsay gestured at the controls. "Hurry up."

"Fine." Ryan rolled his eyes, and started to type. The security station was locked with a password, a password he broke in thirty seconds. He began to go through the security footage, starting from when the outbreak had been first reported.

After several minutes, he paused. One particular footage displayed the emergency ward, with twenty people waiting in the lobby. Some were coughing, others were talking. Two nurses were standing at the reception. A second later, they just disappeared. No sign of them at all.

Ryan rubbed his chin. "This does not make sense at all."

"What?"

"These people...they just disappeared. If someone had messed with the footage, there would usually be telltale signs—a brief second of static, or items moved in different spots. Unless they're someone very good." He took out his laptop and turned it on.

"What are you doing?"

"Transferring this to my laptop. I have software that can work on this better." Within seconds, the security feed was embedded in his video software. He replayed it, this time at half-speed. He spotted something—a blur moved across the room, and the people disappeared. He slowed it down even further as Lindsay stood behind him. As they watched, a black blur attacked the people in the lobby, tearing them apart and then eating up the remaining chunks. The blur then licked up the fresh blood on the seats, and the walls. Only one man was still sitting. As Ryan watched, the black blur latched onto his face, then abruptly left him. The man then fled into the adjacent lobby, before coughing and collapsing onto the stretcher. The same man that attacked them earlier.

"Holy..." Lindsay whispered.

"All of that happened within three seconds," Ryan said. "Faster than we can even see."

"We have to warn the others," Lindsay said, and turned on her radio. "Stephan, do you copy?"

"Stephan, do you copy?"

In the basement level, Matt approached a closed metal door. Even if they couldn't locate the source of the noise, they might be able to turn on the power. Stephan pressed his ear against the wall. "I can't hear anything," he whispered. "But stay sharp." With a frown, he opened the door. It appeared to be a storage room, but right in front of them was a collection of white eggs, giant in size and pulsing in and out. Between the eggs, they could see various black webbing. Matt tried not to gag. The smell was terrible.

"What the…" Stephan breathed.

There was another burst of static from his radio. *"Guys, do not go into that room,"* Lindsay warned over the radio.

"Too late," Matt replied. He looked around. All the hairs on the back of his neck were standing on end, but for the life of him he couldn't see anyone else in the room.

"Get out of there right now," Lindsay ordered. *"There are creatures in this hospital that can move faster than we can react. One blink and you're dead."*

Suddenly they heard a small *crack*, and one of the eggs started to hatch.

"It's breaking!" Stephan warned, and raised his assault rifle.

"Get out of there!" Ryan shouted.

"I concur, Matt. Withdraw immediately," Jeff said.

Stephan wasn't listening as he studied the egg and readied his weapon. "It's opening…"

"Wait—this might be a bad idea. We don't know what that thing is," Matt said, reaching forward to stop him. "It could be something animal—"

"It's a monster, mon ami."

For some reason the air felt a lot colder. Was it just his imagination, or did he feel something breathing down his neck? "Do you think it's really a good idea to shoot at it? Isn't there some kind of rule—"

"I told you. There are no rules," Stephan said, and pulled the trigger.

"Shit," Ryan said, watching on the surveillance camera as Stephan fired. "Go after him."

"But—"

"I'll be fine here. Go! They need your help," Ryan replied.

Without another word, Lindsay grabbed her weapon and ran out the door.

Ryan barely noticed, too fixated on the footage taken minutes after the attack. As he watched, the door opened, and a woman stepped through. Due to the grainy black-and-white footage, he couldn't make her out too clearly, but she had light hair and wore a light dress. She stepped through the lobby.

"Who are you?" Ryan said out loud, and followed her with the footage. "Why aren't you scared? There's no one in emergency. Doesn't that seem unusual to you?"

Apparently not, as the woman ignored the reception and walked to the left. Ryan switched to the next camera, then the next. He watched as the woman entered the hallway, stepped onto the elevator, and arrived at the third floor. Finally, she approached a door that was fifth to the right. She paused, looked up at the camera, and waved her hand once. Abruptly the footage dissolved into static.

"Lindsay—" he began, but of course, she was gone. He reached for his radio, and hesitated. They had enough going on. He could investigate this on his own.

As Stephan fired, the egg shattered into a dozen pieces, and black goo spilled out. He proceeded to destroy the other eggs.

Matt felt something brush past him, moving as fast as a whisper, and when he looked back, Stephan was eagle-spread on the ground. His guts had been ripped out and were dripping along the floor, and his throat had been slashed. His eyes were open in a mask of shock. He was killed so fast he didn't have a chance to scream.

Before Matt could react, something knocked him backward. His arm hit the doorframe, almost to the point of breaking, as he slid back against the hallway floor. He aimed his gun at the seemingly empty room.

Nothing happened.

Matt took in a deep, shaking breath, and with a strangled cry ran forward and slammed the door shut. He lifted his ear to the door, and could hear a small noise, almost like a snort. Then nothing. Heart pumping in his chest, he crawled backward and lifted his gun at the door. He never fully believed Jeff, but after seeing something like that…

It might have been minutes, or hours later when he heard feet pounding against the floor. Startled, he glanced behind him. Lindsay was approaching, her gun raised.

"Where's Stephan?" she asked.

Matt struggled to his feet and wiped the sweat away his forehead. He was covered in it from head to toe. He was not ashamed to say that what he saw scared him shitless. "Dead. It all happened so fast."

"I know," Lindsay said. "Come on. Something's in this hospital with us, moving faster than we can react."

"It could have killed me," Matt said as they returned to the stairwell. "Why didn't it?"

"Ryan's found something," Jeff said over the radio, startling them. *"He's on the third floor."*

Both of them had their guns drawn as they ran up the stairs, but didn't see anyone. Matt looked around, terrified. Even if there was something around, odds were that it would kill them before they could even react. He tried his radio. "Ryan, where are you?"

"In here," Ryan called out just to the left, making him jump. "Come on—you have to see this." He led them inside some kind of storage area. They could see a body lying on the ground. An elderly man in a hospital gown. A knife was protruding from his chest.

Lindsay moved to search for a pulse, but Ryan shook his head. "Dead," he said. "Dead for at least a day."

She glared at him. "You could have called for back-up."

"Aw, were you worried about me, Lindsay? Are we having a moment here?" Ryan asked sarcastically. "Wait—where's Stephan?"

"Dead," Matt said flatly.

"Damn," Ryan muttered.

"Did you know him?"

"We're D.R.E.X," Lindsay replied curtly before Ryan could. "No one is supposed to know each other that well."

"That's right," Ryan echoed softly, glancing at Lindsay. "No one."

Matt studied the corpse. "How did that guy die?"

"No idea. Stephan was the medical expert. If I had to guess, though, I would assume it's from the knife wound in his chest. He didn't seem to bleed out that much, though," Ryan said.

"I think I know where the blood went," Matt said, pointing to the wall with his flashlight. He could see a message written in red. "Where is Jake Burns?" he read out loud

"What the hell?" Lindsay said.

"Who's Jake Burns? Have you ever heard of him?" Matt asked.

Ryan shook his head. "Not a clue."

"*I have,*" Jeff said, surprising them both. "*A chopper is on its way. Mark the building, and get to the rooftop for extraction. We're destroying the building.*"

"Wait, what?" Matt asked.

"*I'm not going to risk those things getting out,*" Jeff said. "*You have your orders.*"

"No," Matt protested. "There might be people that are infected. We can still help them!"

"Matt." Lindsay gripped his arm, surprising him. "We're a recon team only. We assess the threat. Other people in D.R.E.X do clean-up. We've done this before."

"This isn't clean-up!" Matt protested. "This is a massacre."

"*This is containment,*" Jeff said coldly. "*You have your orders. If you want to be part of this, Matt, you'll follow my orders. If not, feel free to leave. And good luck getting out of the quarantine zone.*"

Lindsay and Ryan were silent, watching him. Matt felt like tearing his hair out. He left the room and glanced at the empty hall. In the distance, he could hear somebody sobbing. "I want to help them."

"*And you will. But not by infecting the rest of France,*" Jeff said. "*Get to the roof.*"

"Matt," Ryan asked. "Are you coming?"

Matt closed his eyes, but only briefly. "Let's go."

A few minutes later, they made their way upstairs to the outside roof. The air was bitterly cold. Matt clung to his jacket. Ryan set up flares around the perimeter of the rooftop, in an x-shape. He waved the final flare at a chopper approaching.

Matt glanced at Lindsay. "Is it always like this?"

Lindsay shook her head. "We don't normally lose people. Those things killed Stephan before we could do anything. Jeff is right—we can't let them leave this building."

The next day, Matt took dozens of tests to make sure they weren't exposed to anything at the quarantine zone. While he was waiting for his blood work to come back, he flipped on a television and switched to the news. According to the latest reports, the hospital had perished due to someone smoking while there was a gas leak. With a quarantine in affect, firefighters could not be dispatched to put out the blaze. He sighed. "It's not right. The victim's families deserve to know the truth."

In a nearby bed, Lindsay raised her eyebrow. "According to this report, the victims likely died instantly. Would you like to tell them they were ripped apart? That their skin burst open and they suffered? Due to some kind of creature that might still be out there? And multiplying?"

Matt glanced at her. "So you believe that the public shouldn't be told the truth?"

They were alone in the room, but Lindsay glanced at the open doorway to make sure no one was approaching. "I don't think that decision is up to us," she said hesitantly. "And...I heard rumors. One time someone from D.R.E.X did tell the public the truth. He regretted it."

Before Matt could reply they heard footsteps, and an old, slightly overweight man with thin hair entered the room. "Blood tests are clear, agents. You're free to go. I heard Jeff wanted to see you."

"Thank you," Matt said. "Doctor—"

"Doesn't matter," the old man said with a dismissive shrug. "I only just arrived yesterday, and I don't care to meet new people. I have a habit of forgetting names. Now, kindly get out."

Matt shared a bemused look with Lindsay, and they went to the command center. Ryan was already there, typing on his laptop. He nodded at Matt. As Lindsay sat down, Jeff entered the room. He was reading a folder.

"Morning," Jeff greeted, sitting down. "I'm happy to report that all three of you are in perfect health. Which tells us this infection isn't passed through air or touch."

"Whatever attacked Stephan could have killed me very easily," Matt said. "We weren't a match for those things in the hospital, yet we're still alive."

Jeff nodded in agreement. "So that means what happened in Paris was a demonstration. A message. To us, or to the government in France," he said.

"We got our butts kicked in that hospital." Matt folded his arms. "Just how high is the mortality rate in this organization, anyway?"

Ryan stopped typing and glanced at Jeff. Lindsay's face was expressionless.

"We had a lucky break," Jeff said calmly. "The explosion at the hospital incinerated most of the creatures, but we managed to fully recover one of the bodies. My lab techs have done some preliminary testing last night. The results look promising."

"How are we supposed to fight something like that? Jesus Christ, it killed Stephan before I could even blink," Matt said.

"We're working on it."

Ryan chewed on a pen. "What about the people they infect?"

"Apparently these creatures release some kind of toxin into the bloodstream which boils the internal organs. There doesn't seem to be any rhyme or reason as to how long a victim has. Sometimes it's a few hours. Other times, a few weeks."

"That woman downstairs—"

"She's dead now," Jeff said flatly.

"What about that chick in the hospital?" Ryan demanded, pulling up the image. "The one I saw on the security footage."

Jeff leaned back. "We've been able to ID her. Her name is Samantha Wishart, and she is a University student from Boston. No significant background that would tie her to the hospital, or anything else unusual, for that matter. She's been missing classes for the past week. Called in sick. I have people trying to find her."

"You said you know who Jake Burns is?" Matt asked.

"Yeah, he was one of the eight hundred people who used to live in Devon fifteen years ago," Jeff said, displaying a photo from his laptop. It showed a young man with short brown hair in a police uniform. "This picture was taken during that time."

"I thought everyone who lived in Devon was killed," Lindsay commented.

"He was one of three unconfirmed kills. If several creatures could escape the kill zone, why couldn't the civilians? Though how he could survive both the military attack and the long walk in the desert is beyond me," Jeff said. "Trust me, the military went to great lengths to find this guy, and so did D.R.E.X. Eventually, both of us reached the conclusion that he died in Devon, and his body was simply beyond recovery. It was a missile strike, remember."

"Someone believes he is still alive," Matt pointed out.

"His only living relative is a brother in Colorado Springs. Find out what he knows," Jeff ordered. "Also, you're close enough to Boston. Dig up what you can on this Samantha Wishart."

CHAPTER 6

A quick check told Matt that Samantha had spent the last two years as a student at Boston University. Along the way, Matt bought some casual clothes with D.R.E.X's seemingly limitless credit card—somehow, he didn't think black Kevlar was going to fit in the campus very well.

While Lindsay and Ryan searched her room, Matt asked the local students about her. It didn't take him too long to find two students who were happy to gossip.

"Samantha was a loser," one girl said, happily rolling a joint between her fingers. "And I mean that as nicely as I can. Everyone tried to be friends with her, but she thought she was better than anyone else."

"Where did she usually hang out?" Matt asked, leaning forward on bench.

"In her dorm room," the boy replied. "I tried to hit her up once—I mean, that is some nice ass she had. Thankfully I found something better." He smiled at the girl, who returned it.

"So what did she—" Matt began just as his cell phone rang. He took it out, a little shocked. He had been fitted with a radio, but this was his personal cell phone, one that he had kept for years. Carol had tried to call him a few times, and he ignored it. It was probably her again. He rejected the call. "Sorry about that. So what did she say?"

The boy grinned. "She blew me off. Whatever. Last week, I saw her pack up her bags in her dorm room. She said she was leaving the University and moving on to someplace better. Good riddance."

"How were her grades?"

"I dunno. Okay, I guess." The girl shrugged. "What's with all the questions? Are you her dad or something?"

Matt smiled and handed them a hundred dollar bill. "Something like that. Thanks for your time."

The door to Samantha's room was locked, but one flash of their identification got them through campus security. Lindsay glanced around in the room, not without some astonishment. The entire room had pink wallpaper, and pink blankets. Several statues and crystals adorned the ledges of the windows, and on top of the small table near the bed. The room was very...pretty.

"Great. New age crap," Ryan remarked as he surveyed the room. "Wind chimes, crystals, tarot cards, Buddha statues, crosses, Chinese meditation balls...instead of choosing one religion, she's trying to choose them all."

"Dare I ask what kind of religion you are interested in?" Lindsay replied, picking up a Wicca spell book.

Ryan laughed as he grabbed a pink laptop from the bottom of the bed and opened it up. "Atheism. It's the only way to go. "

Lindsay shook her head. "I hope for Stephan's sake you're wrong."

Ryan shot her an irritated look. "I gave up on being anyone's devoted follower a long time ago. You know why."

Lindsay frowned, but reluctantly decided to drop it. She studied the floor, looking for any sign of a struggle—a drop of blood, someone else's hairs, or anything that appeared out of place. Nothing. "Can you get into that okay?"

"I think I can handle hacking into a teenage girl's laptop, thank you very much."

The door opened, and Matt stepped through. "Find anything?" he asked.

"Nothing," Lindsay said with a shrug. "No signs of any struggle. Or foul play. You?"

"The girl was socially isolated by her classmates, and didn't seem to fit in anywhere. She could have run off."

"Here's something interesting," Ryan said, his eyes glued to the laptop screen. "A whole bunch of e-mails from this group called the 'Blue Power Core'. This is the last one. 'Do you feel like you have no control over your life? Are people walking over you? Is a potential love interest not giving you a second glance? It's time to take back your life! Learn how to control your internal energies and become a powerful, dominating force on the planet. Blue Power Core will show you basic tricks such as telepathy, telekinesis, healing, and manipulation of other people's energies. More advanced students can learn to communicate with the astral plane, opening the way to another level of existence'." Ryan started to type. "They have a meeting in a week. In Winnipeg."

"So she isn't looking for a religion," Lindsay remarked. "She's looking for power."

"Most teenagers do at her age," Matt commented.

"*Ryan, send me a copy of that flier,*" Jeff ordered.

"Done," Ryan said, and closed the laptop.

Matt looked around. "Anything else in here?"

Lindsay shook her head. "Nothing. She clearly left of her own free will. Maybe she went to Winnipeg."

"And this 'Blue Power Core' group might be exploiting her somehow. But why was she in the hospital in Paris? What's the connection?" Matt asked.

"*I'll have someone look into it. Could be a lead. If you're done here, proceed to Vermon as soon as you can.*"

"Another plane trip?" Matt asked.

"You get used to it around here," Lindsay said with a rare smile.

Anna opened her eyes to the overwhelming smell of hay and cows mooing in protest. She lifted her head and a small groan escaped her lips. Had she fallen asleep in the barn again? Must have, judging by the stiffness in her legs. She stretched them for a little bit, removed a bit of hay from her short red hair, and shivered. It was just after winter, and the morning frost lined the old wooden walls. Rubbing her arms, she got up and milked the cows, then proceeded to feed the chickens.

As she spread the seeds across the wet mud, she knew with a sickening feeling that this might be the last time she did this for a while. Fortunately, she had a neighbor who was happy to take over for a couple of days—a little payback for helping her last year when the much older woman had gone on a once-in-a-lifetime Mediterranean cruise.

Having fed the chickens, Anna retreated to her barn, where her computer was set up. She turned on a small hand-held radio as she powered up the computer.

"*What's your situation?*" Jeff asked after a few minutes of static.

"*Nearly approaching Vermon,*" Matt replied. "*Do you have the address of Jake Burn's brother?*"

"*Let me check…1317 Henderson Road was his last known address, apartment 121. Probably a good idea to have Lindsay take a sniper position at the next building,*" Jeff replied.

She glanced at the photo on the shelf above her computer, one that had her and Lisa smiling. She picked it up and closed her eyes, feeling a brief twinge of guilt. She had no business keeping that damn radio on.

"*We're landing right now,*" Matt said. "*We should get there in a couple of hours.*"

Anna bit her lower lip. She stood, and grabbed her brown leather jacket from the chair.

After a very long flight, Matt sat behind the wheel of a rental car in the town of Vermon, silently marveling at the climate change. He had traveled a great deal during the war, but that was several years ago. He was used to sunny days, even during the month of January. Now he had shifted from sunshine, to snow, back to sunshine in Boston, and now to eight meters of snow here. It was getting difficult to adjust to that, or the various time changes. The rare time he could sleep it usually happened on the plane, or if he was extremely lucky, a cheap hotel room. Was this the life that most D.R.E.X operatives lived?

Was this his life now?

He felt a sudden pang as he watched a man, woman, and a girl of maybe eight years old holding shopping bags in their hands. The little girl smiled and waved at him. Matt couldn't help but smile and wave back.

Ryan walked out of the corner store and entered the car, holding two coffee cups in his hand. He passed one to Matt. "Here. Got the heat on?"

"Yep," Matt said, and sipped from the coffee. "Lindsay in position?"

"Yep."

After a few minutes of silence Matt asked, "So how did you get into this? D.R.E.X, I mean?"

Ryan smirked at the question as he opened a bag of Twizzlers. "I was kidnapped a year ago—literally. You could say I'm trying to ransom my way out."

Chicago, Jan 5, 2013

Ryan should have known something was wrong.

Since moving into one of the cheapest apartments in one of the worst parts of the city, he usually heard music cranked on way too high, screaming, or people screwing themselves senseless. Usually it would get to a point where Ryan would turn up his IPod way beyond normal levels. The very idea of sleeping in this dump was laughable.

But today, nothing.

Shaking his head, Ryan removed his headphones and unlocked his door. He had moved in at the beginning of the month, and the place was a mess. Garbage and clothes were scattered everywhere.

No food, though. He couldn't remember the last time he had eaten a full meal.

He went to his fridge and grabbed a red bull. As he did so, he glanced at the table. A single, white envelope rested against a plate. He already opened the letter, and read it yesterday. Even so, he read it again, then studied the envelope. No return address, not that he expected one. It was the same with all the other envelopes.

All of a sudden, he had a strange feeling that he wasn't alone. He turned around in his cluttered apartment, but didn't see anyone. The door was still shut. Ryan threw the envelope back on the table, then opened his drink. A flashlight light on the answering machine told him he had a message, and he turned it on.

"Yo, Ryan. It's Mark. When are you going to change your message? It's just you rambling on stoned. I'll tell you one last time dude— CHANGE YOUR MESSAGE."

Ryan grinned as he sat down next to his computer and got it out of hibernation mode. A few seconds later, he accessed the internet, and flicked to the National Coast Bank website. Out of all the banks he had hacked into, this one was the easiest.

"Anyway, we're having a party tonight. Usual place. You remember Gloria? She's been asking about you. Don't forget to bring beer! I'm not picking up your tab this time."

Ryan picked a credit card account at random. With a few keystrokes, the credit card went from $25,000 to $300.00 in an instant.

Ryan paused as he looked at the reflection from the monitor. He could have sworn he saw something...move. He half-stood out of the chair, just as a hand grabbed the back of his head and slammed it down on his keyboard. Blood dripped over the left side of the white keys as he reacted entirely on impulse and elbowed his unknown assailant. The blow was easily dodged as a black hood slammed over his head, and he felt the sting of a needle in his neck.

"Bring some munchies too. So yeah, give me a call. Hope you show up! Bye."

Adrenaline surged through his veins as he struggled forward out of his chair, only to fall to the floor. He had to run. Find help. Trouble was, it also felt like he just had ten beers, and it was hard to crawl forward. In fact, it felt much easier just to put his head down on the cold, dirty floor. "Help! Fuck, somebody help me!"

Before he passed out, it suddenly occurred to Ryan why the entire apartment was so quiet...

In the car, Ryan took another sip of coffee, remembering that day. The one last time he was free. "I have my own deals going on with Jeff right now. He caught me doing some illegal activities."

"Like what?" Matt asked.

"I transferred some funds from a bank account."

"That doesn't sound so bad."

"It wasn't my bank account," Ryan supplied, glancing at the road. Still no sign of anyone.

"Oh." Matt paused. "Why?"

"Does it really matter? Substitute any reason you want—I wanted a new pool for my mansion, I wanted to pay off my huge drug habit. Whatever." The smile didn't quite meet his eyes. "Jeff needed a hacker, and he's keeping my ass from doing twenty years in jail. That's our arrangement." He shook his head. "Look, Lindsay is right. The less we know about each other the better. We're not exactly in a job with good work safe compensation. You saw what happened to Stephan. That could happen to us anytime."

"Yet you and Lindsay seem to know each other pretty well," Matt mentioned.

"Yeah, well, we're the exception to the rule. We go back."

"So what's her deal?"

"She's a bitch." Ryan shrugged.

"Yeah, but what is she to you?"

"A fucking annoying bitch." He waved a dismissive hand. "Look, can we just drop it please? Believe me, Lindsay is not worth talking about."

Lindsay sat perched on top of the snowy rooftop of the building, covering the back in case someone tried to enter that way. Every now and then, she inspected the front of the building, and observed the car Matt and Ryan were sitting in. Finding nothing amiss, she moved to the back again, rubbing her arms to keep them warm. This was not the best vantage point for a sniper. The sky was overcast with heavy snow. It was almost impossible to see anything out of her scope. In addition, both the front and back had narrow alleyways. Anyone could duck out of sight. Shaking her head in irritation, she sat down at the edge and took a deep breath, feeling the cold snow under her skin. If she concentrated hard enough, she could pretend she was back in the Yukon, hunting moose. She loved the solitude. Being out among people...she despised it.

From the command center, Jeff listened to them talk. Most D.R.E.X operatives often forgot that their radios were turned on. As a result, he often learned and heard things he shouldn't have. He sipped his coffee, and watched the screen. Or rather, three screens. The first one had their satellite location, which pinpointed their location with incredible accuracy. The second screen had their basic health functions—heartbeat, pulse, body temperate, and signal strength. The third was a hacked camera feed, which also showed where they were. Matt and Ryan had been there for a few hours. This might take a while.

Jeff turned to a junior operative. "Call me if something happens."

"Yes sir," the operative replied.

He left the command area and entered the elevator. It trembled as it reached the lower floor, and the lights flickered once. Jeff shook his head. He had a considerable amount of power and influence, but it paled in comparison to what he had fifteen years ago. When D.R.E.X was first created, he had a new building with a full staff. Now, with reduced funding...it was a struggle to get hot water for his coffee on most days.

He got off on the seventh level and entered a makeshift hospital area. Half of the medical bay had been transformed into a quarantine area. A man in his early fifties was washing a bloody scalpel in front of the sink. He was slightly underweight with thin, white hair. "Mister Lumley, I assume?" he said over the noise of the faucet. "Louise Drager. I would shake your hand, but I'm a little indisposed at the moment.'

Jeff folded his arms. "You're not the doctor I recommended."

"That pretty little blond? She didn't pass the final screening. Our mutual benefactor sent her packing back to Czechoslovakia and called me instead." He turned off the sink and tossed away his plastic gloves. His piercing blue eyes studied Jeff, as though he was nothing more than something to be dissected under the microscope. Finally, he snorted. "I knew your father. Long time ago."

"It's nice that we have some family history," Jeff stated. "Otherwise one would think our benefactor is spying on me."

"Do you need to be spied on, Jeff?" Louise asked, his face perfectly serious.

Jeff met his gaze evenly. "I assume your clearance checks out. And that you have the required qualifications."

Louise laughed and turned away. "I have my necessary doctorate in biology and multiple degrees in science and medicine, which I won't bore you with. My files are all in order. And, I have been in the espionage game long enough to know how this works. I've completed the autopsy reports on the sample we brought back." He gestured at the quarantine area.

"I'd like to see it. The specimen."

"Sure. Get suited up first, though. There's minimal chance of exposure, but one can never be too careful. That's why we're both here, isn't it? Someone wasn't careful."

Jeff ignored the attempt to bait him and got into a biohazard suit, which took him a considerable about of time. Finally, they both stepped into the quarantine room. The creature was spread eagle on the table and completely dissected, with its missing organs likely in the fridge. Jeff stared at the creature for a moment. Its appearance was quite similar to a black dog, but rubber-like skin and larger teeth and claws. "What do you have?"

"The specimen is quite impressive, actually. Its skin is similar to rubber, making it bullet resistant. Main attack seems to be from five-inch claws and a spit from the tongue which releases a black enzyme." He touched a small yellow tip on the creature's tongue. "You've seen the results. It essentially boils the internal organs and turns them into soup."

"But we had that woman in our cell for three days. Did it really take that long? She didn't seem to be in pain." Jeff felt a slight twinge of guilt as he spoke. If she were actually in pain, he would have done something sooner to help her

"No. Death was instantaneous. My guess is that the enzyme is dormant in the body for a short period of time. Something triggers it to be deadly."

"Like what?"

"Still working on it," Louise replied curtly.

Jeff said nothing for a moment. "Okay—anything else?"

"See any eyes?"

Jeff searched. He could see two black eyelids, but that was all. "Did you take them out?"

"No, and those aren't eyelids. It's another set of nostrils. Effectively they are blind, and they move by acute smell. They each have a pungent aurora around them, which identifies their own kind. Also its brain is relatively small—about two and a half inches."

Jeff frowned. "That is small."

"Exactly. I don't think it has the intelligence for elaborate thought. Your monster is really an animal."

"Anything else?"

"Yeah, one more thing." Louise looked up at him. "This one doesn't have any reproductive organs."

Jeff blinked in surprise. "Matt saw eggs when he was there."

"My science team has checked multiple samples on site. The ones we found only have one gender, and they don't have any egg sacs, or fertilizer for egg sacs. Nothing's there." He shrugged. "Matt is not mistaken, though. We do have samples of the eggs and are studying them now."

"Impossible," Jeff said. "How are they reproducing?"

"That's why I'm here," Louis said. "To figure out the impossible. Maybe it's only one of them doing it, like an ant queen."

"Let me know either way," Jeff said. "Thanks for your time, Doctor." It was time he got back upstairs.

"Oh no," Louis said, his face completely serious. "Thank you for giving me a reason to leave retirement and suddenly have seven figures a year."

After a few minutes of mutual silence, Matt turned to Ryan. "Okay, let's talk about something else. I'm curious about D.R.E.X."

Ryan shrugged. "I don't know much more than you do, buddy."

"How many agents are there exactly?"

"I don't know," Ryan said, turning up the heat in the car.

"What do you mean you don't know?"

"D.R.E.X is part of a network of agents," Ryan said patiently. "You, me and Lindsay belong to one network. We'll probably spend the rest of our lives without meeting any other networks."

"Doesn't Jeff know? Isn't he in charge?"

"Jeff?" Ryan snorted. "No. He's just a handler."

Matt frowned. If Ryan was right, then D.R.E.X was a hell of a lot bigger than he thought. "Then who—"

Ryan suddenly leaned forward. "Hang on, there he is! That's Jake Burns!"

Matt followed his gaze, and saw a man in a police uniform parking his patrol car near the apartment building. It was the spitting image of the photo…but the photo was taken fifteen years ago. Only one way to find out. He turned on his radio. "Lindsay, eyes on me."

Lindsay watched as the police car pulled up, followed by the door opening. There were two other people sitting in the back, other police officers. She focused back on Matt and Ryan. "Something's wrong," she muttered under her breath.

"*What is it, Lindsay?*" Jeff asked, always able to hear her no matter how low her voice.

She shook her head. "It's almost rush hour. There should be more sound, like traffic. Or in the apartment building—I don't see any other lights on, or people talking. It's too quiet."

Matt watched as the man got out of the car, then took a cigarette from his pocket. "Let's go," he said, getting out of the car.

"Officer Jake Burns?" Ryan asked as they approached, and flashed his D.R.E.X identification. The man was leaning on his patrol car, which had two other people inside.

"No," the man replied, glancing at both of them with a frown. "He passed away several years ago. But I'm his brother. Richard."

"Oh—sorry. You look really similar to your brother, or what he looked like a long time ago," Ryan said. "I'm sorry for your loss."

"I am the younger brother, yes. How do you know that?" Richard asked. "Look fellas, I'm still on duty. I just ran in to grab some lunch. Is this important?"

"My partner and I are from D.R.E.X," Matt began.

"Never heard of it," Richard replied.

"It's a branch of government, kind of like the FBI," Matt explained. "You're not in any trouble. We just want to ask you a couple of questions."

"Okay," Richard said. "Sure."

Then, he took out a gun and shot Ryan several times in the chest.

Through her scope, Lindsay watched as Ryan was shot. His face was a mask of shock as he fell backward.

Lindsay was already screaming out his name, but a different part of her already grabbed the sniper rifle and shot right at the man who had just murdered Ryan. Even though she fired within a second, another officer stepped in the way of her shot, and his head exploded in red. Lindsay swore. Where the hell did that guy come from? Her eyes lifted, and saw that the second officer was firing at Matt and chatting on the radio. No doubt calling for back-up.

Ryan fell, rebounded against the back of the car, and hit the ground. He didn't get up again.

Desperately Lindsay aimed the rifle again. By this time, Richard Burns had ducked back into the alley, out of her sight. Matt, meanwhile, had taken out his own gun and fired back, also out of her line of site. She instantly aimed at the man shooting at Matt and fired. Seeing him fall, she lifted her sniper rifle. She didn't have eyes on either Matt or Ryan.

She had to get down there.

As soon as Ryan fell, Matt reacted entirely on impulse. He backed away, whipping out his own gun and firing back as Richard shot at him. Somehow, Matt evaded his bullets and ran into the opposite alleyway. The bullets hit the concrete wall beside him.

"Shit," Matt said. Suddenly two arms broke through the window behind him, grabbed him, and hauled him backward. Matt was too shocked to mount an effective defensive as the frame smacked against his head. He landed ungraciously on the floor, and jumped back to his feet a second later.

A woman with messy blond hair, wearing a nightgown, grabbed a knife and held it up. Seeing him, she breathed a sigh of relief. "You're here. The heralds have come," she said.

'Is everyone in this town goddam crazy?' Matt thought, taking out his gun. "Stay back!" he bellowed. "I don't want to hurt you!"

Instead of retreating, the woman grinned at him, and raised her knife. "Bring me to the light." She ran screaming toward him. Matt shot her straight in the head and instantly glanced at the window he had just broken through. Next to the police car, Ryan lay unmoving on the ground, partially buried by snow. Alive? Dead? He didn't know. There was still no sign of Richard...or Lindsay.

"*What the hell is happening?*" Jeff demanded.

Matt turned on his radio. "Jeff, get vitals on Ryan and Lindsay. Are they okay?"

"*Something's wrong,*" Jeff said, followed by static. "*We're losing your signal. I—*" The static became too loud to hear him.

"Jeff?" Matt demanded. "Fuck."

Another police car pulled up, and three officers stepped out—two men and a woman. They took out their guns and fired at the open window. Matt jerked away as the bullets ricocheted off the windowsill. He drew his own gun and fired back. Dammit, he couldn't get a clear shot at any of them, and he was running out of bullets fast. There were spare guns in the car, but it was impossible to get to them. .

Suddenly, he heard a soft 'ping' as something rolled into the room. A grenade! Matt immediately ran out the door and into the hallway, which thankfully appeared empty. A second later, the explosion blew the door clear off its hinges.

Matt struggled to breathe. Behind him, the grenade had caused a fire, and the damn cops continued to fire from the next window. He quickly entered another apartment and slammed the door shut. He needed to get out of here. There had to be a back way out!

The side door to the bedroom opened, and a young couple stepped out, also with knives. "Kill him," the man whispered. "It must become stronger." With a collective howl, they ran straight for him.

Matt didn't hesitate, and fired three times. They collapsed to the ground. Matt looked at the bodies and trembled a little. It stuck him like a lightning bolt that he was killing people. Sure, he did the same thing during the war, but that felt like a lifetime ago. He coughed as he reentered the hallway. Smoke gathered around him, burning his vision. Why couldn't he find the exit?

The floorboard above his head trembled as someone ran above it. A second later, a man fell down the steps, screaming and clutching his bloodied head. He didn't get up again.

Lindsay walked down the steps. "Come on!" she demanded.

Matt followed blindly after her. She led him into a room on the third floor and he shut the door. "We can't stay here for long," he said. The floorboards burned under his fingertips, and already he could see smoke.

Calmly, Lindsay grabbed two towels, doused them in water, and placed them under the door.

Matt tried Jeff on the radio, without any luck. He turned it on again. "Ryan, do you copy?"

No response.

"Shit, he might be dead."

"No, he took it in the chest. His Kevlar would have stopped that," Lindsay said, opening the window with a grunt of effort.

"They probably noticed that and finished him off," Matt said.

"Fuck you. We have to find him!" she said, looking at him with such anger that he was caught off-guard. When Stephan had died, she barely batted an eye. But this…

"Why? Why do you care so much? I thought you hated him!" Matt demanded.

"Fuck off. Now's not the time to get into it!"

"Lindsay!" Matt snapped, gripping her shoulder.

"He's my brother, okay!" she snapped. "So with or without you, I'm checking. And if he is dead, then those cops will not leave here alive."

Matt took a deep breath. He had a feeling there was more to this story—much more—but now wasn't the time to pry. "Okay. Let's find him."

They both climbed out the window into the adjacent metal grating of the fire escape. Matt breathed in the cold, crisp air, never more thankful to be out of there. They both ran down the steps onto the snowy concrete, and he looked up at the burning building. He couldn't hear any screams, but he was sure people were dying. "We have to try and help them."

"We're not part of the fire brigade," Lindsay snapped. "Let's focus on our own problems."

Matt said nothing, torn with indecision. Lindsay did have a point, the people did attack them first. Feeling sick, he stepped forward.

"Help me," a tiny voice pleaded.

Matt stopped, and glanced to the left. Pressed up against a closed window was a kid, the very damn kid he had seen earlier with the shopping bag. He didn't look very different from his own daughter. She was sobbing, and appeared to be alone. Behind her was a wall of fire.

"Matt!" Lindsay snapped,

"Can you get the window open?" Matt asked.

"The latch is stuck! I can't get it!" the girl cried out, panicked, then started to cough.

"Get back from the window," Matt said. As she hesitantly stepped to the right, he grabbed a nearby brick and smashed it open. He gestured. "Come here, sweetie. It's going to be okay."

Sniffing, the girl ran toward him, and he helped her out of the window. "You'll be all right. I'll help you find your parents—"

Too late, he saw the girl grab a gun from her belt. "It has to feed!" she screamed.

"Get away from him!" Lindsay screamed.

Matt moved to stop her, just as the gun went off. The next thing he saw was a bright flash.

Then pain.

Lindsay's hand automatically reached for her handgun and she aimed it at the girl. But no matter how hard she tried, she just couldn't do it. She couldn't murder a child. Instead, she angrily took three steps forward, grabbed the gun from the girl's hand, and slammed the butt of her own gun against the girl's forehead. The girl fell soundlessly in the snow and didn't get up again.

Guilt seeped through her body as she stared at Matt. She was supposed to protect them, and have their backs. First Stephan, than Ryan, and now Matt. "Fuck," she whispered, running toward him. "Matt? Are you okay?"

Matt wasn't conscious. The fucking kid had aimed at his head. Lindsay felt for a pulse. He was still alive, but his head was bleeding. She glanced nearby and saw a bullet casing in the snow, with a few drops of blood. Thank God. If the bullet had entered his skull, Lindsay was sure he would be dead.

"There they are!" a voice shouted behind her. Lindsay turned around, where a single man was pointing with a baseball bat. She raised her gun, and his body jerked forward as bullets impacted his body. He fell.

Lindsay blinked in surprised. She didn't do that.

A woman stepped over the man and walked toward her. She wore blue jeans, and a brown leather jacket. Her short red hair was tied back in a ponytail.

Lindsay aimed her gun. "Stay back!" she warned. "Or I swear to God I will kill you."

The woman, whoever she was, put her gun away and raised her hands harmlessly. "You're D.R.E.X, right? It figures. Newbies."

"Who the hell are you?" Lindsay demanded.

"My name is Anna. I'm not here to hurt you." She gestured right behind her. "My truck's right over there. I can get you out, but if you don't hurry, we're going to get overrun."

Lindsay swore, but knew she was right. Already she could hear shouting in the distance. "My brother—we need to help him too."

"Where is he?" Anna asked.

"At the front of the building."

The woman shook her head, the movement causing clumps of snow to fall from her hair. "No. There are too many of them. If he is there, then he's dead." She placed a hand on Lindsay's shoulder. "We need to go."

Lindsay stared at Matt's body, torn with indecision. A flash of anger struck her as she thought about Ryan. But Matt was right in front of her, bleeding and unconscious. Reluctantly she stared at Anna, and nodded. "All right. I'll trust you. For now."

"I'm so glad," Anna said sarcastically.

Ryan opened his eyes to the red-and-blue flashing of a police cruiser. Instantly he closed them again. He wasn't able to see much, but he was lying right beside the front tire. There were three cops in front of him, talking. Despite probably being out for only a couple of minutes, a few good centimeters of snow had piled on him already. He could see his gun in the snow, on the opposite site of the car. He might be able to get it if he crawled under the car. Might. As tempting as it was, he didn't try it. He didn't move at all.

"What a fucking mess," one of the cops said. "Anyone ever heard of D.R.E.X?"

"I think I have," a woman's voice replied. "Years ago. Does it matter? The end of days is here." She paused. "Do you think more will show up?"

"Fuck yeah, especially if we don't catch those other two. The more the merrier, I say. What about the Kat-su?"

"They won't find it," the woman replied. "If they try—"

"The whole city will take arms," the third replied. "We might not win, but the Kat-su will have enough power." The man hesitated, and repeated more firmly, "Yeah, there'll be enough. Let's deal with the body."

Ryan could hear the crunching of snow toward him. His right hand was still in plain sight, and he once again overrode the overwhelming temptation to move it. He had landed on his left hand, however, which was obscured from view. Very slowly, he reached for the knife in his belt.

Abruptly, he felt a sharp sting in his leg as someone booted him experimentally. He didn't react at all. As he grabbed the hilt of his knife, Ryan heard a sigh from the woman and two hands reach for his chest. "Wait, where's the blood?"

Ryan opened his eyes and saw her briefly—a young, blond woman in her twenties—before plunging the knife right into her throat. His aim was slightly off, and he buried the knife in the tender area between her neck and her shoulder instead. He yanked the knife away as she fell back, choking. Blood gushed between her fingers. "Check there."

As another cop reached for his gun, Ryan threw the knife at the second man's chest just as the third man opened fired. He dived on the opposite side of the police car as glass exploded above his head. Quickly he crawled underneath the car, toward his gun. Just as he reached for it, a foot clamped down on his wrist. The third man had a gun pointed right at his head.

"You're dead, motherfucker," the man said.

Quick as a flash, Ryan reached for a switchblade in his pocket and slammed it into the man's ankle. The man howled in agony and fell backward into the snow. His hand free, Ryan grabbed the gun from the snow and aimed. Without hesitation, he fired.

The police stared at him with an almost puzzled expression in his eyes, a bullet hole between his eyes. Then he fell backward.

Breathing hard, Ryan surveyed the area, but didn't see anyone else. He struggled to his feet. "Damn," he whispered. It was getting hard to breath. He opened his bulletproof vest, and touched his black shirt. The bastard had shot him not once but three times. There were going to be some good bruises forming tomorrow, assuming he lived that long. He looked around for Matt or Lindsay, but didn't see either. He did notice, however, the blond woman stumbling toward an alleyway, her shirt covered in blood.

Ryan walked toward her, stopping only to grab a spare gun from the ground. The woman gave a small cry as she stumbled into a pile of trashcans, and braced herself against the wall. She whimpered in pain. He caught up with her easily. "Look, I really don't want to hurt you more than I already have," he said, wiping away the sweat from his head. "But I need to know what's going on here."

"What's going on?" the woman echoed, and gave him a sickly grin. "You will cause the end of days, you and your friends." She gripped the wet stone behind her. "Everyone knows this. But you won't make it out of here. The Kat-su will burn you alive." Screaming, she lunged at him.

"Cheerful," Ryan said, and pulled the trigger. She didn't get up again. With another wince, he tried his radio. "Lindsay. Matt, can you hear me?"

Nothing but static answered back.

"Fucking useless equipment," Ryan muttered, and looked up at the burning building. "I sure hope Jake Burns wasn't in there."

After getting off the main streets, Ryan approached a warehouse with an empty parking lot. He kept his gun drawn and pressed his ear against the door. Nothing. He kicked down the door and entered a car shop. A quick sweep of his gun and flashlight told him that the staff had definitely gone home for the day.

His radio didn't work. He took out his cell phone, which still flashed 'No signal.' He was completely cut off from D.R.E.X. He checked his ammo. Five bullets left.

He slid down to his knees, again feeling the bruises against his chest. According to his watch, it was three-thirty. If he tried to get out of the town now, someone could easily spot him. He would barricade the door, and rest a few hours until dark.

Matt awoke to the overwhelming smell of wet hay, and the tapping of rain against a wooden roof. He opened his eyes, and found himself lying in a barn.

A hiss of pain escaped his lips as he sat up and touched his forehead, where he could feel a few stitches poking out under a small plastic bandage He wasn't entirely sure what hit him, but it hurt. A lot.

The only illumination came from a lamp on top of a desk. A woman with short red hair was typing on a laptop. She wore a leather jacket and a white scarf, with blue jeans. Matt blinked, astonished for a moment. Who was she? How did he get here? His instincts kicked in and he looked for his gun, but didn't see it anywhere.

The woman stopped typing for a moment, long enough to lift a gun from the table. His gun. She put it back down.

Matt swallowed. Since it was painfully clear that she knew he was awake, he decided to talk. "Who are you?' he demanded. "Where am I?"

"Forty-eight miles from Devon, in my farmhouse," the woman replied. "I was able to get you and your friend Lindsay out."

"Are you a doctor?"

"I'm a lot of things," she replied, turning to face him. "I know who you are. What you are. Did Jeff ever tell you the reason why D.R.E.X closed down?"

"What?" Matt whispered, astonished that she knew so much. "Um…no."

"Well, that figures." The woman turned off the computer and stood. "I used to be part of D.R.E.X. Spent a good ten years there." She paused for a moment. "I'm sorry for your loss. Lisa spoke highly of you, Matthew."

"How do you know my name? Or hers?"

"I was at your wedding. The whole team was." She shook her head, her eyes glowing with amusement. "Not that I expect you to recall. We were the catering service."

Matt shook his head. "I remember that. The food sucked."

"I didn't say we were good caterers," the woman stated with a small smile.

Matt turned around, looking at the barn. "So why are you here? How did you know *we* were here?"

"It wasn't intentional," the woman said. She handed him his gun. "I…have a D.R.E.X radio that I left on. An old keepsake. You can imagine my surprise when I started to hear voices on it again a few weeks ago. It didn't take me long to realize that D.R.E.X was back, and headed toward Vermon." She rubbed the back of her hand. "I've suspected that there is something wrong with that town, which is why I wanted to warn you first. Unfortunately, I arrived too late. I'm sorry for your third friend—what was his name?"

"Ryan, and I haven't given up on him yet," Matt stated. "Why did those people attack us?"

The woman turned away, disturbed. "Honestly, I'm not sure. I've been there a few times for groceries, and I don't like going there myself. Sometimes the town feels too quiet. Other times... well, I know the people there, and some of them pretty well." She sat down in a wooden chair that creaked from the motion. "Or at least, I used to. But over the past few years, they seem 'barely there', if that makes any sense. They've made no effort to contact me. Whenever I try to see them, they always appear exhausted. Whatever friends I had in that town, we quickly fell out of touch. Then, when you arrived, the whole town went dark, according to my readings."

"What do you mean?" Matt asked.

"Well, the cell phone tower was shut down an hour ago, and road blocks are set up everywhere. And there's this." She moved her laptop around so he could see it. "Unusual power readings, all over the town. What exactly did you guys do?"

"Nothing—I mean, we were looking for someone. His name was Jake Burns, and we met his brother. When we asked about him, it seemed to work the entire town into a frenzy, all at once." He glanced back at her. "Where's my other friend? Lindsay?"

"Out back." The woman smiled. "She's barely left your side all night."

Matt frowned. "Wait—all night? How long was I out?"

"In total? Almost a day," the woman said.

Matt's eyes widened as this sunk in. He had to get back to town. Immediately. He grabbed his jacket and put it on. "If you were part of D.R.E.X one time, why didn't Jeff contact you? He must have known you were here."

The woman turned down the lantern. "We had a falling out. Years ago. He likes to pretend that I don't exist, and that works pretty well for me." She glanced at him. "Take some advice, Matt— you can't trust Jeff. And you can't trust D.R.E.X." She looked away. "Being in that place for too long...it's unhealthy."

Matt considered this. "What's your name?"

"I don't like giving people my name," the woman replied firmly.

Matt couldn't help but smile. "Well, I have to call you something. If you don't tell me I might have to call you something silly."

She hesitated, and finally sighed. "All right. My name's Anna."

Matt struggled to his feet. "So what do you normally do? Besides living in a barn, I mean?"

"Actually I live in the adjacent house, and I make a damn good living as a farmer," Anna snapped. "It is nothing to be ashamed of."

Matt raised his hands. "I didn't mean anything by it, Anna. I used to go door-to-door selling lights, before all of this all happened."

Anna blinked. "A salesman? I hate it when they call me."

Matt smiled. "So do most people."

Suddenly, the radio turned on. *"Matt? Are you there?"*

"It's Jeff," Matt said, almost in relief.

"I'll give you a moment alone with Jeff," Anna said. "I have chores to do anyway."

Matt hesitated, and turned on the radio. "Yeah, I'm here."

"Good. How are you doing? Lindsay tells me you took one hell of a clip to the head."

"Yeah, I'm fine," Matt said. "I'm at some woman's house—"

"Anna Bell. I'm surprised that she came to help, but she's a friend. You can trust her completely."

"She mentioned she used to be a member of D.R.E.X?'

"Yes, but it was a long time ago. Now she's retired. Knowing her, I'm sure she would like to keep it that way. Things must be pretty bad out there."

"It was a damned ambush. The whole town went crazy as soon as we mentioned Jake Burns," Matt replied.

"There's some kind of interference in that town. We can't get through it with our radios. The cell phone towers are out, and so are the landlines and the power. What the hell is happening? I read you

about forty miles from Devon. How did that happen? And where's Ryan? We still can't find him at all, and it's been over a day."

"He was caught in the cross-fire when the local police started shooting at us. I don't know if he's alive or dead."

"Okay. Matt, I want you to get out of there. I'm sending reinforcements."

Matt felt a twinge of irritation. "Negative on that. I'm going to find him—alive or dead."

"This is not your responsibility. You're not the leader on this, Matt."

"Someone has to be," Matt said.

For a moment, he thought Jeff would disagree. *"Okay, but you've got twelve hours. Otherwise, plan B."*

"Thanks," Matt said, and turned off the radio.

Anna closed the door, surprising him. He didn't hear her come in. "It's suicide to go back. For some reason they want to kill you in that town, and you could use more time to recover from your wounds."

"Probably," Matt agreed. His days in Afghanistan echoed back at him, days when the Taliban would fire non-stop at his men, and the only thing that kept them alive was a thin wall of concrete. "But I don't leave anyone behind. Ever."

Without waiting a reply, he left the barn.

He spotted Lindsay perched against the fence, watching the sunset. She barely glanced at him. "How are you feeling?"

"Better," Matt replied. He patted a cow to the right, which mooed slightly in protest. "Thanks. For staying behind with me. I'm ready to head out anytime."

Lindsay didn't reply.

Matt followed her gaze. "So Ryan's your brother, huh? I'm guessing not by blood?"

Lindsay snorted. "Please. He married my sister about two years ago. They separated about six months ago, but they are not officially divorced yet. So yes, technically Ryan is my brother-in-law."

Matt studied her. Lindsay was a tough woman to read, but he needed to try. "Is that why you hate him so much?"

"No," Lindsay said, and sighed. "I don't really want to talk about it."

"Okay," Matt said. "Then tell me how you both joined D.R.E.X?"

"Also something I don't want to talk about," Lindsay snapped, turning to leave.

"Lindsay," Matt touched her shoulders, making her tense. "I barely know anything about you. Give me something, okay?"

Lindsay studied him, and finally broke free of his gasp. "I don't like anyone touching me. *Especially men*," she said.

"I…sorry," Matt stammered.

She lifted her hands to her face. "No, don't be. I didn't always live like this, Matt. I used to be a real estate agent, and a damn good one. I was on my way to the top." She smiled, briefly. "And, I used to be an artist. Not a terribly good one, but a few of my pieces ended up in shows. Every now and then, I sketch on the plane to pass the time."

"Then what happened?"

Lindsay's gaze hardened. "Then my husband broke my arm and called me a nigger cunt, and I couldn't draw for three months. One of many wounds over the three years we were married." She smiled, but there was no mirth to it. "It's funny, given the world today. Yet, old racism, like the color of your skin, can still exist. I broke ties with my abusive husband, after a couple of years, and everyone else. I traveled to the Yukon. It seemed…quiet. Nice. No one could bother me anymore." She frowned. "Until my sister called."

Yukon, February30, 2013

It was a clear, perfect day in the Yukon, and Lindsay could see the field of white for what seemed like miles. She braced herself down on a cold snow bank and aimed her rifle at a buck, which was occupied with eating a bush. Unfortunately for him, it was the last meal he would ever eat. The thought of killing the animal didn't give Lindsay any regret. Food was scarce around here. She lived in a small cabin a few miles from the city, and didn't interact much with the locals except for a Native American reserve where she would occasionally trade supplies. The buck alone would be a lot of work, but it would keep her going for at least a week.

Suddenly, her satellite phone rang. She swore at it, and looked down her scope. Fortunately, she was far enough way that the noise didn't startle the deer. She glanced once at the call display, and turned it on. "Suzanne. Not the best time."

"*How are you?*" Suzanne asked. Her estranged sister had barely spoken to her, besides the occasional Christmas holiday, an event in itself that was incredibly awkward for Lindsay.

Lindsay adjusted her sniper rifle. "I'm fine. Why did you call me? I'm sure it's not to make a social call. What's wrong?"

"*Do you always have to be so…can't you just be happy to see me?*"

"The battery on this phone is running low, sis. I'm not sure how much charge it has left."

"*It's Ryan,*" Suzanne finally admitted. "*I think he's missing. He hasn't contacted me in weeks.*"

Lindsay frowned. The buck was almost in her sights. Just one move to the left… "Are you sure he isn't trying to run out on his bills?"

"*We both know what's at stake,*" Suzanne whimpered.

That much was true, Lindsay silently conceded. Despite her hatred for her brother-in-law, it really didn't sound like Ryan. She pulled the trigger, and the buck fell. "So you need a tracker."

"*I need a sister willing to look for her brother!*" Suzanne snapped. "*Doesn't family mean anything to you?*"

Lindsay holstered her weapon and walked towards the kill. The buck glanced lazily at her, a line of blood running from his chest. She aimed for his heart, but missed slightly and now he was suffering. She leaned forward with her knife and cut his throat.

"He barely qualifies," she muttered, and snapped her knife shut. "But I'll do it."

"*Thank you,*" Suzanne said. "*Thank you. Thank you!*"

Lindsay smirked. "The way you're going on, sis, one might think you're actually worried about him. We both know why we need him."

She hung up before Suzanne could reply. She knew what her younger sister would say anyway.

Lindsay hated Chicago. In the Yukon, one could track easily with a boot print in the mud or snow, or a broken twig. One could seldom interrupt Mother Nature without leaving a mark. But in the city, anyone could override any signs a person made. Concrete effectively wiped away any boot prints, someone's intoxicating perfume could destroy a target's scent. Not to mention, Lindsay just hated the thought of so many people crammed together, about to explode. Chicago was the worst place for claustrophobia. And there was just something in the air that made her wince in distaste. The smog, perhaps. How could her brother live in a place like this? For that matter, how could anyone else?

Not that she knew much about Ryan, and she preferred to keep it that way. The one time she had met him at a family gathering, he had shown up drunk out of his mind. That told her everything she needed to know.

Suzanne had provided her with the address: a run-down apartment among a hundred other run-down apartment buildings in a twenty-block radius. She walked up three steps to the glass door and peered through. The interior hallway had a web of cracks along the wall, a dirty carpet, and a woman smoking a joint near the mailbox. With an irritated sigh, she approached the back door instead.

"Hey baby, got a smoke?" a homeless man outside the alleyway asked.

Not in the mood to be civil, Lindsay flipped him the bird. If he tried to attack her, she would break his arm. Fortunately for him, he didn't make any more advances toward her. She focused on the locked door. A simple hairpin got her inside.

Within minutes, she arrived at Ryan's apartment. Inside was everything she expected from her brother—a single, cheap, bachelor pad with a trashcan filled with empty cans of beer and caffeine. The fridge was almost empty except for condiments. Nothing had been cleaned, at least not for a while. Clearly, Ryan hadn't achieved much in the world.

Lindsay stood in the center of the room. She studied the obvious, but Suzanne had brought her here to study the not so obvious. Her eyes zeroed in on the carpet underneath the computer. A single impression was in the floor, one made from a chair in a fixed position. Yet the chair itself was a couple of feet away. She moved next to the computer and inhaled. She could detect a strong odor of chemicals—someone had cleaned the computer recently, in a room where nothing was clean. The smell itself was more potent near the white keyboard. She picked it up, and spotted a single brown spot between the 'w' and 'e' key. Could be blood.

As she studied the stain, it slowly dawned on her for the first time that her brother might not have left the apartment voluntarily. But why? She turned around. It might take some time, but the tiny cramped apartment had now become her blueprint to answering that question, probably containing dozens of secrets she had yet to discover.

Just because she hated tracking in the city didn't mean she couldn't.

Matt helped Lindsay lift a box onto a blue pick-up truck parked near the front of the house. Even though the box was heavy, Lindsay handled the load without any complaints at all. He watched as her muscles rippled against the strain. "So you actually tracked down D.R.E.X?"

"It took me a few months. They are professionals, but things happened after his disappearance, which provided even more clues.

Eventually I pieced some of it together. I finally caught up to Ryan in…Volos, I think," she replied as they loaded the box into the back.

Matt scratched his head, but couldn't recall his geography. "Where's that?"

"In Greece. He was working a case for Jeff. I found him while he was chasing these horrible creatures. I try not to think about them. It didn't take me too long to get wrapped up in D.R.E.X, the portal, and everything else." She smiled a little, but it was a bitter smile. "I was happy in the Yukon, and Ryan took me away from it."

"Is that why you hate him so much?" Matt asked.

"One of many reasons, I suppose, but not the main one," Lindsay said, but did not elaborate.

After a few moments of awkward silence, Matt decided to try another question. "So let me get this straight—Ryan never actually volunteered to join D.R.E.X?"

"No one does," a voice said behind them. Anna. "Jeff usually recruits people by blackmailing them somehow. What does he have over your brother?"

Lindsay glanced at her, annoyed. "I appreciate the help, but I really don't know you. So why don't you mind your own fucking business?"

Anna studied her. "So it's the same thing he has over you. Okay."

Lindsay frowned. She opened her mouth to say something, but Matt decided to interrupt.

"We're wasting time," he said as he closed the back. "Thanks for the weapons, but I'm going to need the truck as well. I'll make sure D.R.E.X compensates you."

All of a sudden, Anna gripped his arm. "Lisa thought the portal might open again. Has it?"

"Not yet. That's what I'm trying to prevent," Matt replied. "You could help me."

Anna shook her head and folded her arms. In the distance, they could hear a rooster crowing. "Why should I? You have nothing to offer me, and I really don't need any help from cannon fodder. That is really all you two are, you know. It's the reason Jeff hired you."

"Have it your way," Matt said with a shrug. He got into the driver's seat and felt a sudden wince of pain. It felt like his head had been pounded twenty times by a sledgehammer, but he had to keep going.

Anna opened the door, making him jump. "Move over. I'm driving," she said.

"I thought you said—" Matt began.

Anna gave him a furious look. "Let me make one thing clear. I don't care anything about your friend or your situation."

"Then why are you doing this?" Matt asked as she started up the truck.

Anna shifted to first gear. "This is my favorite truck. It's going to take us two hours to get back. Let's hope your friend can last that long."

CHAPTER 7

Ryan stirred to consciousness, and his eyes focused on a dark, half-disassembled Porsche right in front of him. It was quiet, and the air reeked of oil. Right. The machine shop. He didn't mean to fall asleep. He glanced at the watch, and his eyes widened as he saw the date. "What the hell?" It was a day later, but that couldn't be right. The watch must have skipped ahead or something. He stood, and his limbs cracked from the motion. Suddenly, he was aware of something on his face and wiped it away. Dried blood. A nosebleed? He never had one for as long as he could remember. He turned on the radio. "Jeff?"

Nothing but silence answered back.

With a shake of his head, Ryan stood up and opened the door.

The street to the left and right were empty. He stepped outside cautiously, expecting to be sniped at any moment. Much to his shock, he couldn't see anybody, or hear anything. "Crap," he whispered. This was more than just too easy. It felt like the entire town had vanished, which couldn't be a good thing. Well, there was nothing to gain from waiting around, but he also had a sneaky suspicion he was walking into a trap.

He kept to the shadows as he walked down a couple of blocks, indirectly backtracking to the original location of the apartment building. As he expected, the whole building was now a charred mess, and barely stood on exposed metal beams. Fortunately, the fire didn't seem to spread to any other buildings. The firefights must have done a good job, which would make more sense if he were actually asleep for a day and not a few hours.

Ryan tried not to think about it. Where was everybody? Ryan whirled around, but he couldn't see a light on in any single building. "What the fuck?" he whispered in astonishment.

He drew his gun as he heard a sudden noise from behind an exposed beam. He circled around to see a woman with blond hair hunched over a pile of ashes. She wore a black skirt, a white blouse, and didn't appear to be armed. As Ryan watched, she released a deep sigh and stood.

"Turn around," Ryan ordered. "Hands where I can see them."

She obliged, yet didn't look afraid. If anything, her green eyes were full of amusement. "Nice gun."

"Who are you?" Ryan demanded.

"Catherine Simone. I'm a journalist. Are you a cop?"

"No," Ryan replied.

"So why are you holding a gun?"

"Look lady, I ask the questions around here, all right?" Ryan snapped. He gestured at the wreckage. "What are you doing here?"

Catherine shot him an *'are-you-kidding'* look. "This used to be my home. I was on assignment in Serbia for two weeks. When I came back…" She gestured and sighed. "Where is everybody?"

Reluctantly, Ryan lowered his gun. "That's what I'm going to find out."

"Who are you?"

"Adam Anderson," Ryan said. Lies and aliases came to him so easily nowadays. "I just moved in too. Lost everything. Bad time to forget to sign up for tenant's insurance."

Catherine folded her arms, amused. "So again, why do you have a gun?"

"Because most people in America do." Ryan put away the gun. "Look Catherine, I'm sorry for doing that. I'm just a little jumpy, but something strange is going on here."

"Strange?" Catherine raised an eyebrow. "What do you mean?"

He ignored the question as he spotted the rental car they had driven into town. He opened up the truck, but the weapons were gone. "You should get out of here. Willows is only a half-hour drive—"

"Uh-uh. No way. This is the story of the lifetime. I'm going to find out what's happening here, with or without your help. Not even you pointing a gun at me is going to change that."

Ryan swore under his breath. The safest thing to do would be to knock her out, tie her up, and stash her somewhere out of the way. He had done it before, when people were too curious. But as she gave the white ashes a horrified glance, he couldn't help but feel a tad responsible. Besides, someone local might be useful. "All right. But the nearest sign of trouble, you bail. Clear?"

"I'm a journalist, Adam. I wouldn't get much of a story if I fled from danger," Catherine said. "But I'll take what you said under advisement."

Ryan made a mental note to destroy her cameras after he was done with her. "Let's start at the police station. Know the way?"

"Yeah," she said. "That your car?"

"I would rather walk, if it's all the same to you," Ryan said. Attracting noise would be a very bad idea.

Catherine was about to say something, then thought better about it. "All right then. Follow me."

For a few minutes, they walked in silence. While the streetlights were on, every single shop and building was pitch-black, without any signs of life. Ryan thought of sticking to the alleyways, before giving up. Either someone would attack him or they wouldn't. He almost hoped they would. The silence was getting on his nerves.

"Why do you want to go to the police station?" Catherine asked, breaking the silence.

"I'm looking for a man named Jake Burns. Or his brother, Richard. He's a police officer."

"Jake Burns? Why are you after him?"

Ryan shot her a quick look. "Do you know who he is?"

Catherine ran a hand through her blond hair. "No…not really. I only saw him once, near the grocery store. He looked like a homeless guy, so at first I didn't pay much attention. But the man looked terrified. Before I could ask if he needed help, his brother Richard drove up and told him to get in the car. Richard gave me a dirty look too, but then, he was usually an asshole anyway."

Ryan touched his chest. "No arguments there," he muttered under his breath.

"It took me a while to piece the family resemblance. What's your interest in him?"

"I have a couple of questions I want to ask him about the fire," Ryan replied evasively.

"Why? Do you think he's responsible?"

"Something like that." He glanced at her. "Have you always lived here?"

Catherine studied the dark, empty street. "Not until recently. What about you?"

"Seattle," Ryan said. Another lie, but a much smaller one.

"Why did you move here, of all places?"

"I needed a change of scenery. Took a job as a mechanic," Ryan said.

Catherine blinked in surprise. "Huh. I didn't think Sedwick would hire someone else. But then, he is getting pretty old."

"That he is," Ryan agreed, without knowing who that person is.

"So are you seeing someone?" Catherine asked.

"Huh?" The question caught him off guard.

"Sorry—this place is making me a little nervous," Catherine said with a smirk. "I'm just making conversation."

Ryan thought about it as they passed a bookstore. "No one I really consider important to me," he said carefully.

She laughed. "You really can't seem to give me a yes or no answer, Mister Anderson. Are you always this vague?"

"I guess you got me there," Ryan admitted. *Ah what the hell.* "I'm working on getting a divorce with my wife. There is really nothing between us anymore. But other things keep getting in the way. What about you?"

"Single. I've had plenty of boyfriends, though, which isn't a bad thing." Catherine said.

Suddenly, they heard the sound of glass breaking. Catherine jumped as Ryan drew his gun. It came from a bookstore they just past.

"Stay here," he ordered. The door to the bookstore was locked, but it was easy enough to break into. He opened the door and entered a two level pitch-black room. To his left was a till, followed by several rows of bookshelves. No sign of anyone else, but he could hear...a strange creaking. Back and forth. He slowly looked up, and could see five bodies swinging on the rafters by their necks. Three women, a teenager and a boy. Dead.

Suddenly gunfire rang out, making him jump behind the till. Someone was above him! He fired back, but without a fixed target he was shooting blind. And he was running fast out of bullets.

A man appeared on the ledge, with brown grizzled hair and a beard. "What are you doing here?" he shouted, thumping the ledge with his hands. "It's time to go!"

Ryan aimed carefully at the man's shoulder and squeezed the trigger.

"Fuck!" the man shouted in pain, dropping the gun over the side. He disappeared back into the darkness. Ryan ran forward, grabbed the discarded gun, then hurried up the small staircase. He could see a small puddle of blood on the ground, but where...

He saw a flash to his left, and dodged as the man slammed a fire axe into the bookcase. Swearing, the man struggled to dislodge it.

Ryan aimed his gun. "Drop the axe!" he shouted. "Drop it!"

The man laughed hysterically. "*You* want me to live? I know what you are!" With a final tug, he dislodged the axe. Before the man could bring it to bare on him, Ryan shot him twice in the chest. The man slid to the ground.

He felt a light tap on his shoulder, making him jump. Catherine. "Are you all right?" she asked.

"Dammit, I told you to—" Before Ryan could finish the man chuckled, blood trickling down his mouth.

"The heralds," he whispered. "The heralds are here."

Ryan stepped forward. "Why the fuck do you keep calling me that?"

The man's dying brown eyes studied him. "It knows who you are. You and your friends. The herald who will save us, and bring the end of days. In the darkness, when there is nowhere left to run, you will know what to do. You will grant us…power." With a final sigh, he lowered his hand, revealing a grenade.

Ryan didn't think. "Get back!" he shouted at Catherine, pushing her off the railing. He managed to run to the left behind a bookcase as the grenade exploded. For a split second he could see burning wood flying at him, then he fell as the floor underneath gave away. He hit the back of his head, and blacked out. When he could see again, he had no idea where he was in the building or how bad he was hit. He couldn't move. Debris landed on top of him, and he could feel heat slowly building up. Suddenly, he was dragged backward. He felt weak, too weak to do anything besides keep his eyes open.

Catherine was dragging him past a burning, charred mess of wood. Around him, he could see several books on fire. The whole place would be up in cinders before too long. Strangely, Catherine's face was calm. Ryan struggled to breathe, and got a lungful of smoke for his efforts. Oh god…he needed fresh air, and fast.

All of a sudden, a woman screamed and ran toward them, holding a knife. Catherine dropped Ryan, whose arm landed with a small thud, dug into her purse, and took out a gun. She shot the woman once in the shoulder.

Ryan's eyes widened. *That's not my gun*, he thought. *Where did she…where…*

The woman fell out of his line of sight, and Catherine walked toward her. Suddenly Ryan heard a distinct ripping noise, and the woman screamed. Catherine laughed.

Everything went dark again.

"I need eyes on Vermon. What is causing the interference?" Jeff asked calmly from his underground command bunker in Devon. In front of him were three rows of computers with almost twenty operators in total. Men and women dedicated to one thing only—finding a way to access the damn town. "Some kind of lightning storm?"

"Negative, sir," one of the operators said. "Forecast is clear."

Jeff joined him. "Pull up the satellite imagery and cross-reference with thermal. Put it on the main screen." He studied the image, and gripped his mug tighter. Either the majority of the town was on fire, or something else was causing radically different heat levels.

He heard the door open behind him. "That's not normal," a voice remarked. Louise. "The patterns aren't consistent with a fire."

"Shouldn't you be working on the creatures found in Paris?"

"Smoke break," Louise said, taking out a cigarette and a lighter. "Do you mind?"

"Actually I do," Jeff said.

"Too bad." Louise lit up.

"Overlap it with the street map. See where the hottest point is," Jeff ordered the technician. He glanced at the new map. The hottest point seemed to be coming from the police station. He walked over to Louise. "Is our benefactor curious to see if I crack under stress? Is that why you're checking in?"

"I am a doctor, among other things," Louise said casually. "Just making sure your blood pressure can handle it. Are you going to bomb it?"

"What?"

"Vermon. Are you going to bomb it like you did Paris?" Louise exhaled a cloud of smoke.

Jeff shot him an irritated look. "Contrary to what you think, I don't destroy a town at the first sign of trouble. Especially with my people still in it." He sighed. "Right now I don't have nearly enough information to figure out what the hell is going on."

"Sir!" a female operator said. "I have access to the town's cameras."

Jeff turned around. Finally, a break. "All of them?"

"For now, sir. With the levels of interference we could lose the connection anytime."

"Triangulate on Ryan's satellite signal. See if you can find the closest camera."

She nodded. "I think I have it."

Jeff watched as she put the image on the screen. The camera footage was black and white with no audio, but he could see Ryan walking with a blond-haired woman. "Who is that?"

"She's got a name tag," Louise commented with a nod.

"Zoom in on that," Jeff ordered, tapping the operator's shoulder. A second later the title CATHERINE SIMONE-CSB WORLD NEWS was enlarged.

"Sir, there's no Catherine Simone listed in the CSB database," an operator to his far left reported before Jeff could even ask.

"Okay, I want a search through all of Vermon's government records—birth certificate, marriage, divorce, any employment anywhere. The rest of you not doing anything comb through the CIA database, FBI, NSA, Interpol and the rest. See if Catherine Simone is an alias to something else. I want this woman identified in ten minutes." He frowned as he stared at the camera footage. They were talking, but he couldn't figure out what they were saying. It didn't help that the footage was grainy. What were they saying to each other? "Record that and send it to be analyzed."

"I can lip read," Louise spoke up. "Hard to tell, but it looks like they are planning to go the police station."

They watched as they both stopped outside the bookstore. Ryan took a gun out, then walked in. Thirty seconds later Catherine stepped inside, just as the camera dissolved into static.

Shit, Jeff thought. At least he was still alive. "Do whatever you can to get control of the cameras again. You now have eight minutes to figure out who Catherine Simone is." He glanced at Louise. "My blood pressure is just fine, thank you."

For a time, all Ryan could see was red. His nose bled. Not just a small trickle, but gushing down his clothes, forming in a puddle below him. It wouldn't stop. Something had to be wrong with his brain. Ryan didn't mind. It was time for him to go—

"Gah!" Ryan's eyes snapped open to someone rifling through his pockets. With one hand, he shoved Catherine backward. With the other, he aimed his gun and removed the safety. They were outside, thankfully, and he drank in a cold breath of air. "What the fuck are you doing?"

Catherine raised her hands, but didn't look terrified. If anything, she appeared amused. "I was looking for your ID. Can't blame a journalist for being curious."

Absentmindedly he wiped his nose. No sign of any blood. Good. "I already told you who I am," Ryan said.

"Oh, please. You've been lying to me since the beginning." She smirked, her pink lipstick reflecting in the light. "I wasn't entirely sure until I tested you. Sedwick is only nineteen years old. Far too young to be in charge of a car shop, but he inherited early. If you really worked for him, you would know that. I'm almost glad in a way. You're too cute for a name like Adam Anderson."

Ryan struggled to his feet, keeping his gun level. "I'm not the only one who's lying. You're not just a reporter. Not with those instincts." He couldn't fully explain it, but nothing about this woman seemed real.

Catherine didn't seem the least bit worried. She laughed. "Adam, I'm sure that I'm more of a journalist than you are a welder."

"Who are you, really?" Ryan asked.

"Who are you?" Catherine retorted. "What's your real name?"

"You first," Ryan snapped. "Jesus, are you C.I.A? They're just the type of people to pull off this bullshit!"

-pulse-

Ryan screamed as a sharp pain ran up and down through his head. He couldn't help it. What the hell was happening to him? "Did you hear that? What the fuck was that?"

"You're sick," Catherine said, her eyes bright. *Too bright,* he thought. "You've been in this town for too long."

"What are you talking about?" Ryan said. The hand holding his gun trembled.

She stepped forward, her high heels echoing. "Since you're running out of time I'll make things very easy for you. I know you work for D.R.E.X, and I know why you are here. Maybe even better than you do."

Ryan frowned. "I'm looking for Jake Burns, to take him into protective custody."

"No, Adam. You may think you're looking for Jake Burns, but you're really not." Her hand gently brushed the gun to one side. "I am going to be as honest as I can be. I'm trying to help you."

"Why?" Ryan demanded. "Why do you want to help me?"

Catherine laughed and touched his cheek. "Now that, super spy, is something you need to figure out for yourself."

As Anna drove past a sign saying 'VERMON TWO MILES', Matt breathed a sigh of relief. The endless farmland gradually transformed into industrial buildings. He tried his radio again. "Ryan, do you read me?"

"I can't see anything," Lindsay murmured, glancing out the window at the dark street. "Not a light. This place is dead."

Nothing but a shrill whine answered back. Matt glanced at it in irritation. "Where did D.R.E.X get these, Lindsay? The toy store?"

"The problem isn't your equipment," Anna said. "Remember when I said there were unusual power readings coming from this town? It's causing electrical problems with everything—lights, cell phones, laptops, even the temperature."

"Oh my God," Lindsay suddenly said.

Matt looked out the window, and followed her gaze. "Anna, stop the truck!"

Anna obliged, and the three of them jumped out. Matt turned on his flashlight and lifted it up to confirm what he was actually seeing.

Three people were hanging from the telephone wire. Below the bodies, he could see three separate ladders, discarded on the road. He could just imagine what would happen once the power came on. Their bodies would just twitch and jerk until someone found them. Assuming someone ever did.

"Why would someone do that?" Lindsay asked.

"I…" Matt whispered, at a loss for words. "I don't know."

Through the binoculars, Ryan studied the police station.

It wasn't easy to get to a rooftop across from the one-story building. Twice they had to stop because of a migraine. He never got migraines, ever. Both times Catherine appeared amused, and she also looked…satisfied? He didn't get it, and his head was pounding too hard for him to figure it out. He just wanted to find Jake Burns and get the hell out of here.

"Damn. I don't see anyone," Ryan said, looking at the empty police station. "The lights are off."

"You feel like you have to go inside, don't you?" Catherine asked.

Ryan lowered the binoculars slightly. It was true, as much as he wanted to deny it. Even though he was looking at an ordinary, dark building, he couldn't shake the feeling that he had to get down there, and right away. "Is that where he is? Jake Burns?"

"Yes," Catherine said. "And the Kat-su."

"The what-what?" Ryan asked.

Catherine smirked. "The item which Jake Burns brought back from the portal years ago. That's what everyone wants, not him."

"Okay, why? What is it?"

"Only the most powerful and important object on this planet," she explained, looking through the binoculars. "Not to mention the most dangerous. Even now it's feeding."

"Feeding," Ryan echoed dubiously.

"You've felt it. Everyone in this town has. Especially when someone dies." She paused. "The Kat-su has been here for many years, soaking up energy from this town. Worse, it can reach out and touch the minds here, controlling them. And when someone dies…it gets a burst of power, power it needs."

Ryan took the binoculars again. "So you're saying…this thing down there can control me?"

"No. At least, not yet. But that will change the longer you are here, Adam. It'll grow stronger, and you'll grow weaker. After a while, you'll be just like everyone else. Wanting to die so it can feed." She glanced at him. "D.R.E.X's arrival has forced its hand. It wants to get as much power as it can, as soon as possible."

"For what? Why does this…Kat-su need all this power?"

Catherine didn't answer, but shrugged.

Ryan glanced back at the police station and decided to let it go for now. "No wonder we haven't seen anyone in this town. Jesus Christ, they're too busy killing each other." He glanced at her. "How do you know all this?"

"I'm one hell of a good journalist," Catherine stated.

"Uh-huh. Funny how you're not affected by any of this," Ryan noted.

"Yes," Catherine echoed. "Funny."

Ryan shook his head. "Is there any way I can save this town?"

"Yes," Catherine said. "I know your name is not really Adam. You don't trust me, but if you want to save the town, we need to get the Kat-su as far away from here as possible. It can't be near any living being."

Ryan glanced at the station again. "Look, lady, you want me to trust you? All right. Stay here. This is way too dangerous. I'll find Jake Burns, and this…Kat-su. After that, we can figure out a way to get out of this town. Together."

Catherine frowned. "Are you sure—"

"Yes." Ryan could feel the whispering in his mind, persuading him to go to the police station. The longer he waited, the more it gave him a migraine. "I'm sure."

A few minutes later, Ryan approached the police station. The parking lot was completely empty, even of patrol vehicles. The inside lights were switched off. Not good. He drew his gun and opened the door.

Inside he could see an empty reception desk, and several adjacent cubicles, which appeared to be empty. "D.R.E.X officer! Come out with your hands up!" Ryan demanded, but not one person answered. He instantly shifted to the left as two papers flew off the desk, then looked away. Even though the windows were wide open, the police station wasn't cold at all. If anything, it felt hot and murky. Experimentally he touched one of the walls, which burned against his skin. As he pulled his hand back, he noticed gray paint on his fingertip and realized the wall itself was melting. His heart pounded against his chest. Something definitely felt wrong.

His instincts screamed at him as he entered the next hall leading to the jail cells. All of them were open and empty. He shined his flashlight through one of them. An orange jumpsuit was neatly folded on the bench, but he didn't see anything else. At the very end of the hall, he could see a closed door with a padlock on it. The words 'EVIDENCE LOCKER' were highlighted above it.

He touched the door handle, which almost boiled to the touch. Ryan exhaled a red breath. God, this felt like some horrible nightmare. Worse, it felt like there was an electric—

(pulse)

—current running through the place. Ryan bit his lower lip. He slid the lock back and opened the door, revealing several rows of dark lockers.

At the very end of the room was a man—or what Ryan figured used to be a man. He appeared to be eighty years old, and didn't have a shred of fat on him. Ryan's flashlight only caught a glimpse of him, but long enough to see that his skin was yellow and sagging. There were also black patches on his face. From what, he couldn't tell. The man also appeared to be chained to the wall and holding something in his hands. That was all Ryan could see before nausea overloaded his senses and he almost collapsed to the ground. He braced himself against the wall. One time when he was a teenager, he had drunk twenty tequila shots and had to be taken to the hospital for alcohol poisoning. It felt like he was back in that situation, only much worse. He drew in a wheezy breath. "Jesus, that—"

Two hands grabbed his shoulders and hurled him backward. Before Ryan realized what was happening, someone grabbed his hair and slammed the front of his head against the bars to the open cell. For a second, Ryan's head exploded in stars as he slumped to the ground. Dazed, he took out his gun, which was kicked away.

Richard Burns was standing in front of him, staring at him with indifference. "You just couldn't stay away. You and your—" his mouth twisted in disgust, "—organization."

"Who..." Ryan tried to talk as he scrambled backward, which was far more difficult than he thought. "Who is that?"

"My brother. The man you were looking for. Jake Burns. I lied before. He never died," Burns said with no emotion in his voice. "I know. He looks more than a hundred." He studied his sibling for a moment, before closing the door to the evidence room. "I like to think one day he can forgive me. But honestly, there was no other alternative."

Desperately Ryan crawled toward his gun. Blood dripped from his head as he reached for it. "What the fuck do you mean?"

Richard booted him in the stomach, followed by kicking his weapon. The gun slid at the other end of the hallway. "My brother was a hero. Not that you could understand. All his life, he wanted to do something important. And he *stopped* it. Don't you understand? He stopped the portal."

Ryan gripped the metal bar of the cell and used it to stand up. "You mean back in 1999, in Devon," he said.

"Yeah. He went up that godforsaken mountain, and he saw things…monsters that threatened to destroy his sanity. He told me the story once. Want to hear it?"

"Not really," Ryan said honestly, and Richard grinned as he picked up a metal pipe.

"Sure. Bashing your brains in sounds just as fun." Richard lunged at him with the metal pipe. Ryan dodged to the left, and the pipe rebounded against the bars. Richard's arms trembled from the contact. Ryan turned away and lunged for the gun.

"You might be the herald, you might not. Doesn't matter either way. The end result will be the same. Everyone here will die tonight."

Finally, Ryan thought as he reached for the gun and brought it to bare. Just as he fired, Richard swung with the pipe, connecting with the gun in his hand. It went off in his hands, missing Richard entirely. Richard swung the pipe at Ryan's chest, and Ryan blocked with his arm, feeling something crack. Ryan lunged at Richard and punched him. Even though such a blow would normally knock out a man, it seemed to barely affect Richard, who grabbed him and head-butted him. Effortlessly, Richard tossed him to the floor.

"Everyone here *needs* to die tonight. The Kat-su needs the energy, immediately." He studied Ryan, perhaps wondering if he would try to get up. Deciding that he wouldn't for the time being, he began pacing. "Now let's talk about what happened in Devon so many years ago. My brother saw many creatures, some of which he could not even describe. One of those creatures spoke, and Jake said it felt like…maggots digging through his mind. He told me his body was trembling. He felt sick. His buddy, Ian, fainted on the spot, but my dear brother pressed on."

"Either the creatures didn't see Jake, or they didn't care. In the center of the cave, Jake saw this portal to another world. He told me the archway looked like 'devil's wings', ones that moved whenever he blinked. As for the inside…" Richard paused for breath.

By this time, Ryan had gotten his second wind back, but he was held entranced by Richard's story. How often would he hear an eyewitness account?

Richard sighed. "For the longest time my brother would not talk about what happened. Jake…you have to understand. Jake lost most of his sanity when he came back." He shot Ryan a look full of hatred, tears brimming in his eyes. "The trauma forced him to regress back to a child, and he stayed awake for weeks at a time. The rare time he did sleep, he would scream non-stop. Nothing I gave him would work. He didn't lose his mind from looking at those creatures. No, it's what happened next. On a pedestal in front of the portal, he saw some kind of book, glowing with power. The military bombarded the top of the cave. He said all of the creatures inside were screaming. The cavern shook, and Jake seized his chance. He ran to the portal, and grabbed the book."

"The Kat-su?" Ryan asked.

Richard didn't look at him, but he nodded. "Jake described what it felt like. Time and physics just weren't right. He said it was like his arms were stretched to an unimaginable degree. He could see his reflection in the portal, and it was laughing at him. He only had a brief glance at the other side. Another world, and dear god, it killed his mind. Most of it."

Richard glanced at him. "To this day, I still don't know why he brought it back here. Maybe he thought he was keeping it safe? Instead, he damned us. For so many years, the Kat-su fed on us. You would think that was bad…but it wasn't. Especially when someone died. Ben was first, I'm sure of it. That eighty-year-old coot's heart gave up when he was riding on a bicycle. But when he died, we could all feel it, followed by something powerful." He paused. "I…want to die too. I have to." He glanced at Ryan, a mixture of despair and longing dancing in front of his brown eyes. "What's happening to me?"

"Listen buddy," Ryan said. "We can stop this. Let me take it out of here—"

"Nah, I don't think so," Richard said. "You're here to ruin everything. I think I'll kill you instead." He paused. "Yeah, that's a good plan."

As he reached forward to boot him again in the chest, Ryan grabbed his ankle and twisted, forcing him to fall. Both men struggled to their feet, and Ryan grabbed his knife. It was damned hard to fight with a pounding headache, but he wouldn't go down so easily. Not by a long shot. As Richard reached for him, he swung wide with the knife, slashing the older man's arm. Richard screamed and backed away. Ryan lunged at him again with the knife. At the last second, Richard twisted, and the knife slammed into his shoulder instead of his chest. His eyes glowing with hate, Richard kneed Ryan in the head and punched him. Ryan drew back as pain exploded in his jaw. Richard jumped on him from behind.

"It can't leave town!" he shrieked insanely. "*Dakudus! Mortin!*"

The words meant nothing to him. "Get the fuck off me, you lunatic," Ryan snapped, slamming him backward against the wall. Richard's head snapped with the concrete. Ryan twisted around and choked him.

Richard struggled in his grip, but Ryan held on for what seemed like hours. Finally, the police officer gagged, then stared at him with dying brown eyes. "It's part of us all." He sagged in his arms, dead. Ryan released a red breath and lowered him to the ground.

-pulse-

Ryan cried out, but this time he could feel a brief surge of power, followed by pain in his head, and longing. The Kat-su had fed again by Richard's death, he was sure. And he was connected to it.

"I need to die," Ryan said quietly, but the words were disconnected from his mind. He wasn't thinking them, merely repeating a statement that was undoubtedly going around town. He still had control, for now.

For a moment, he sat there, overcome by fatigue. He had to keep moving. With a sigh, Ryan struggled to his feet and opened

NATASHA BENNET

the door to the evidence locker. Jake Burns didn't react at all to his brother's death, even though it was only meters away. He didn't even look up at him.

"Look, I know you probably can't understand me," Ryan began, and kicked open a chain-link gate next to him. He grabbed a backpack from a nearby shelf, along with a couple of guns. "But what I'm doing is for your own good. Trust me."

Jake didn't reply. Ryan glanced down at the book in his hands. The Kat-su. At first glance, it looked like nothing more than a closed book with a lock and a blank, brown cover. Ryan knew better. He reached his arm slightly, and his hand tingled with power. This was more than a simple book. Much more.

Ryan took the book from Jake, who offered no resistance. A small vibration ran through it, and through his body.

Suddenly Jake gave him a jaw-splitting grin, making him jump. Then, he slid to the ground. Ryan reached forward and felt for a pulse. Dead. Ryan stared at him, not without pity. Richard was right about one thing. This guy might have stopped the apocalypse years ago.

He deserved better.

He ran his hand over the Kat-su experimentally. It really did feel like a leather book, with a metal lock that ran around it. There wasn't any room for a keyhole, but it was a strange, circular design. It was probably a good idea not to open it either way. A small current of power was running through it. This thing was apparently responsible for opening the portal.

What else could it do?

Ryan didn't know, but he needed to get the Kat-su out of the town, and right away.

CHAPTER 8

They were approaching the city limits. Matt glanced to the left and right, but couldn't see anyone nearby.

"Matt, can you hear me?" Jeff's voice came in through the crackled radio.

Matt turned it on. "Go ahead."

"*You're almost…Zssss…out of range. We have a serious problem,*" Jeff said. "*We have some access to the cameras monitoring the town. The town is experiencing unexplainable temperature fluctuation, and it seems to be getting hotter by a few degrees. At first, I believed they were random, but now I've noticed a pattern. I've seen a few people commit suicide, and immediately following that the temperature fluctuates and goes up a few degrees. I think the two events are connected.*"

Matt frowned and turned on his radio. "What's causing it?"

"*Not sure yet. Ryan is alive, but all reports indicate that he is headed to the police station now, where the thermal readings seem to be the hottest. He might already be there. Go after him, but if you want my advice, don't kill anyone. Something tells me that will make things worse.*" Matt could hear more static on the radio. "*Also, there is…someone not…*" The rest dissolved into static.

"Jeff? Hello? Damn." Matt glanced at Anna. "Do you have anything non-lethal?"

She shrugged. "I have a stun-gun in the glove box when I needed to deal with Jehovah's Witnesses, but nothing else."

"Lindsay?"

"D.R.E.X doesn't usually take anything alive," Lindsay replied. "We did have a couple of options, but they were in the trunk of the rental."

"Shit. I'm sure they're gone by now." He turned to Anna. "You've been here before. Any gun stores?"

Anna tapped the steering wheel thoughtfully. "Yeah, one a few blocks from here. Hopefully your friend can hold out a bit longer."

Gun drawn, Ryan ran back into the reception area, and stopped dead in his tracks. Standing just outside the door, almost pressed against the glass, were people. Dozens that he could see, including children. They weren't trying to force open the door, which he knew for a fact he had left unlocked. They didn't appear angry at all. They were just…standing there. Waiting.

Ryan froze. He wasn't the type to spook easily, but after seeing them like that, he wanted to scream in terror. Something about that just felt so wrong. Worse, he knew he was a ridiculously easy target. But they could afford to be patient—he had nowhere else to go besides out. Once he opened those doors, they could very well tear him apart.

"The herald," one man whispered. His lips were white.

"The herald," a woman echoed.

"The herald," a child added. Soon they are all chanting.

"The time is here!" another man shouted. "The time is now!"

Ryan ran back into the opposite hallway. He felt an irrational sense of relief as the door slammed shut and he slid to the ground. Quickly he reached over and locked it, then glanced back at Richard's still body. He released a deep, red-tinted breath.

'It's not the first time you've murdered before,' a voice whispered in his mind. 'You killed Simon Jones. The man was guilty of a lot of things, but not killing Matt's wife. Yet you slit his throat like a pig, put him in the trunk of a car, and lit it on fire. You've killed others, people more innocent than him. How many more crimes will you commit, Ryan? In her name? All your life you've done more harm than good.'

Ryan trembled. He knew this had to be the Kat-su, working on him. He wanted to get up, to run out of the hall. Yet, he couldn't find the strength in his legs. He was trapped in the dark, with a rotting corpse, and no way out.

And he knew what to do. Or rather, what the Kat-su *wanted* him to do. He lifted it in horror, blood dripping from the closed pages, onto his hands. Thankfully, he was wearing gloves, but even though his bare skin hadn't touched the damn thing, it felt like his proximity was enough. He knew it wasn't an actual book, not really. This Kat-su, or whatever it was, burned against his body. D.R.E.X had procedures for touching an unknown artifact. Most involved running the hell away, which wasn't really an option right now. He knew it wanted him to open fire on the crowd, killing as many people as he could. But he would save one bullet, so he could shoot himself in the head. With so many deaths at once… the Kat-su would gain insurmountable power. More than enough.

But enough for what?

He didn't know. He wasn't sure he *ever* wanted to know. But it would happen soon.

The door pounded once. They were trying to break in. Tears of frustration ran down his eyes. Kill, or be killed. There was only one other option. Kill himself now, and minimize the chance of casualties.

"God help me," he whispered, looking at his gun. He wouldn't kill these people. No matter what.

Ryan tried his radio act. Last desperate act of a dying man. "Matt? Can you hear me?"

At first he couldn't hear a reply, but then he heard… something. He tried again. "Matt?"

Suddenly he screamed as he heard a noise that was a higher pitch than anything that seemed possible. It wasn't coming from the radio—it was from the Kat-su! Above him the glass shattered and exploded, showering him with shards. He slammed his hands to his ears as blood dripped from both of them. '*What the fuck is that?*' was the last coherent thought before he fell to the bloodstained concrete floor, praying that the sound would just go away. After what felt like an eternity, it did.

Ryan shakily stood to his feet, aware that he couldn't hear anything, not even the snapping of his own fingers. "Fuck," he whispered, and stumbled toward the stairwell. He needed to get out of here!

The door to the roof was locked, but one good kick took care of that. He walked to the edge of the roof. He knew it would be bad, and he wasn't disappointed. Almost fifty people were standing below him, looking up. At first, he couldn't understand what they were shouting, but gradually his ears began to clear. "*Shoot us! Shoot us! Shoot us!*"

"Shut up!" he snapped, and tried the radio. "Matt?" he asked in a small voice. "If you're out there I could really use your help."

No response. The radio was completely fried.

To his horror, he realized that people were dying even if he didn't do anything. As he watched, a man whirled around and began to strangle his wife. He raised his gun, but didn't have a clear shot with the crowd. The woman slipped to her knees and didn't get up again.

"Ugh," Ryan whispered as a charge built up from the *Kat-su* and through his body. He would give anything to just drop it and run. Where he would run to, Ryan had no idea, but anywhere was better than here. But it felt like being tied to an electrical current—he just physically couldn't do it.

The book in his hands was not just bleeding, it was gushing bucketfuls of the stuff, which formed in pools around him, and on his clothes. As he watched in horror, the lock around the book started to spin, and with a solid click, the book unlocked. As the pages spilled open, Ryan could see the air above him start to sparkle.

Below him, the young D.R.E.X officer could hear more people screaming in pain. He barely noticed as he stepped back and stared at the pages. Words he couldn't understand were written in dark, red ink. Or perhaps blood. He was confident that despite his ignorance of the language, he could still speak them, and something would happen. It wasn't enough that these deaths were happening. Someone still had to speak the words. But which page—

Suddenly, Ryan felt something connect against the back of his shoulder—a flying kick. He wasn't prepared for it at all and went sprawling to the ground. The Kat-su flew out of his hands. Ryan jumped to his feet a second later, and took out his gun.

"I said you would need my help," Catherine said in front of him, calmly picking up the Kat-su. Where had she come from? "You can't form a portal here," she added. "Certain conditions have to be met, and they're not. Still, to speak those words from the book... even one of them, would be disastrous."

Ryan aimed his gun, having no idea what she was talking about. "What are you...I wasn't...give it back!" he stammered.

Catherine seemed to be reading his mind. "Are you saying that because you honestly want to save this town, Adam? Because if you do, then having this book is the last thing you want."

Ryan honestly couldn't answer.

"Thought so." She stepped forward. "I like you, Adam, I really do. But I can't let you bumble around with this any longer."

Ryan shook his head, as some of his thoughts began to clear. "You're not human. Are you?"

Catherine smiled, a sad smile. "No." She reached forward and kissed him. For a moment, his mouth was filled with the taste of watermelon from her gum. Then, with a smirk, she pushed him off the roof.

Ryan expected to fall straight into a crowd of people who would tear him from limb to limb. What he did not expect, however, was to land in the back of a pick-up truck. He rebounded painfully against the sharp metal. Somehow, a path had been cleared around them, but there were several people who were running toward the truck. Instantly he grabbed his pistol and fired at them. A couple fell off. He could feel the surges of power still, but his connection to the Kat-su was further away, in Catherine's arms. An old man grabbed his jacket, and he fired at the man's face, exploding in red.

He tumbled backward, pulling Ryan with him. He wasn't prepared for it, and they both fell off the truck.

A red-haired woman in the driver's seat tossed a tranquilizer gun out of the window, and a gas mask. "Take this! You're going to need it!"

Ryan caught it, and fired at two more with her gun. Two people fell and didn't get up again. *Of course.* It was the only way to stop powering up the Kat-su. He stared at the gas mask in confusion for a moment, but not for long as the parking exploded with a loud BANG, followed by a flash. Tear gas. He quickly put on the mask as the rest of the townspeople around him started coughing and crying. Some of them fled. Others still tried to fight, but without being able to see, it was a short battle.

He could see Matt start to tie up some of the people who were down. "We need more zap-straps. Should be some in the police station." He glanced at Ryan, who was pacing backing and forth. "Are you all right?"

Ryan didn't respond, rubbing the back of his neck. Where was the Kat-su?

"Are you all right?" Matt repeated.

"Yes!" Ryan snapped. "It just...my god...it feels like I've been in town for ages. Where were you guys? And who's that?" He gestured at the woman.

"A friend," She said, rubbing her hands over her flannel shirt. "You're welcome, by the way. My name is Anna—"

Ryan aimed his gun at her. Surprised, Anna had hers out in a split-second.

Matt took out his as well, having no idea what was going on. "Ryan, what the hell?"

"I see you Catherine," Ryan said. "Come out. I'm in no mood for games."

Catherine stepped out from behind a cloud of smoke. Not to Ryan's surprise, she wasn't affected by the tear gas at all. "Ryan, huh? So that's your name. How did you know I was here?"

"Didn't. But I knew *it* was there," Ryan said.

"Then it's gotten too powerful of a hold over you, Ryan. You know I have to leave with it," Catherine said. "That's why I came here."

Matt held his hands out. "Okay, time out. Can someone please explain to me what the hell is going on here? Preferably before they cause us a problem again?" He gestured at the coughing townspeople.

"She has the Kat-su," Anna said, her eyes wide. "The artifact responsible for opening the portal years ago. I've heard of it in fragmented eyewitness accounts…drawings…most assumed it had been destroyed. All this time, Jake Burns had it?"

"And it's also been driving this town bat-shit crazy for the past fourteen years," Lindsay added.

Catherine nodded.

"And who are you?" Matt demanded.

"Her name is Catherine. But you're not human," Ryan stated. "Are you?"

Catherine smiled, and her form began to change, stretch, and grow taller. She transformed into a tall, bald man with dark skin. "Does it matter what I am?"

Ryan swore under his breath. "Perfect end to a perfect day," he muttered.

"You're a Rachi, aren't you?" Anna asked behind them. Her eyes flicked to Matt. "A shape changer. You consume human beings in order to maintain your form. I thought D.R.E.X wiped out your kind."

The form melted back to Catherine. "You almost did. There is only a handful of my kind left on the planet. We are almost extinct here."

Hearing this, Matt tightened his grip on the assault rifle.

"So why did you help me?" Ryan asked. "What was that all about?"

Catherine smiled at him. "I *wanted* to help you. Not everything which left the portal is a terrible creature."

"Bullshit," Lindsay said. "You kill people as a snack."

"Well, we all have our weaknesses, darling," Catherine said with a laugh. "I wouldn't mind eating you."

Matt opened his mouth, about to speak. Nearby a woman on the ground began to stir.

"We don't have a lot of time," Catherine said.

"Will the people here…be okay now?" Ryan asked.

"Honestly? I don't know. But getting it away from here is a good start for them. Bad luck for someone else. It doesn't matter where you take it." Catherine waved a hand at the town. "What you have seen here today could easily happen in France, China, even your own base. The artifact feeds on energy, soaks it up until there is nothing left but a shell. And I am quite certain its power and range is growing."

"Fine," Matt snapped. "We'll destroy it."

Catherine laughed. "Other people have tried, believe me. Throw it in a smelting pit or a metal compressor as many times as you want. It doesn't do anything. This is going to kill you—all of you. The only option is for me to take it."

"You must be joking," Lindsay said.

Catherine scowled. "Believe me, I'm not fond of this either. But the Kat-su cannot fall into the hands of the Brache."

"Who?" Matt asked.

"The ones that wrecked that hospital in France. All they do is conquer and destroy!" Catherine snapped. "Hasn't your organization been paying any attention?"

"Fine," Matt said. "We'll deal with this ourselves."

Catherine stared at him. "The Kat-su will slowly kill any part of the world you take it to. Are you really this dense?" Seeing Matt's determined face, she shook her head. "Ryan, I saved your life more than once. I am immune to the Kat-su's effects. You know this is the right decision. The only decision. Please."

Ryan studied her. It was hard to think about anything with the whispers in his head. Reluctantly he lowered the gun. "I think—"
Bang!

Catherine gripped her bloody chest, staring at them in shock. "You—" she whispered, then pitched forward to the concrete. She didn't get up again.

Matt glanced back at Anna, who was holding a gun. "Anna, what—?"

Anna briskly stepped forward and grabbed the Kat-su. "Let's get out of here."

"You killed her!" Ryan accused.

"No I didn't, and it wouldn't matter if I did." Anna pushed her red hair behind her ears and gave him an irritated look. "You want to get out of here? The ride leaves now. D.R.E.X can send someone else to clean up here."

For the next couple of minutes they drove in silence. In the passenger seat, Matt took off his gas mask and thankfully breathed in the cold night air. He tossed the mask away.

He glanced at Anna, who was smoking a cigarette out of the open window as she drove. "Why did you shoot that woman?" he asked.

"Like I needed a reason," Anna snapped. "She was a Rachi."

"She helped me," Ryan pointed out. "Helped the entire town."

"Yeah, well, the Rachi are pretty renowned for destroying towns, Ryan, and entire cities," Anna said. "Do you remember hearing about that hurricane near Port Alberny in the news?"

"Yeah…I think so."

"That wasn't due to a hurricane." Anna switched lanes. "I don't honestly know why she helped you, but I've never met one that was interested in helping D.R.E.X, especially since we destroyed most of her kind here. Mark my words, she was going to fuck you over later. We did not have time to puzzle it out."

Matt sighed as he leaned back against the seat, then studied the Kat-su on the dashboard. On the surface, it looked like an ordinary book. It was no longer dripping blood and was locked again. He touched the air above it, and could feel static electricity. "Let's get this back to D.R.E.X."

For several moments, they drove in silence. Matt watched the rain splatter against the windshield and felt his eyelids get heavy. How long had he been awake? More than twenty-four hours, at least. "I think I'm going to take a nap," he said.

Anna grunted but didn't add anything more. Behind him, Lindsay was already slumped against the seat, her eyes closed. To his right Ryan also barely appeared to be alive. His face was pale. This might have been a concern to Matt, but he needed to…

Needed to…

Matt knew he was dreaming. In one world, he was sleeping in the passenger seat of a car, with the back of his head lightly touching against the headrest. In another, he was standing in his own driveway, holding a briefcase in one hand, a briefcase that carried fliers about environmentally friendly lamps. Until the afternoon of November 28th, that was his entire world.

But he wasn't here in the afternoon. Matt breathed in the crisp morning air, and knew—just knew—that he could prevent this catastrophe. He dashed to the front door, reaching for his keys. Before he could grab them, the door opened on its own. Lisa stood in the doorway, a glass of water in her hands and a toothbrush in her mouth. She was dressed in her fuzzy pink pajamas, the ones he loved so much.

Matt opened her mouth, about to warn her. Except nothing came out but a strangled choke. He didn't even know what to say. A second later, it was irrelevant, because a man dressed in black brushed past him, and shoved the door open with one hand.

Startled, Lisa dropped the glass, which bounced against the carpet but didn't break. Matt didn't think. He lunged forward toward the man. A second later, he hit an invisible wall and rebounded. He couldn't get close.

The man punched Lisa, and she went sliding backward. The toothbrush slipped out of her pink mouth and she turned on her belly.

"Run to the study!" Matt tried to say, but could only make the same strangled noise. "You have a gun there—I saw it!"

Instead, she ran up the plush white staircase, toward their daughter's bedroom. She made it halfway before the man caught up with her. He gripped her ponytail and pulled her backward. Lisa fell, smashing her tooth in the process. Blood exploded from her mouth.

"No!" Matt screamed silently. "No!"

The man dragged her back toward the couch. Lisa gripped the carpet with a claw-like grip, which stopped the advance until she was kicked in the ribs. She screamed, and could only hang onto the carpet limply until the man picked her up and dragged her back to the couch.

"Why are you doing this?" Lisa asked weakly. "Is it for money? I have money in the safe. Just, please…don't hurt my daughter."

In response, the man lifted his gun and fired three times. Lisa gasped, jerking back. Then, the light faded from her eyes. A small puddle of blood formed on the couch as she slouched over the side. "Time for the kid."

Matt fell to his knees. "No," he gasped, tears running down his face. "Please, no more."

Surprisingly, the man turned toward him. He was bald, and Matt noticed that he had a blue tattoo of a sun on his face. "Tough break, kid," he said. "There are no rules."

He aimed the gun at Matt, and pulled the trigger.

"Gah!" Matt said, his head jerking up. Instantly he knew something was wrong. Both his nostrils were dripping with blood, and through the windshield he could see the car was headed right for a tree. Anna was fast asleep, her head lightly braced against the steering wheel. Matt grabbed the wheel and turned it to the right, and at the same hit the emergency brake. The truck jerked sharply as it hit a ditch.

"What the—?" Anna said, her eyes jerking open as they impacted against the dirt. She screamed as her body pitched forward.

"Ow!" Ryan snapped, hitting the back of the car seat. "Seriously, what the hell?"

Matt didn't respond. He grabbed the Kat-su from the dashboard, got out of the truck, and flung it away as far as he could. "That almost killed us," he said as the others climbed out of the truck. "We can't take it back to D.R.E.X. We won't survive the trip." He shivered, and not just from the cold air.

"So what do we do?" Lindsay demanded.

"I don't know," Matt snapped, pacing back and forth. "We have to hide it somewhere. A place no one else will find it, for now. Then we get the hell out of its range and try to reach Jeff."

"I know just the place," Anna said. "Grab it. Get in."

Matt hesitated, then went and grabbed the Kat-su from the muddy ground. He ran back to the car. "This place better not be far."

CHAPTER 9

Outside of Winnipeg, Andrew Parkland stuffed his hands inside his pockets and kicked the snow out of his path. It was below freezing, and according to the forecast, it wouldn't get any better. Normally on a night like this he would stay in a shelter, fighting for a bed. But not tonight.

The payphone rang next to him, just like he said it would. Just like it always did. Andrew picked it up, wincing as the cold plastic touched his ear. "Hello?"

"Are you ready for this?" Jeff asked.

Andrew shrugged. "I guess." Jeff was a stranger to him, and the less he knew about the man, the better. But whenever he helped him, thousands of dollars would find its way to him in a brown envelope.

"The address is 1162 Dale Avenue, right across from where you are. It's a building called the Blue Power Core Reception Hall. I'll call back on this phone in three hours. Tell me what you see. You'll be paid the usual way." The phone clicked dead.

Andrew stared at it for a moment, then hung up with a shrug. He waited as a car passed by very slowly along the snow, then crossed the street. He could see several cars parked outside the building, but no one outside.

He peered through the window, and could see about twenty people inside, talking in different groups. Most were near a long buffet table, eating finger food—cheese, crackers, dips, and vegetables. The only thing that seemed out of place was their attire. The ladies wore blue dress with gold trim, while the men wore black suits with blue armbands. Still… "Doesn't seem like a bad place," he muttered.

"Hey!" a voice shouted behind him.

Andrew turned around. "Ah, hell…" he swore. Walking down the street was Lawrence Gale, his favorite personal dickcop.

"What's going on here, Andrew? Not soliciting these good people, I hope? Rumor has it you've started talking to Marlo again," Lawrence said, referring to a cocaine dealer.

Andrew raised his hands. "I'm not into that crap anymore, trust me." He glanced at the window. "Hey, what's up with these people, anyway? Why are they dressed that way?"

Lawrence barely gave it a glance. "Staff party, maybe? Who knows. They pay their bills and don't bother me, which is more than I can say for some people." He narrowed his eyes. "So what are you doing here?"

Andrew shrugged. "Just keeping warm, Lawrence."

"Hm." Lawrence's eyes narrowed. "Well, just don't freeze to death. You want a ride to the shelter?"

"Thanks." Andrew kept his gaze to the ground. "But I've got things to do."

Lawrence said nothing for a moment, likely trying to think of something to charge him with. "Fine. But don't make me come back here."

Andrew watched him walk off. "Prick," he muttered, then turned around and peered back into the window.

The hall was empty.

Andrew gasped. No way that just happened…maybe they went out the back? "What the hell…?"

He circled back to the front door. The man on the phone probably wouldn't be too happy if he didn't get more information. He tried the doorknob, which was unlocked, and a blast of hot air hit him as he opened the door. Even though he had snow-covered boots, he almost slipped on the tile floor. Seeing no one around, helped himself to the food. Licking his fingers, he looked around. Now where did they go?

A thump below him made him jump. Curious, Andrew crouched down on his knees, and pressed his ear against the concrete floor. What was that sound?

For a few seconds he couldn't hear anything. Then, the sound of laughter. They had to be in a basement somewhere. He shuffled along the floor, then noticed a painfully obvious bulge under a red carpet. He moved it aside, revealing a trapdoor handle. Andrew hesitated, then shook his head. No. That wasn't even remotely safe. He should—

A hand touched his shoulder, and he jumped. A small woman with blond hair and blue eyes looked down at him. Like the others, she wore a blue dress. "Can I help you?' she asked politely.

Andrew licked is dry lips. "Sorry miss, I didn't mean to impose. I—" He thought fast. "—just popped in here to get warm. I didn't mean to interrupt anything. I'll just be on my way."

The woman studied him, and gently gripped his arm. "Please, stay with us tonight." She invited. "If nothing else, we can give you a better night than out there. Let me guess—you're homeless, right? Assuming your poor life hasn't been swept away in drugs, no one ever helps you, do they? Or when they do talk, they have such loathing in their eyes?"

"I…" Andrew stammered. He knew it would be a good idea to run, but couldn't. "I…"

"Join us. The chicken is especially good tonight. We brought some downstairs." She winked. "We might pass along some religious mumbo-jumbo, but it's not going to kill you, I promise. We don't have to go down that way. There's a stairwell around the back."

Reassured, Andrew nodded. "Sure…sure, okay."

He followed her downstairs to a dimly lit room with several people sitting on benches. At the very end of the room stood a tall man with curly brown hair. He wore jeans, a black t-shirt, and had a cross hanging his neck.

The woman dressed in blue kissed the man on the cheek, then backed away. He grinned at all of them. "Welcome, everyone, and thank you for coming on this miserable night. I know what you're thinking. We've had our food, but now comes the boring part, right? Where I quote the bible for a couple of hours while we twiddle our thumbs and go home?"

Several people laughed. The priest smiled.

"I've met most of you, but it's been a while, so let me introduce myself. My name is Father Robert Jacobs. Ex-father, I should say. I wasn't much of a talker. I had a church able to house a hundred people, and most Sunday mornings only ten would show up. For me the religion, the passion, wasn't in my heart. One night, I prayed for the Lord to give me a reason to believe." Jacobs grinned. "Something did answer, but it wasn't the Lord."

For a moment, Jacobs seemed lost in thought, then he stared right at Andrew. "I know you," he stated.

Andrew gulped.

Jacobs paced the stage. "I know your story. Some of you are teenagers, here because your parents denied you the freedom you so rightfully deserved, and reaped upon you abuse upon unspeakable abuse. Others are adults." He gestured at the man sitting at the front bench. "I had a lucky opportunity to talk with this individual here, before the session started. His name is James, and he gave me permission to tell his story. His wife and child were killed by a fire while he worked at a sawmill. He knew it was arson, but the police didn't have time to listen to him."

James bowed his head.

With a sigh, Jacobs touched his shoulder. "This world is twisted. Which is why the Blue Power Core was created. Blue symbolizes healing, and we have to heal ourselves before we can do the same to the world."

Fascinated, Andrew continued to listen.

Jacobs shrugged. "I'm sure I can spend the next few hours boring you to death with a book you can easily read. We can all say Halleluiah and go home. But why quote it?" He smiled. "Tell me, can a sermon do this?"

Jacobs lifted his hand, and the pedestal in front of him lifted upwards. Suddenly the room trembled. Alarmed, Andrew gripped the bench. Several people gasped.

"I have power now," Jacobs said, his eyes glowing with light. "I have belief. And most importantly of all, I feel safe." He blinked, and the light faded from his eyes as the trembling stopped. "I want all of you to share the feeling, so that people like James—" He spread his arm. "—never have to go through that ever again." He turned to face him. "James, if you want to walk out of here, I understand. But I offer you this power, and I ask you to trust me. Will you do so?"

James stood, tears forming in his eyes. "I…I guess," he whispered. "Sure."

Instantly he was lifted upwards, as though gripped by an unseen force. His body jerked once.

"Jacobs doesn't claim to be, but he is the one true God," an old woman next to Andrew whispered quietly. "And believe me, this one lives in the real world. He is far more understanding than the last one."

Andrews watched them. Both the priest and the woman had a predatory look in their eyes.

Finally, James opened his eyes. "Oh my god," he whispered. "It's true. The pain…it's gone. I feel like I can do anything."

Jacobs patted him on the shoulder, then turned to the audience. "This is just the beginning. My friends, I want to help all of you take back control of your life again." He raised his hands. "Will you accept it?"

Several people ran toward him, arms outstretched, perhaps asking him to take away their pain. Andrew stood. Now might be a good time to get out of here, and talk to Jeff. With all the chaos going on he should be able to slip away from the crowd. He hurried through an empty hallway and back toward a small set of stairs, which would lead to the back door.

"Are you leaving?" The blond-haired woman stepped casually into view. "Jacobs, it appears we have a disbeliever in our midst."

"A disbeliever, and a spy, Samantha," Father Jacobs said, taking her hand. "If I were still a Christian I would call that a double sinner."

Andrew raised his hand. "Please," he said. "I mean no harm. I was just looking for some warmth…a little food…but I don't believe in your 'power'."

Father Jacobs smiled. "You're smarter than you look, Andrew. I genuinely want to offer you a better path. Isn't enlightenment better than a measly thousand bucks?"

Andrews blinked. "You don't know anything about me, sir."

"Oh, I know that D.R.E.X hired you to spy on us and report back," Jacobs said, running his hands up and down Samantha's arms. "They will know our truth, but not yet."

Jacobs stood alone in his private room with a slight frown dancing on his lips. Ever since Ethan had visited him in the chapel, things had gotten a little fuzzy. Well, perhaps visited was the wrong word. *Joined* would be a better term for it. Most of the time he felt normal, aside from a sensation similar to being high. But other times…he stared at his hands in wonder. He, or rather Ethan, had the power to do *anything*. It was simply a matter to ask, and most of the time Ethan provided. Walking on a lake or turning water into wine were things he could do, but after a couple of times the novelty soon wore off. Still, Jacobs gave a couple of swimmers the shock of their lives. The memory still made him giggle.

But sometimes…the feeling of fuzziness would increase, to a point where Jacobs couldn't think clearly. Eventually it would overwhelm him to a point where he passed out. "Why does that happen to me?"

A calm voice spoke in his mind, *"Being joined with you can be taxing. You possess a strong will, Father, but even you can sometimes be overwhelmed. I hope you don't mind that I take over. It will do neither of us any good for you to faint in front of your followers."*

"What happened to that stranger in the basement? The homeless one?" Jacobs murmured. "I don't remember."

"*I told him that if he didn't leave I would call the police, so he did. That's all.*"

Jacobs stared at his fingers, which started to tremble. It was hard to focus again. "Are you sure that's the only thing which happened?"

"*You doubt me? See for yourself.*"

Jacobs gasped as, for a split second, he saw Ethan standing next to the window, wearing his familiar cowboy hat that covered his eyes. A second later, he was gone.

Ethan walked over to the window, and pulled the curtain back. He could see the homeless man walking in the snow. Shivering, but away from the building.

Jacobs breathed a sigh of relief. "Thank you," he whispered.

"*Don't mention it,*" Ethan replied.

Matt opened the door as Anna stopped the truck. "Wait here," he ordered Ryan and Lindsay, and walked toward a large, abandoned parking lot which belong to a mall—or what used to be a mall. The building itself was massive and spanned three levels. Matt could see a couple of flickering lights, one of them being a bank sign. Most of them were dead, however, and he noticed several piles of debris and collapsed holes. All of the windows were boarded up. "So why is this place safe?"

Anna shoved her hands in her pockets as they felt a bitter chill. "This place used to be a golf course. Then some contractor tried to make it into a shopping mall. For fifteen years, they fought the courts. Both sides lost. Eventually, they stopped caring, and neither side has touched it since. Believe me, this has been abandoned for a long time. Nobody comes here anymore."

"What about squatters?"

"The mall was picked clean years ago, and too far away from town." Anna glanced at him. "It's not a perfect solution, but the best I've got."

Matt kicked open a boarded window, entered the unfinished mall, and helped Anna inside. She was right. There was no sign of any used syringes or sleeping bags lying around. The interior hallway was pitch-black, and he could see several doors taped off with large green letters: 'CLOSED FOR RENOVATIONS. LOOK FOR US IN FALL 2008!'

"Pass me the book," Anna said as she cleared away a pile of rocks near the entrance of what used to be a bookstore.

Matt grabbed it from the ground. As he touched the leather, a brief surge of power ran through his fingers, and for a split second he had a mad impulse to try to open it. Shaking his head, he tossed the book into the makeshift hole Anna had made. That done, they spent twenty minutes piling as many rocks as they could find on top of it. As Matt put down the last rock, he released a sigh of relief. It felt as though a huge weight had been taken off his shoulders.

"I'll give you a ride to the airport," Anna offered as they both stood. She gripped his arm. "Matt, you cannot trust Jeff. Not now, not ever."

Matt was suddenly aware of how close their proximity was, and the fact they were both covered in sweat. Mentally chastising himself for even thinking about that, he stepped back and glared at her. "But I can trust you?"

"That man lied to me every day I was at D.R.E.X. He does not give a damn about you. And if you ever cross him, even once, he will take away everything you have, including things you didn't ever believe possible," Anna said.

Matt shook his head. "If it weren't for Jeff, I would be in prison right now, serving time for the murder of my wife and child."

"And what did Jeff do to fix that? Destroyed evidence against you? Framed someone else?"

Matt didn't reply.

"Yeah, exactly," Anna said. "I know how the man thinks, Matt. Look, I...I need to show you something. It's important."

As they drove through the night, Matt was relieved to see the welcoming highway signs leading to the next town. Everyone else in the car appeared more awake, and aware. Lindsay and Ryan were even back to arguing with each other. Hopefully, their exposure to the *Kat-su* would have no lasting side-effects. Would it be the same for Vermon? He tried his radio again. "Jeff, come in," he said. "Are you there?"

"Yep. Good to hear from you. What happened? Where is the Kat-su now?" Jeff asked.

"I'm sending you the coordinates," Matt said. "It can't easily be transported and slowly kills whoever touches it. I don't know how to get it back to D.R.E.X."

"Don't worry Matt, I'll figure out something. In the meantime, we'll arrange for a patrol to monitor it from a safe distance so no one else tries to take it. What about the town?"

"We left quite a few people alive, but the Kat-su has been feeding on them for several years. I think they'll need some help getting back to normal."

"I'll see what I can do. Good work. Take the next plane back to the base," Jeff said.

"Got it," Matt turned off the radio, and glanced at Anna. "You said you had something important to show me?"

"As long as you don't mind missing the next plane," Anna said dryly.

They drove for the next eight hours and finally arrived in front of a house. Anna got out of the car, and Matt followed her.

"Nice house," Matt muttered, even though it wasn't true. The two-story building was in sad need of repair. Most of the paint was peeling away, and garbage littered the driveway. It looked like there had been an attempt to make a garden, once, but all of the plants were dead.

Anna knocked on the door, then rang the doorbell.

"I'm coming. God, hold your horses," a voice said.

The door opened, and Matt's breath caught in his throat. A man sitting in an electronic wheelchair stared coldly back at him. The man had horrible burns across the side of his face, starting from his cheek and ending at the top of his scalp. Several patches of brown hair were burned away, permanently. He was dressed in a blue bathrobe and wore glasses.

The man, whoever he was, stared at them in irritation. "Yes, I know I'm not pretty. Thanks for the gaping looks. Can I help you?"

"Jeremy," Anna said, getting his attention.

The man's face immediately lit up. "Anna! Good to see you! Oh my God, it's been...how long?" He gestured at the other D.R.E.X members. "Who are they? Do I need to shoot them for you?"

"No—they're members of D.R.E.X."

Jeremy squinted his eyes in confusion. "No they're not. I don't recognize them. Unless...oh. You mean that Jeff—"

"Uh-huh," Anna said.

"What a fucking idiot." Jeremy drove his wheelchair in reverse. "Follow me," he said.

Perplexed, Matt entered the house. It wasn't any less messy inside. Several plates of half-eaten food were littered on the ground, with plenty of fruit flies circling around the remains. The smell was disgusting.

"Excuse the mess," Jeremy said curtly. "Because of my... condition, it's hard to find work. I can only pay for a housekeeper once every couple of months. This is bad, Anna. Very bad."

"Go easy on them. They're young," Anna replied.

Ryan raised his hands. "I'm sorry. I don't understand."

Jeremy turned around in his wheelchair. "I was a member of D.R.E.X, years ago, and part of Anna's team. She brought you here, in a not-so-subtle attempt to illustrate what a poor mistake that can be."

"What happened to you?" Matt asked.

"A grenade in my face," Jeremy said. "The resulting shrapnel did a number on my spine too. Coffee?"

"No, we're—"

"Sure," Lindsay said automatically, and Matt flashed her an irritated look.

"Matt and I ran into each other, but I was on my way to see you anyway, Jeremy," Anna said. "Are you still getting the news?"

"Should I be?" Jeremy asked as he plugged in the coffee maker and switched it on.

"A few months ago, Lisa was murdered in her home," Anna stated, then gestured at Matt. "This used to be her husband. She's not the only one."

Jeremy's eyes flicked to both of them. "My God. Who else?"

Anna spread three files on the coffee table. "Collins, found murdered in his home a week ago. Someone tied him up and stuffed a grenade in his mouth. The end result wasn't pretty. Hanson was found shot in the head. No suspects."

Matt glanced at Anna in astonishment. Other D.R.E.X members were dead? Why didn't Jeff tell him?

"Jesus," Jeremy said as the kettle boiled. "Excuse me for a moment." He went into the kitchen, and came back a minute later holding a tray of three cups of coffee. "So it's just the two of us left."

"And them," Anna said, glancing at Ryan, Matt and Lindsay. "And whoever else Jeff has recruited since then."

As Jeremy reached forward, the tray trembled and the cups overturned. Matt and Lindsay caught theirs just in time. Ryan wasn't quick enough and the coffee spilled against the carpet.

"Shit," Jeremy whispered. "Sorry about that!"

"It's all right," Ryan said, waving a dismissing hand. "I've got it."

An awkward pause punctuated the room.

"I tried to phone you three days ago," Anna said.

"I stopped paying the phone bill a long time ago," Jeremy replied.

"You can't stay here. You and I are being targeted. It's not safe."

Jeremy smirked as Ryan cleaned up the mess. "Let them come, Anna. There is nothing left to kill."

"That's not true," Anna protested.

Jeremy glanced at Matt. "Did you tell them the real reason why D.R.E.X shut down?"

"No, and I'm not going to either," Anna replied.

"Oh, this is fucking bullshit." Matt suddenly slammed the cup on the table, surprising everyone. He stood. "Do you people get off on holding secrets and acting mysterious? Do you think it's cool or something? Let me tell you something—I spent last night being shot at the entire time, and I am no closer to finding out why my wife died. If you have something to tell me, great. Otherwise, don't waste my fucking time."

Without waiting for a reply, he stood and stormed out of the house. He slammed the screen door shut and sat down on the porch with a sigh. Much to his irritation, his radio beeped. "Hello?"

"You missed your flight," Jeff said, and didn't sound too happy. *"Something wrong?"*

"No, we're fine," Matt said, rubbing his head. "We'll catch the next flight, no problem."

"You know, Matt, in a spy organization it's never a good idea to lie to your boss," Jeff said.

Matt blinked. "What? I don't—"

"Seriously Matt, this isn't hard. Listen to me very closely. Whatever Anna is telling you right now, just remember, she cares only for herself. She has no problem manipulating you for her own ends."

Matt laughed. Jeff was really one to talk. "She seems to be the only one who is being honest with me, Jeff."

There was a pause. *"Really? She's my ex-wife, Matt. Did she mention that?"*

"No," Matt said in astonishment. Awkward.

"Yeah," Jeff said, as though reading his mind. *"I know what I'm talking about. Get back as soon as you can. We've had some new developments. Lives are depending on you."* With that, the radio clicked off.

A hand touched his shoulder. Anna was standing over him.

"I don't want to keep secrets from you, Matthew," Anna said, and sat beside him.

"Are you really Jeff's ex-wife?"

Anna sighed and zipped up her brown jacket. "Yes. The marriage didn't last very long. Maybe about six months."

Matt shrugged. "Doesn't matter. It's none of my business, anyway."

"Matt, I am not like Jeff or any other member of D.R.E.X. I want to tell you everything."

"So why don't you?" Matt demanded, looking at her.

Anna played with her hands. "Because I care about Lisa. We were friends since before you two even met. She never wanted you to be part of this."

"Then why was *she* part of this?" Matt demanded.

"Because there are things in this world that can be very ugly. She knew this, and wanted to make it better. But Matt, that used to be *her* life, not yours. You have only scratched the surface of what is really going on here, and I guarantee you it will not get any more pleasant. Leave. While you still can."

"I have to find the person who killed her," Matt said. "That's the only reason I'm here." He stared into her cold blue eyes. "What did she do? Why did the team split apart? Why did D.R.E.X become obsolete?"

"Respect her memory, Matt. Please don't ask me that." She took a deep breath. "Whoever killed Lisa is going to come after me next, and Jeremy. I can feel it."

"So come with us. I can protect you," Matt said.

"I'm not part of this anymore," Anna said.

"Yes you are, whether you want to be or not," Matt said. "My wife was shot. Your friend had a grenade stuffed in his mouth. Do you want to end up the same way?"

Anna frowned. He expected her to slap him. Instead, she looked away, shivered, and finally nodded.

"Okay. Let's get out of here." They stood and entered the house. Matt glanced at Ryan, who was typing on his keyboard. "What are you doing?"

"Trying to book us plane tickets," Ryan said, and glanced at Jeremy. "No offense dude, but your connection sucks. When was the last time you paid your bill?"

Jeremy shrugged as he drank his coffee.

"Forget about it. We can phone it in. Let's go," Matt said, and glanced at Jeremy. "I wish…"

"What? That things didn't turn out this way for me? I don't need your pity, kid," Jeremy said, focusing on him. "I am dealing with this my own way. If you really feel sorry for me, do me one favor—quit D.R.E.X. Run and don't look back." He raised his eyebrow. "Or do you think Jeff gave me any compensation for this? Once I stopped becoming useful, he cut me off financially and denied I ever existed."

"What?" Lindsay whispered.

"Jeremy—" Anna began.

Jeremy laughed. "If anyone kills me, Anna, it'll be a favor." He smiled and waved his hand at her. "Go on. I'll be fine."

CHAPTER 10

The next day all of them were on a chopper, heading toward D.R.E.X.

Lindsay and Ryan sat across from each other, irritated. Anna heard from Matt that they were brother and sister, and got on each other's nerves. She had no idea what set them off this time, and frankly didn't care. The less she knew the better. It was nothing personal, but both of them reminded her too much of D.R.E.X. She knew they had secrets they probably thought were important. Perhaps they even had secrets from each other. It was all trivial in the end.

She noticed Matt staring at her. "Yes?"

"Thank you," Matt said. "For coming with us."

Anna shrugged. "I'm here for one reason only, Matt. I want to find out who's killing my friends. After that, we never have to see each other again."

Matt studied her. "You say that like it's a good thing."

Anna said nothing, considering. She could still remember when Lisa had asked her to be a caterer during their wedding, which turned out to be a disaster. Saving the world a dozen times over from a supernatural creature was a cakewalk compared to cooking for over a hundred people. They even dropped the wedding cake at one point. Any other couple would have screamed at them, but Matt had been understanding. He even gave them money to buy a cheap ice-cream cake from the store. They both laughed about it afterwards. He was a decent guy.

She hoped D.R.E.X didn't destroy that.

"We're landing," Lindsay murmured.

Anna glanced out the window. Seeing the familiar strip in the desert, her body tensed. She never wanted to come back here.

"Home sweet home," Ryan said.

No, this wasn't. Home was a hundred miles away, in a tiny farm where she could forget about the world. Anna shook her head, but didn't bother to correct him.

The chopper landed on a metal strip meant to camouflage itself with the rest of the desert. The pilot murmured something into the radio, and with a small click, the entire pad descended into the underground complex. Anna took a deep breath as the scorching heat was instantly replaced by gray walls, and filtered air conditioning. There was no escape now.

Finally, the pad stopped, and the pilot turned off the lights. The rest grabbed their gear. Anna was the last to leave the chopper.

Not surprisingly, Jeff was waiting just outside for them. "Hello, Anna," he said. His face revealed nothing.

Anna straightened. It felt like the air between them had become electrified. She struggled to keep her face just as unreadable. "Jeff."

Jeff put his hands in his pockets. Years ago, that simple gesture had reminded her of a ten-year-old boy. At the time, she thought it had been cute. Looking back at it now, she had no idea why. "Matt seems to be pretty adamant that we need your help, but I don't think so. I *can* put you in witness protection, if you think that you're in danger."

Anna shouldered her backpack. "Over the years all of us tried to hide, Jeff. It didn't help my friends." She sighed. "While I am here, I expect the same clearance as before. And my same room."

"Of course," Jeff agreed. "But I would like to speak to you for a moment. In private."

"See you later, Anna," Matt murmured. She smiled briefly in gratitude, a smile that vanished as soon as the three of them left.

Jeff said nothing, his blue eyes unreadable. Anna blinked, remembering a time, and not so long ago, when they shared the same bedroom. Those same blue eyes looked at her while they were making love.

Anna remembered how much hurt both had caused the other. "What do you want?" She folded her arms. "Is this the point where we make fuzzy wuzzy conversation about our relationship?"

"Why are you really here, Anna?" Jeff asked.

"Do I really need to explain my reasons again, Jeff? Someone is killing my friends, and I'm going to find out why."

Jeff's eyes widened a little, and she could see the gears working very quickly. She used to love that the most about him. "And you think it's someone on Matt's team, don't you?"

"Could be one of them. Could be all of them," Anna stated flatly. "Whoever killed my team had to know their location—that requires hacking into their confidential records. A tracker would have been useful, and it would have required someone capable enough in hand-to-hand combat to beat them. So no, I seriously doubt that one person did it alone." She shrugged. "So all of them could have."

"That's ridiculous, Anna, even by your standards."

"Why not?" Anna asked. "I did a little hacking of my own and checked your files. Lindsay and Ryan weren't on any missions when my former team members died. And Matt wasn't part of the team at that point. All of them had opportunity."

"But not motive," Jeff countered. "Anna, everyone on Matt's team only joined recently. They've never even met any of your team before."

Anna sighed and shook her head. "Jeff," she said patiently. "Anyone who's read the file on Owphiyr would have a motive to kill us, believe me. All of us."

Jeff considered that, and looked away. "I'm still in charge here," he muttered, looking again like a ten-year-old boy. "You know what happens if you don't follow my orders."

"You also used to be my husband," Anna said, raising her eyebrow. "Believe me, I know all the things you *can't* do."

Without waiting for a reply, she turned and left.

"Where are you, Matt? Help me!" Lisa cried out, followed by a gunshot.

Matt jerked up in bed, his heart racing against his chest. Another nightmare. He trembled, his body was covered in sweat. He released a slow breath and collapsed back into bed. Part of him wanted to cry, but he couldn't. There were no more tears left. He checked his watch. Close to five a.m. Try as he might, he couldn't go back to sleep. The moment his eyes closed, he could picture his wife screaming. He couldn't relive that dream again. Finally, he stood and left the room.

For a few minutes, he paced the quiet D.R.E.X bunkers. Some people were working in the command room, but most people were still asleep. He eventually found himself walking towards Anna's room. The door was closed. He listened, but couldn't tell if she was awake or asleep. Finally, he knocked on the door. Finding it unlocked, he opened it.

Anna sat in a metal chair next to a desk, pointing a gun at him. A book was in her other hand. For a moment, Matt could only stare at her, struck by how she different she looked dressed in black.

"Sorry," Matt said, raising his hands. "I can't sleep."

Anna relaxed and leaned back in her chair. "It's pretty rare that someone in D.R.E.X gets to sleep in a bed. You should enjoy it while you can."

"You can't sleep," Matt pointed out.

Anna sighed. "No, I can't. Too many memories here."

"That's why I wanted to talk to you." Matt stepped forward. "I need to know something. What was it like? Working with Lisa? I mean, I used to feel like I knew her, inside and out. And now... there's such a large chunk of her life which I don't know about."

Anna studied him. Then she smiled and patted the bed beside her. Matt sat down.

"Things were different back then," Anna began. "D.R.E.X was more organized, and had a lot more people. We were…young. We had a sense that nothing could hurt us. Let's see…Collins was our team leader. Hanson specialized in demolitions. I was a medic. You already met Jeremy. He used to be a hacker. And Lisa was a sniper."

Matt blinked. "A sniper? You can't be serious? My wife, a sniper?'

"She had a passion for it." Anna grinned. "Believe me, if she didn't get a clear shot on our missions, she wouldn't talk to us for at least a week." She laughed. "She had a carefree soul."

"Definitely two sides of a coin, then," Matt replied, leaning back in his chair. "The Lisa I knew…was very conservative. Always making sure the housework was done on time. She was pretty anal about it."

Anna glanced at him. "Lisa would talk about you quite a bit, Matt. It got to a point where we would beg her to stop. She loved you more than anything. She wouldn't want you in this job."

"Maybe," Matt said. "But whoever killed her is a part of this."

"Because Jeff told you?" Anna asked, skeptical.

"Yes, but more than that. I can feel—" Matt began, and was interrupted by a knocking on the door. He turned around as the door opened.

"Hey," Lindsay said. "Jeff wants to see us. Now."

Concerned, Matt joined the rest of the team in the briefing room. Ryan was already there, along with the old doctor…what was his name? Matt thought about it, before it finally clicked. Louise. Jeff had told him at some point. The man in question stood near the screen, clutching yet another cup of coffee. His face appeared worried—not a great sign.

"You remember those creatures you found back in Paris?" Louise said, smoking a cigarette. "None of them have any eggs or reproductive organs, so we couldn't figure out how they were breeding for the longest time."

"There were eggs in that hospital," Matt said, taking a seat. "Stephan and I saw them."

"Stephan?" Anna murmured.

"A former member of D.R.E.X.," Ryan supplied. "He's dead now."

Anna's eyes burned at Jeff. "Huh. Another one."

Jeff returned her gaze without flinching. "I can assure you, Stephan's death had nothing to do with a conspiracy and everything to do with stupidity. And not following my orders."

"At any rate," Louise interrupted. "I figured out how they were doing it. The creatures aren't reproducing by themselves. Humans are lending a hand."

"Humans?" Lindsay echoed.

Louise dabbed his cigarette into the ashtray. "These creatures—let's call them Blinkers, launch themselves onto a human, and force a liquid down their throat. This liquid contacts microscopic eggs that are then attached to a subject's stomach lining. The conditions and internal body temperature seem to be ideal for the eggs to grow, and digestive acids don't seem to have any effect. Eventually, the eggs are ready, and a human regurgitates them back up."

"Ew," Ryan said.

Louise smiled a little. "I do have some slides, if you're interested."

"No, that's fine," Matt said. "But they were destroyed in Paris...right?"

Jeff shook his head. "They showed up in Paris. It doesn't mean they came from there. Somehow this Blue Power Core is connected. We do have a problem. Remember that tip on Samantha Wishart?"

"Yeah, that mysterious woman in the hospital," Matt replied.

"I paid an informant to check out this Blue Power Core seminar. He hasn't checked in at the scheduled time. According to my sources, they rent out a hall in Winnipeg. We need someone to—"

Suddenly, Matt's cell phone rang, and he gave everyone an apologetic look. Was it Carol again, begging him to talk? He was surprised to see the display come up with a blocked ID. "Give me a sec," he said, and turned it on. "Hello?"

"*You need to turn back,*" a computerized voice said. Impossible to tell if it was male or female. "*If you don't listen, what happens next is on your head.*"

"Who is this?" Matt asked. Behind him, Jeff snapped his fingers several times at Ryan, who began typing.

The phone clicked dead.

Jeff glanced at Ryan. "Anything?"

Ryan shook his head. "It ended too soon. I couldn't trace the call."

"What are we going to do?" Anna asked.

"It's time we pay a visit to the Blue Power Core," Jeff replied. "Get on the next plane to Winnipeg."

"Oh great," Ryan said. "More snow. Any idea how we can destroy these 'Blinkers', if we run into them? Or how we can avoid them?"

Louise shook his head. "Still working on it."

"That's reassuring," Matt muttered under his breath.

After the meeting, Ryan hurried to his room and packed a duffel bag full of clothes—nothing too fancy, just enough to get him through the next couple of days. Their plane left in two hours. It was pretty rare to stay in one place for too long. Story of his life.

He turned around, and was surprised to see Lindsay standing in the doorway. "What do you want?"

"Can't a sister be worried about her brother?" she asked. "You almost died in Vermon."

"So?" Ryan snapped. He brushed past her. "We've got a plane to catch."

She grabbed his arm, hard enough to stop him. Her face, however, revealed nothing.

After a few seconds, Ryan got irritated. "What is it you want, Lindsay?"

Lindsay ran a hand across her braided hair. "I don't know! Just be careful. I just have a bad feeling about this one."

Ryan rolled his eyes and stepped back. "Let's get one thing straight, okay? I don't care about you, and I know you don't care about me. We both know why you want me to stay alive."

"Fuck you, Ryan. Why did you lose her?" she blurted out.

"Why couldn't you find her? You're the fucking tracker!" Ryan shouted, and bit his lip, trying to keep his temper under control. It wouldn't do him any good, not now. He backed away. "We are going to get through this mission the same way we always do. By being smart, staying the hell away from each other, and not talking to each other if we can help it."

Lindsay looked hurt, but he didn't care. He left without a backward glance.

Matt knew something was wrong with Lindsay as soon as they boarded the plane. She sat apart from everyone else and her hands were tightly clenched on the armrest. He moved out of his seat to join her. "Hey," he prodded gently. "Are you all right? I need you to be focused."

Lindsay nodded, her brown eyes sharp. "You don't need to worry about me."

His eyes glanced at her backpack. "I wanted to ask you something. Back when I first met you, I thought I saw you drawing something. Can I take a look?"

Startled, Lindsay blushed a little. She took the pad out of the bag. "It's nothing really. Just something to pass the time." He handed him a sketch of an elk.

Matt stared at it, amazed at the detail. "Wow. That's pretty good."

Lindsay snorted. "I've been drawing ever since I was a kid. Guess I could never give it up. Heck, I might have a future in it. If I ever manage to escape D.R.E.X., I want to give it a try. Shocking, I know."

"What is?" Matt asked.

Lindsay frowned, then shrugged. "Very few people think they have a life outside of D.R.E.X. What we do is so dangerous, that no one really makes lifelong goals." She glanced at him. "What about you?"

Matt shrugged. "I'm only here to find out who killed my wife, and why."

"And then what?" Lindsay asked. "What comes after that?"

Matt hesitated. He honestly didn't know how to answer that.

They arrived at the Blue Power Club just after four in the morning. Late enough for most of the streets to be empty, including the nightlife. The hallway was only one story, and Matt couldn't see any lights on inside. No thermal readings on the binoculars either.

He walked across the street, shivering. He turned on his radio. "Jeff."

"Matt," Jeff returned.

"How's the signal?"

"Loud and clear. What do you see?"

"The place looks abandoned," Matt said, as he walked past the window. He gave it a passing glance, but couldn't see anyone moving inside.

"Appearances can be deceiving," Jeff replied. *"Keep an eye out for my contact. He's African-American, with short black hair and a beard. He looks homeless…probably because he is."*

Matt approached the front double-doors and tried the handle. Locked. He took out a lock pick and got through it within seconds. Inside, the lobby appeared deserted, with an empty podium and a guest book. Lindsay flipped through it.

"No alarm," Ryan remarked as they entered.

"I'm scanning in some names, Jeff," Lindsay said, taking pictures. "Let me know if they mean something."

"Got it. Thanks," Jeff said.

Matt strained to hear any noise, but didn't. The adjacent hallway also appeared to be empty. Raising his gun, Matt gestured for the rest to follow and proceeded next to the banquet hall.

Inside was everything one would expect form a cult. A dozen folding chairs were set up in front of a small stage that had musical instruments. Above the stage, a large, blue banner held the words 'power belongs to you!' Matt could see several crystals latched onto the ceiling. He glanced to the right, and saw an empty banquet table.

"There's a trapdoor hidden underneath the carpet," Lindsay remarked, kicking it aside. "Pretty obvious."

Matt opened the trapdoor, that led to a dark stairwell. He scanned it with his gun and flashlight, but didn't see anyone. That did not reassure him. It was too damn quiet. "Anna and I will check it out. You and Ryan search this floor."

Ryan nodded. "Got it."

"Right behind you," Anna said.

They climbed down the ladder, and Matt didn't have to look far to find Jeff's missing contact—the man was sprawled over the steps. A bullet hole was burned out of his forehead, and blood had dried around the wound some time ago. Matt touched his skin. Stone cold. He scanned the room, but couldn't see anyone.

"Jeff, looks like your friend was killed," Anna reported in.

"*He's not my friend,*" Jeff corrected. "*Just a paid informant. Keep looking.*"

"Find anything?" Lindsay asked Ryan.

Ryan shrugged. "Nope. Looks like the cultmobile came and went." He opened a door at the end of the hall, which led to an adjacent alley. A homeless old woman stared at them sleepily. Ryan closed the door. "Maybe we should come back during normal business hours."

"*You could, but I don't want you preaching about finding your inner teenage power,*" Jeff said dryly.

"Ha ha. Don't worry, boss man, cults give me the heebie-jeebies." He opened another door, leading to a storage closet. "I don't see anything here."

"*The analysis of the names is starting to come back,*" Jeff said. "*All of them are people that have been reported missing, but in most cases the police concluded they left voluntarily. A lot of these names are teenagers.*"

Lindsay didn't reply. It felt like she was missing something. She watched as a paper napkin flapped a little from the breeze, but it wasn't from Ryan opening and closing the door. The direction was wrong. She looked behind her, at the wall. "There's a secret door there," she said.

Ryan followed her gaze. "I don't see anything."

"You're not supposed to," Lindsay curtly reminded him. "Give me a hand."

The two siblings moved away a tea cabinet that blocked the wall, and Lindsay cut away a banner of the Blue Power Core that was hiding the cracks along the door. She kicked a small pressure plate in, and the door opened. Both scanned a narrow, dark hallway with their guns, but didn't see anything.

The hallway only led to one door. Ryan opened it as Lindsay covered him. Inside they could see a small office with a plain oak desk, a whiteboard, and a chair. Nothing more. Lindsay wondered why it was hidden.

"Holy…" Ryan breathed as he examined the whiteboard.

Lindsay followed his gaze. Several photos were taped on it—photos of Matt, Ryan, Anna, and herself. Underneath each photo was their name and place of birth. Pinned on the whiteboard was a map, with several locations circled with lines through them—Paris, Boston, and Vermon.

"*Ryan, Lindsay, what is it?*" Jeff asked.

"It's…us," Ryan said and swallowed. "Our names. Where we've been. What we've done."

"Somebody's been tracking us," Lindsay said as she opened a folder on the desk. It contained pictures of what appeared to be past members of D.R.E.X as well, judging by the names on the file—Collins, Jeremy, and Hanson.

"*No, that's not possible,*" Jeff said.

Lindsay didn't listen as her flashlight searched at the upper right of the white board. Pictures of the destroyed mall. "Jeff, they know where the Kat-su is."

"*What?*"

"We have to tell Matt," Ryan said.

"*...hsss...what did you say...?*" Jeff asked.

Lindsay frowned as she heard a burst of static on her radio. "Jeff, do you read me?"

There was a long pause. "*Yeah, loud and clear,*" Jeff replied. "*Sorry about that. Signal interference. Found anything else?*"

"Hang on," Ryan said, flipping through another folder of papers from the desk. "This looks interesting. A lot of receipts for excavating supplies—bulldozers, blasting equipment, concrete, contractors. The list goes on and on. All of it under the Blue Power Group's business account and most of it dating back years ago. It seems to be tied to a specific place."

"What else are they hiding?" Lindsay asked, checking another drawer.

A brick of C-4 with a ten-second timer stared back at her.

Matt frowned as he heard a burst of static on his radio. "Jeff, do you read me?"

There was a long pause. "*Yeah, loud and clear,*" Jeff replied. "*Found anything?*"

"So far we haven't seen anyone." They studied what appeared to be an underground chapel of some kind. "This feels too weird," he said. "Why is there no one here? Where did they go?"

"Do you want to abort?" Anna asked.

"*No—keep looking,*" Jeff encouraged. "*You're close to something. I can feel it.*"

Matt tried the next room, which appeared to be some kind of preparation room. He could see a closed cabinet, and a full-length mirror. Strangely, someone had carved the name 'Ethan' into the mirror several times with a knife. He could see smudges of blood on the glass.

"Ethan?" Matt said. "Who's Ethan?"

"What's in there?" Anna asked, her flashlight spotting another door.

"Let's find out." They tested the room for sound, and Anna shook her head. Matt kicked opened the door.

The room was empty except for a wooden table, but there were several photos of people taped to the wall, people he didn't recognize. They all appeared to be Middle Eastern. All from the same place, perhaps? Blood-red words were also painted below the photos: 'THERE ARE NO RULES.' His eyes moved to the table, which had a device with a timer on it. It was counting down from ten seconds.

Matt turned around. Anna stared at the room in horror. *Not at the bombs, but the photos,* he thought to himself. He grabbed her arm. "Move!"

They both sprinted toward another metal side door. Matt honestly didn't know where it led. Either it was an escape route to outside world, or it led to nothing at all besides death. But all too soon, Matt felt the ground tremble, followed by a flash of heat. He looked up.

Just as the ceiling collapsed.

For a split-second, Lindsay honestly thought they could both escape the blast.

Just as they ran out the door, Ryan shouted 'Get down!' and she felt an incredible heat wave behind her back. She was pushed forward, down the steps and face-first into the snow. A second later, debris impacted against her body—rocks, burning wood, followed by a cloud of smoke. She struggled into a sitting position, trying to peer through the haze. "Ryan?" she called out.

There was no response.

"Ryan!" she tried again, struggling to her feet. She was covered in scratches, but her armor protected her from the blast. She had been lucky.

Others might not have been.

She found Ryan a short distance away, not moving and also covered with debris. The snow around his head was stained red.

She turned him over and gave him a shake. "Ryan?" She inhaled a lungful of smoke and coughed. He was out cold. The gash on his head was bad, and would probably require stitches. Otherwise, she couldn't see any obvious signs of injuries. Like her, very lucky.

She glanced back at the building, which by now was a collection of burning wood and smoke. The fire department would be here any time. Matt...Lindsay. She tried her radio. "Matt? Come in!"

For a few seconds there was static. *"We're alive, Lindsay,"* Matt said. *"The area was rigged with bombs. We managed to get out, but Anna's hurt."*

"How bad?" Lindsay asked.

"Bad. She's lost an arm," Matt said bluntly. *"I'm trying to stabilize her as best as I could but...I'm losing her. Lindsay, you have to help me!"*

Lindsay breathed in horror. "Where are you?" she demanded.

"I managed to carry her out of the building. There's a warehouse to the right. See it? We're in there."

She gave the burning reception hall a final glance. She glanced at Ryan, and hesitated. He was safe for the time being. She gave his shoulder a squeeze, then stood. "All right, I'm on my way."

"Good," Matt said in relief. *"Please...hurry."*

She stumbled toward the warehouse. The cloud of smoke was getting to be too much, and her head was spinning. She looked down at the fresh layer of snow. No footprints? For some reason that bothered her, but she didn't know why. It was impossible to think.

She blindly located the side door and opened it. Inside she could see a pitch-black warehouse with a few crates in the center. "Where are you?"

"Near the crates," Matt replied.

Why didn't he call out to her? Lindsay's senses screamed at her, and she finally realized what was wrong. She couldn't see a blood trail anywhere.

The door behind her slammed shut. *"Goodbye, Lindsay,"* Matt's voice said triumphantly in her ear. *"Nice knowing you."*

The radio clicked off, a noise that made her cringe. Even though the bomb exploded a few minutes ago, her ears perked up as she heard several rocks fall from nearby. All of a sudden, she had a sense that something was…watching her. Lindsay's breath caught in her throat, as she slowly removed the gun from her belt. She could feel something breathing down her neck, causing her flesh to ripple with goosebumps. Swallowing, she removed the safety from her gun, whirled around—

—just in time to see a Blinker right in front of her, on its hind legs. The creature opened its mouth.

And screamed at her.

"Matt? Matt, can you hear me?"

Matt opened his eyes, slowly aware of how much every bone in his body hurt. He could see his bloody forearm half-buried in snow. Beyond that, he could see fire nearby, and smoke. Several rocks were piled around him, and on him. His hand was also tangled in red hair. Anna was unconscious below him. He closed his eyes, wanting nothing more than to go back to sleep. At least they made it out.

"Matt?" Jeff said in his ear, not without some urgency. *"Come on, wake up. You're not hurt that badly."*

'Easy for you to say,' Matt was tempted to snap at him. Anger stirred him to open his eyes again and he tried to move the rocks away, not without some difficulty. He opened his mouth, and breathed in smoke. His vision blurred.

"Wake up, Matt. Come on!" Jeff snapped.

That forced his eyes to open. Fortunately, there weren't too many rocks piled on him, and he was able to push them off and stand. "Jeff. Wha—" He closed his mouth. God, his throat felt so incredibly dry, not to mention the stinging pain in his arm. "What happened?"

"*Not sure,*" Jeff replied, followed by a buzz. "*I'm getting some... interference...*" Abruptly his radio switched off.

Matt frowned, and tapped the Bluetooth in his ear. "Jeff?"

"*Matt?*" Jeff asked after a lot of static. "*Wait...I think... someone...*"

Suddenly the signal turned off completely, then turned on again.

"Jeff, do you read me?" Matt asked impatiently.

For a moment, there was no response. "*Matthew,*" Lisa said, followed by a sob.

Hearing her, Matt's blood turned to ice water. "Lisa?"

"*How could you leave me and our daughter like that? We waited for you to come home. Matt...why weren't you there?*"

Matt was paralyzed. Even though the smoke was still burning his lungs, he couldn't move a muscle. After a moment, he blinked. "No," he said, clenching his fists. This was impossible. Which meant someone else was substituting her voice. "You can't be real. You're not really her. Lisa's dead."

"*Please Matt, stop trying to follow my ghost. You have to let me go. Give up. Go back to Ottawa.*" Lisa continued sobbing.

"You're not my fucking wife!" Matt exploded. "Who are you really?"

Hearing a slight rustle, Matt glanced to the right. Anna was awake, and sitting with her knees against her chest. Her eyes were wide. They both could hear Lisa's voice.

"*Ha-ha,*" Ryan laughed over the radio. "*It would take a hacker to do this kind of thing, wouldn't it? I guess that implies I killed your wife. But what if it's not me? I can be any voice in the world. Millions of people, in fact. Maybe Jeff really did leave you to die. You'll never figure it out, Matt. I'm too smart for you.*"

Matt narrowed his eyes. "Why are you trying to kill us?"

"*Truthfully, I didn't want to kill you. Not until you showed me where the Kat-su was. I knew D.R.E.X had more than enough resources*" *to track it down, and sure enough, we stole it from your little hiding spot yesterday. Oh, do tell Jeff that I'm sorry about the men I had to kill who were guarding it. But now that we have it, you aren't useful anymore,"* he replied. *"As for why I'm doing this...Anna, I think it's time you told Matt our little story. Oh and by the way—"*

"—where's Lindsay?" Ryan asked right behind him.

Matt didn't think. He grabbed his gun and whirled around. Ryan looked shocked, and probably concussed judging by his head wound, but he still was moving. One of his hands deflected Matt's gun as the older man drew it to bear, and with the other hand pulled out his own.

From the ground, Anna gave a startled gasp. He ignored her as he moved to punch Ryan in the head. Ryan dodged it, but didn't recover in time. Matt kicked Ryan backward, who impacted against a tree. The gun flew from his hand. Matt had his gun at Ryan's eye level within seconds.

Swearing, Ryan rubbed his arm. "Jesus, what is your problem, Matt? Are we having some team issues?" he asked sarcastically. "Do you want me to ask Jeff to schedule a staff meeting?"

"Shut up," Matt demanded. He had an easy shot, but...this didn't feel right. Not at all. Still, he kept his voice firm. "You're the traitor."

Ryan raised his hands. "Okay, I really have no idea what the fuck you're talking about."

Matt shook his head in disgust. "It has to be you. You're the only who could do that to the radio."

"Do what?"

"Did you kill her?"

"Kill *who*?" Ryan shouted.

"Did you kill my wife?" Matt screamed.

Suddenly, Matt heard a soft click behind his head. "Drop the gun," Lindsay demanded, her voice cold. "Leave him alone."

He glanced at her from the corner of his eye. Lindsay looked incredibly pale, but appeared unharmed. Her gun was pointed right at his head, but he could probably shoot Ryan and take out Lindsay at the same time. Anna too. Were they all traitors?

Matt…why weren't you there?

"This was a trap," Matt said calmly. "Someone hacked into the com channels. Disguised our voices. I can't think of too many people who can do that. Can you, Ryan?"

"I already told you," Ryan snapped. "We never met your wife! If anyone is a traitor here, it should be you, Matt! You're the newest addition to the team! You have more reason to kill us than anyone." Ryan abruptly looked away.

"What?" Matt whispered. "What do you mean?"

"No," Anna said quietly. "You couldn't know."

Ryan shrugged. "Maybe I read a report or two I shouldn't have, Anna. About what happened. What you did. It seems like we're all paying for it now."

Before Matt could reply he heard a siren approaching.

"The fire department. We need to get out of here," Lindsay said.

Matt swore, but reluctantly lowered his gun. "This discussion isn't over," he said.

"Can't wait," Ryan said sarcastically. Anna's face was pale.

By the time the fire department arrived, they were gone.

Half an hour later, they were in one of D.R.E.X's former safe houses. A long time ago, it might have been a cozy two-story house. Having been neglected for the past ten years however, it was in a sad state of disrepair, and long since picked clean. All of the electronics had been stolen, and garbage littered the ground. In the kitchen, Matt carefully bandaged his arm, but it didn't seem to be too bad.

Nearby Ryan winced as Lindsay applied stitches to his head. "Careful."

"You should go to the hospital."

"I'm fine. What about you?"

"What about me?"

"I dunno, you just seem…shaken up."

Matt suddenly noticed a shadow move in the living room. Anna was walking toward the door, backpack in tow.

"Anna," Matt called out softly.

She paused, one hand on the doorknob. "I found a cache of weapons that the looters overlooked. It isn't much but…I put it in the bedroom."

Matt stared at her, knowing full well that he wouldn't let her leave without hearing her side of the story. "Where are you going?" he asked calmly.

"Out." Anna hesitated, and looked up at him. A car briefly reflected her tear-stained face. "I was wrong to ever come here, Matt. This isn't my time anymore. I just want to go back to my farm. D.R.E.X is…it's poison. You should leave while you still can."

Matt followed her outside into the snow. "You know those people," he accused. "Tell me who they are. Why is someone trying to kill us? What did that message mean?"

"Leave me alone," she snapped. He gripped her arm and whirled her around.

"Tell me why D.R.E.X didn't work! Tell me why someone wants to kill us! Who murdered my wife?"

"What are you going to do? Beat it out of me?" Anna spat.

"Maybe you killed her," Matt snarled.

Anna shoved him back. "Jeff and I have both been trying to protect you, Matt. Once you know the truth, you can't go back," she snapped. "If Lisa was here…she wouldn't want…"

"Anna, I am giving you a direct order. Do not tell Matt anything," Jeff said.

"Lisa isn't here," Matt replied. "I need to know what happened. Even if it costs me everything. Please."

With a sob, Anna walked aimlessly for a moment. "I'm sorry, Lisa," she whispered. Finally, she turned to face him, and wiped away the tears from her eyes. "Okay. This is what happened."

CHAPTER 11

Owphiyr
July 5, 2009

For Anna, the difference between her old D.R.E.X team and the new was a clear difference between night and day. Her old team had a chemistry, a vibe which couldn't be matched. They had seen the worst monsters the portal had to offer, and came out without a scratch. It would only occur to her, much later, that they also had a sense of arrogance as well.

The day had started in a helicopter, a local one they had charted from Israel. She could remember all of them laughing their asses off.

"Okay, worst monster ever?" Collins, the team leader asked.

"Pfft. No contest," Jeremy replied, pushing up his glasses. "The Saimes monster. Every time that damn thing hit me, we teleported to another continent. Or the ocean. Good thing that creature was pretty dumb or we would have never caught it. What do you think, Lisa?"

Lisa was staring at a photo. She didn't reply.

"You're not going to get back to him any sooner by looking at that," Anna reminded her gently.

"Yeah, come on," Jeremy prodded. "What is the worst monster ever?"

Lisa smirked at him. "Maybe it was the sex daemon who wouldn't leave you alone for three days, Jeremy."

Hanson laughed.

"I hate to interrupt," Jeff said, amused. *"But I have the mission briefing ready."*

Collins turned on his radio. "Go ahead."

"We had suspicious activity reported in the village of Owphiyr. Based on Hasida's description, it doesn't sound like one we've categorized this one before."

"Hasida?" Anna murmured in surprise.

"Yep, she was the one who phoned it in. The good news is that the village is aware of D.R.E.X's activities, and they know we're the good guys. The village is also far enough away from the insurgency that I don't expect any trouble from the locals. Hasida spotted a stranger walking into their village two nights ago. He didn't stick around for long, but Hasida was suspicious enough to call us."

"Why?" Jeremy asked.

"I'll let her fill you in. According to her, the man fled into the desert and she lost track of him. Bag and tag, people." The radio clicked off.

A couple of minutes later the chopper approached a crudely made runway near the village. Anna grimaced as the bright light hit her eyes and she put on her sunglasses. She always hated the desert heat, and the dry air. As they landed, a blond woman wearing a camouflage uniform was waiting for them. She smiled as Anna exited the plane.

"Hasida," Anna greeted.

"Anna." The older woman gave her a hug. She, like the rest of the village had discovered her involvement with D.R.E.X. But Hasida had also seen Anna destroy a monster, which, three days prior, had murdered and cannibalized several villagers, including a baby. Someone else might have gone to the press, but so what? D.R.E.X had twenty-three employees dedicated to wiping away their identities over the internet, disclaiming news report, and planting false evidence. The few times a civilian did report their activities it usually did not end well for them.

"I thought you were working for the IDF," Anna said.

"Still am. I'm on leave right now," Hasida replied, waving a dismissive hand. They both walked toward the village. "I wasn't planning on staying here for this long. Things are...tense right now."

"Aren't they always, here?" Anna asked.

Hasida smiled. "Jeff talked to my superiors, however, and they've granted me leave to stay here until we sort this out."

"That's nice of the IDF," Anna said.

"Israel needs all the friends they can get. Including the strange ones," Hasida said as they approached the center of the village. Several people spoke in Hebrew. Anna could only catch a few words here and there. Hasida shooed them away. "But enough about me—how are you doing? Are you and Jeff still together?"

"Yep. It's going good," Anna said, smiling. She glanced briefly at Lisa, who was conversing with someone else in Hebrew. She didn't know how Lisa could manage to have a relationship with Matt, and lie about her work, but somehow it worked for her. Personally, Anna liked things to be simple. At least Jeff was honest...most of the time.

"Jeremy, report," Collins ordered, bringing Anna back to the present.

Jeremy typed on his notebook and gave a shrug. "Not a good place for electrical. There are pockets of brown spots everywhere. Communication with Jeff might be tricky."

"Let him know. Lisa, patrol the village. Let me know if you find anything." Collins turned around. "All right, Hasida. What have you got?"

Her face turned serious. "Two days ago, I was having a smoke outside, and I saw this man approaching the fountain. He was pale, far too pale to be healthy. And his eyes were bright green. I called out to him. He turned to me and spoke in a language I didn't recognize."

"That doesn't sound unusual," Jeremy pointed out. "I can barely understand the people in half the places I've been to."

Hasida frowned at him. "But it was the way he said it. His voice was…echoing around me. When he did, everything felt so quiet and still. Like I was moving in slow motion. He looked directly at me and his mouth…it was folded in different directions. If I didn't know better, I would have sworn that I was going crazy. Especially since he looked perfectly normal otherwise."

"Describe his other features. What does he look like?" Collins asked.

Hasida shrugged. "He was skinny, with black hair and green eyes. He looked Palestinian."

"So what did you do?"

"I shot the ground in front of him, and he ran. I didn't see him again," Hasida said. "Why is this thing here? Are my people being threatened again?"

The radio burst to life before Collins could answer. "*Collins, are you there?*"

Collins turned on his radio. "Go ahead, Lisa."

"*I found some tracks outside the village. I think we can trace them.*"

"There are caves outside the village. It's the only smart place to go on foot," Hasida said.

"Do you mind showing us where?" Collins said.

Hasida nodded, and spoke a few Hebrew words to the villagers nearby. "Definitely. We'll get you a jeep. We also have lodgings set up in case you need to stay the night."

"Thank you, Hasida…as always," Anna said.

After a few minutes, they drove through the desert and picked up Lisa. Four more of the locals drove nearby in a similar jeep.

"We don't need back-up," Hanson said, looking at them.

Hasida laughed a little. "They're not here as back-up. They just want to see you slay a monster. You didn't answer my question. Why is this thing here? Why is my village a magnet for trouble?"

Collins shrugged. "There is no definite reason why these creatures decide on where they want to live. Usually it's something pretty simple, like the climate. If a creature has a bit more intelligence than the usual lot, they may like the people. Or the energy around a place. Usually we don't have time to ask."

Hasida narrowed her eyes. "Your organization does not try to bring them back alive?"

"That's not our mandate. Besides, when we deal with the unknown, we don't know what they are capable of. Some of these creatures can wipe out an entire city within seconds. It's better for our safety if we strike at them first," Collins explained. "We'll try and bring back the carcass for scientific study. But if there's a risk to other people, even when it's dead, then we burn the body."

Hasida was about to say something, then gestured. "The cave is up ahead. I can see it."

"See anything on the thermal, Lisa?" Collins asked.

"No sign of anyone wandering around."

"Nothing on the satellite, either," Jeremy added.

Anna stopped the jeep. "Let's park here, and make the rest of our way on foot." The team got out of the vehicle and armed themselves with their weapons in the trunk.

"Stay here, Hasida," Anna said, as the blond woman was about to reach for a gun.

Hasida bit her lower lip. "I can actually shoot, you know."

Anna flashed her a smile, but the rest of her team had geared up and were ready to go. She gestured at the second jeep as it parked. "I need you to keep the rest of our audience safe. You've done your job. Let us do ours."

Mercifully, she didn't argue, and talked quietly to the rest of the locals.

"Let's go," Collins said, and they climbed a small path up to the cave. Once inside, they made as little noise as possible. Anna slipped on infrared goggles but couldn't see anything.

Jeremy scraped the ground slightly, and flashed her an apologetic look. She shook her head, and they descended further into the cave.

Collins held out his hand, signaling for them to stop. Anna crouched down. She couldn't see anything on infrared besides a couple of nestling bats…but she could hear something else moving. Anna removed her goggles, and could see a set of bright green eyes looking down at them from the ceiling. This creature must be able to camouflage its body heat. She gestured quietly.

Lisa aimed her weapon upwards. At Collin's nod, she released two bullets. The bats shrieked and flapped around them. One tangled itself through her red hair. Swearing, she tore it free and let it flap away. She focused her gun, but saw no trace of the creature.

"Where did it go?" Jeremy demanded, aiming his gun in random directions. "Lisa, you shot it, didn't you?"

Before Lisa could reply Anna felt a rush of air hit her, and she landed on her back as the creature straddled her. It resembled nothing human, with a white body and green veins. Four arms attacked her, which had suckers instead of hands. The creature still had green eyes, however, likely the same brown eyes Hasida described.

Anna didn't think. She grabbed her gun from the dirt and aimed upward. The creature hissed at her, and opened its mouth. Before she could fire, it spat out some kind of green liquid at her face. Anna wasn't sure what it was, only that it smelled vile. Anna ignored it and fired. Shrieking, the creature jumped off her and into the darkness. Collins, Jeremy and Hanson followed it.

Lisa helped her up. "Are you all right?"

"Yeah. It didn't go into my mouth," Anna said, and coughed. In the distance, she could hear multiple gunshots. "Left a hell of a stench though."

"Yeah, it reeks. Come on, let's back them up."

The two followed Collins and Jeremy, but found they didn't need to worry. The creature was dead on the ground. As its white skin broke open, more of the liquid was released, making the stench even worse.

"Didn't put up much of a fight. Looks like we surprised it," Collins said, giving the creature a kick.

"Want to preserve the body?" Anna asked.

"Fuck that noise. I am not dragging that stench back to the hotel," Jeremy snapped. "Let's burn it."

"I agree," Hanson said. "Let's get the gasoline from the jeep."

They headed toward the entrance of the cave, and Anna tried her radio. "Jeff, are you there?" Only static answered back. "We need to clear these caves before I can get a signal."

"It can wait," Collins said, shrugging. "Think Jeff will give us a bit of downtime?"

"I wouldn't mind staying here for a couple more—" Anna began, and looked up at the mouth of the cave.

Five more of the white creatures were shuffling into the cave. They must have multiplied! One of them made a strange clicking noise and raised its sucker-like hand.

"Shoot them!" Collins ordered, panicked.

Anna instantly aimed her gun and shot one of them. As Jeremy leveled his gun, the second charged and overpowered him. She shifted her aim, but couldn't get a clear shot as the two rolled back and forth on the ground. Lisa shot a third creature and Anna could hear a soft 'ping' as Jeremy's grenade suddenly rolled off his belt. Anna's eyes widened. It was live.

Collins shot the four creature, and noticed the grenade as well. "Clear the cave!" he screamed.

In the span of three seconds, Anna reached forward, grabbed the creature on top of Jeremy by its thin, wisp-like hair, and shot it once in the head. The creature made a strange gurgling noise, and died. No time to clear the cave. Anna dived to the ground behind a boulder, doing her best to protect her head.

"Ugh," Jeremy said. Dazed, he began to stand up.

"Jeremy, run!" Anna screamed.

The grenade exploded behind Jeremy with a deafening noise. Shrapnel flew past her head, followed by smoke. Anna looked up in the chaos. Miraculously, Jeremy turned to face her, his gaze tilted at an odd angle. Blood covered his chest, undoubtedly caused by the shrapnel tearing through his body. Yet, Anna knew with a sickening certainty, that the damage would be nothing compared to the damage in the back.

He fell to his knees, his uniform catching on fire. Lisa instantly ran toward him, doing what she could to douse it. Thankfully, the explosion hadn't caused much of a cave in. Collins was nearby but dazed. She had to kill the other two that escaped. Hasida and some of the locals were still outside and could be in danger. She gestured at Lisa. "Come on!"

"Those bastards are going to pay for this," Lisa said.

"Damn right," Anna said as she ran out of the cave. The two creatures were running away. Lisa aimed her sniper's gun, and fired. One of the two creatures fell.

"Good job," Anna said. "The other one's mine. Give me the rifle."

Lisa nodded and handed it to her. Anna focused in on the target through the cross hairs.

"Wait!' Lisa snapped, lifting the gun up just as Anna fired once. The bullet went harmlessly into the sky.

"What the fuck is wrong with you?" Anna demanded.

Lisa studied the fleeing figure through her binoculars. "Is that? My God is that..." she gave Anna the binoculars.

Anna looked through them, and her breath caught in her throat. A five-year old boy was running for his life toward the village.

"I don't understand," Matt said.

"How could we know? How could we have possibly known?" Anna whispered to herself, clutching her jacket tighter. She looked up at Matt. "When we were in that cave...we inhaled something. A powerful hallucinogenic. We thought we were seeing monsters, but they were the villagers." Tears fell from her eyes. "I shot Hasida. She was trying to say something to me, but I couldn't understand her as I...as I put a bullet in her brain."

Matt sighed heavily. So this was the big secret Lisa had been hiding. He gripped her shoulder. "What happened was horrible, but Anna, you can't blame yourself. You had no idea. That wasn't your fault."

"No," Anna said, and looked up. "But what happened next was."

"Fuck, help me!" Jeremy screeched in the cave. His face was covered in burns and blood.

Anna crouched over him, fumbling for a medical kit. "Shit... shit!"

"What's going on?" Hanson asked groggily behind her.

Anna bit back an angry retort. It wasn't Hanson's fault that he was the only person who didn't shoot anyone. "Hanson, there's a stretcher back in the jeep. Grab it."

Hanson didn't argue, and left.

"We killed her," Lisa said. She pushed back a lock of Hasida's blond hair with trembling fingers.

Anna grabbed a pair of gloves and a bottle of saline from the kit. "Jeremy, you have to stay still honey, just for a moment." She poured the saline over the deepest piece of shrapnel she could see, then grabbed a pair tweezers from the medical kit. She willed herself not to look at the doorway as she pulled it out. Jeremy screamed beneath her.

"Stay still," Anna snapped.

"Jesus Christ, we didn't know," Collins said. "How could we?"

She didn't bother to respond as she searched for more shrapnel. There was going to be infection and...gods, she killed Hasida. She released a breath as she stared at her bloodstained gloves. No, now was not the time to think about it.

Collins turned on his radio. "Jeff, we've got a situation. Can you hear me? We need help!"

Thankfully, Jeff answered. *"Got a signal. What's wrong?"*

As Collins spoke quietly, Jeremy gripped her arm, startling her. "Put me out, Anna," he asked, tears gathering in his eyes. "Please."

Anna glanced at the medical kit. No sign of any sedative. Best she could do was morphine. She injected his leg, then took his hand. "You're going to be fine," she said. She glanced up at Collins. "What are we going to tell them?"

Collins didn't reply, looking away.

"Collins, *what are we going to tell the villagers*?"

Hanson ran back into the cave, holding the stretcher.

Collins shook his head. "Anna, you and Hanson get Jeremy back to the chopper. Prep for immediate take-off. Lisa and I will deal with the villagers."

Anna nodded as she and Hanson carefully loaded Jeremy onto the stretcher. "What's the plan?"

"Focus on Jeremy. He needs your help right now more than we do," Collins said. He gave her a comforting smile. "Anna, it'll be okay."

Anna nodded. "All right." She bit her lip, willing herself not to cry. "Jeremy..."

"I know," he said, and placed a hand on her shoulder. "He needs you, Anna. That's why you have to keep it together."

With considerable difficulty, Lisa and Hanson loaded Jeremy onto the jeep. Hanson started it up and drove them toward the helicopter. Anna watched a second jeep take a different path, back toward the village

The jeep suddenly jerked once, breaking her concentration. "Dammit Hanson, keep it steady!" she snapped.

"How bad is it?" Hanson shouted over his shoulder as she continued to work.

"I can stop the bleeding. I don't think his internal organs were hit." Anna glanced up at him, and wiped the blood from her face. "But...I think some of the shrapnel impacted his spine. Back of his legs are pretty burned as well."

"My god," Hanson said. The implications were clear. It was very likely Jeremy would never walk again.

"Anna," Jeremy murmured. "Thanks for getting that damn thing off me. How many creatures are left?"

"He's going into shock," Anna said. "I have to stop this bleeding."

Anna worked silently for several minutes as Hanson drove toward the helicopter. By the time they got there, she managed to get Jeremy into a somewhat stable condition.

"I can't feel my legs," Jeremy said. "Why can't I feel my legs?"

"Don't worry. Jeff will fix them for you. We'll get you the best treatment money can buy," Anna said tonelessly as Hanson parked the jeep. "We're going to have a bitch of a time getting him on the helicopter," she added , and glanced up as she heard the sound of gunfire. She didn't think. She grabbed an assault rifle from the side, slung it over her shoulder, and jumped out of the jeep. "Stay here! Protect Jeremy!"

"Got it," Hanson said.

Anna didn't pause as she sprinted across the desert. Just as she made it to the outskirts of the village, bullets fired again, followed by people screaming. She lifted her assault rifle as she arrived in the center of the square.

Five villagers were lined up against the wall as Collins and Lisa fired again, including the little boy. As Anna watched, blood sprayed from their bodies, and they fell backward into the sand. She didn't think. She aimed her gun above Collins' head, and released a warning shot. Collins and Lisa automatically turned and pointed their gun at her.

"Stand down, Anna," Collins said. "That was the last of them. It's over."

"What...why...?" Anna stammered, and glanced at the wall of corpses.

"We're going to burn the village. Make it look like this was an unprovoked attack from Iran," Collins said.

Anna kept her gun held high, but glanced at Lisa. "Lisa?" she whispered.

Lisa's face was pale and she wouldn't meet her eyes.

Anna switched her aim to Collins. "Why?" she demanded again.

"That kid told the village what happened. They knew what we did! If you or Lisa had just shot him, we could have said the monster killed them all! Instead we have this bullshit to deal with!" Collins snapped, gesturing angrily. Behind him, Lisa recoiled as though slapped.

"So what?" Anna demanded stepping forward. "We could have denied it! Denied everything! We've done it in the past!"

"This is different!" Collins shouted. "This country is on the verge of war. If Israel learned that people from America shot their own people, it might push them over the edge and cause a shit storm we don't need! This is D.R.E.X. We cover this stuff up all the time."

"Even our own goddam mistakes?" Hot tears burned her eyes. "We knew these people!"

"Put down the fucking gun, Anna," Collin said. "I won't ask again."

Anna stared again at the bodies on the ground. She released a breath and lowered her assault rifle. "I want to talk to Jeff."

Collin gave her a disgusted look. "Who do you think ordered this?"

Bullshit, Anna was about to say, when she heard a voice on the radio.

"Anna. Stand down."

Anna fell silent, studying the grass.

"God," Matt said. "Lisa—"

"Was a part of it, yes. Soon after, D.R.E.X shut down. Officially, it was because we found the last escapee from the portal and had done our job. Unofficially though…it was because we blotched the entire operation. Every single member of that team had become a mass-murderer." Anna released a breath, then gave him a smile full of bitterness. "And we all got off scot-free. Not a mark on our record. Jeff ensured that, and to save his reputation D.R.E.X. shut down. To this day, I have no idea how Jeff was able to get it back up and running again."

Matt backed away, stumbling over a rock in the process. Lisa could not be a mass-murderer. He felt sick to his stomach. "No. You're lying to me."

Anna used her free hand to wipe away her tears. She stepped forward, arms outstretched. "Matt, I am so—"

Matt held up his hand, stopping her. He couldn't breathe. "Stay the fuck away from me!"

"I know you're furious, but you have to hear me out," Anna persisted. "We have a traitor on this team! Someone who reported every step we took."

"What?" Matt asked. Everything was turning gray. What traitor? What team? What did it matter? Matt took in a deep, cool breath. His head began to clear and he stood. "Anna, that voice could have been anyone. Someone hacked into our com systems, and they could have had a sample of all our voices."

"Really? Think about it! Someone has followed us from the beginning, tracking our movements. They knew the book was still in Vermon! Ryan could have done it." She shrugged. "I've seen his file. He's guilty of every single crime you can think of. Including murder. So why am I wrong?"

"I can't trust you either, Anna. You may not have committed genocide, but you sure as hell didn't come forward!" Matt felt a flash of wild fury, and fought to keep it in check.

"You think I didn't want to every day since? Jeremy tried to report it to the press. And guess what? Jeff destroyed him. Not just financially, but by the time he was finished he almost went to an insane asylum. He paid for what happened."

"And now, someone else is making the rest of you pay," Matt said. "Give me your phone."

Anna said nothing, her cheeks flushed. Reluctantly she took it out and slipped it into his hand.

"I don't want to ever see you again," Matt said quietly. "Go back to your farm. Take our rental. If I ever see you again, it will be the last thing you ever see."

Anna studied his face, looking for another alternative. Seeing none, she turned and stumbled toward her car.

It was only a couple of seconds later when Anna's words really hit him. *My wife killed innocent people. My wife committed genocide.* Matt made it three steps before collapsing into the dark, wet grass. He wanted to scream. Instead, he threw up.

You look upset honey…are you okay?

Matt touched his face with the back of his hand, not surprised to feel tears falling from his eyes. He was shaking all over, and couldn't seem to stop.

If he had known at the time, what could he have done?

Matt glanced at the safe house. Would that be him in a couple years' time? Unknowingly killing hundreds of people, and Jeff brushing it aside? Matt took in a deep gulp of air. No, he wasn't okay. He wouldn't be okay ever again.

"*Matt, do you copy?*" Jeff suddenly asked over the radio.

Matt felt anger surge in him. Finally, he had a target he could hit back. "Yeah, go ahead. Sir."

"*What happened back there? We only had static for a while.*"

"We can't trust the com systems right now. Someone hacked into it, and might be impersonating other people."

"*Could be confusing,*" Jeff said. "*I'll see if my tech people can fix that. For now though, rest assure that I am me.*"

"Are you?" Matt muttered. "Is anything you told me the truth, Jeff?"

For a moment, there was stunned silence. "*How is your team holding up?*"

"Lindsay and I are fine. Anna…" Matt paused.

"*What about Anna?*" Jeff asked, a bit tense.

"I know the full story, Jeff," Matt said. "Everything. What D.R.E.X did in Owphiyr. What you did. You should have told me."

There is a long pause. "*This isn't the time or place to talk about that now,*" Jeff said curtly. "*Is she okay?*"

"She's fine, but I told her leave. She's not needed on my team anymore."

"*Matt, what happened in Owphiyr was a mistake,*" Jeff said.

"Save it," Matt snapped. "I don't want to hear it. I don't want to hear from you ever again. We're through."

"*Matt, I—*"

Without waiting for a response, Matt tossed his Bluetooth away, and stomped on it until there were only pieces left. Only one thing kept him going. Somewhere out there, a man killed his family. Lisa might have deserved it, but his daughter didn't.

He calmly entered the house. Ryan was typing on his laptop. Lindsay was cleaning her sniper's gun. Neither looked at him. Either they heard his argument with Anna or they didn't. Matt decided they must have, but didn't care. "What are you doing?"

"Running a trace on our com links. If someone did tap us, I want to find out who."

Matt shook his head. He felt a mad desire to laugh and cry at the same time. "Don't bother. I know who it is."

Ryan paused. "Okay…care to enlighten us?"

Lindsay stopped cleaning and stared at him, interested.

Matt took out Anna's phone, looked through her list of contacts, and dialed. He heard the phone pick up. "I know it's you."

There was an odd click, followed by silence. "*No, Matthew,*" Lisa sobbed. "*Please don't do this—*"

"You had a sample of her voice. And you took ours when we were in your house," Matt interrupted. "Jeremy."

Another pause.

"*Pretty brilliant, huh?*" Jeremy asked. "*All the while giving you the impression that I hadn't paid the phone bill in months.*" He chuckled. "*I'm surprised that you of all people figured it out. You're not too bright. How did you figure it out, anyway? And how did you get this number?*"

"The pieces were there. And you were the only one who lost as much as I did," Matt replied. "The phone number I took from Anna's phone. Did you kill Lisa, Jeremy?"

Jeremy said nothing for a moment. "*How can I do anything, Matthew? I'm so crippled I can barely raise my arms. Tell you what,*" *though. Why don't you visit me and find out? I'll tell you all of my evil schemes, I promise—"*

"You're not in your house anymore, Jeremy. I know that much for a fact. You destroyed my life," Matt stated. "My wife had nothing to do with what happened in Owphiyr."

"You can lie to yourself all you want, Matt, but I was there. I see the truth every day. When I try to get a glass of water. When I try to take a piss. You know, after it happened, I did go to the police. The media. Anyone who would listen to me. Jeff shut me down, and destroyed what little I had left. My paycheck, my reputation, my relationship with my wife...not that there was much left after I lost my legs. D.R.E.X has no rules, and no sense of justice." There was a pause. *"Hanson was the only one who didn't murder anyone, and for that he got a quick death. Collins, not so much. And just wait until you see what I have in store for Anna. You can just walk away, Matt. My quarrel isn't with you. And if it makes you feel better, I won't survive this either. In the end, the souls of Owphiyr will finally have peace."*

"The world doesn't have to end with you," Matt said.

"I have no idea what you're talking about."

"No? The Blue Power Core wanted the Kat-su because they want to open the portal again. You knew D.R.E.X had the resources to find it, and manipulated us from the very start. And in return, they committed your murders for you."

Jeremy released a shaky breath. *"The world isn't going to end. They need to see everything...D.R.E.X...the portal. Believe me, I have tried everything else, Matt. Now I'm out of options. D.R.E.X will bounce back from what I plan to do, I know they will. But the world needs to see firsthand what you have seen. Isn't this the right thing to do?"*

"No. You're insane, and I will stop you."

Jeremy laughed. *"You'll never figure out where they are. But go ahead and try. Even if you do find us..."* He paused. *"That just means I can kill you in person."*

Matt turned off the phone. He walked over to the kitchen sink, put in the plug, and turned on the water. "We need to find out where they are. Right now."

"Oh my god, I am such an idiot," Ryan said, putting his head in his arms.

"Don't blame yourself. He gave us quite the performance, convincing us he was helpless. He didn't even have internet at his house. He must have been tracking us somewhere else." He paused as he glanced at Ryan. "I'm sorry."

Ryan gave him a faint smile. "I would have probably suspected me too."

"No, I mean I'm sorry for your laptop."

"Huh?" Before Ryan knew was happening, Matt snatched up the laptop and threw it in the water, followed by the radios. "What the hell!"

"Sorry—I'll get you a new one. That one came from D.R.E.X, and it might have some tracking devices in it. Where we're going, Jeff can't find us," Matt said.

"Matt, I know you're mad," Lindsay began. "But don't you think it would be a good idea to have his resources where we're going?"

Matt shook his head. "All this time, we've had a voice in our ear, manipulating us. And look where that got us."

"Okay, point taken," Ryan sighed. "I think we found out where this Blue Power Core might be. Fortunately, I managed to grab this before the reception hall blew up." He gestured at a folder on the table.

Matt lifted it up. "Receipts?"

"Yeah, get this—in 1999, before the military blew the hell out of the portal in Devon, they took a sample. There's a lot of superstition behind the portal, magical rituals and whatnot. But the actual mineral of the portal was a combination of quartz, copper, and obsidian. And guess what the Blue Power Core is buying huge quantities of?"

"All three. Some of which conduct energy," Matt muttered. "Where?"

"We have a delivery address," Ryan said triumphantly. "It's a warehouse in Missouri that's shut down. Something about workers going on strike, and some footage got leaked out that painted management in a bad light." Ryan waved a dismissing hand. "Either way, it's been closed for years. Odd place for a delivery, don't you think?'

"They're not trying to get to the portal in Devon," Lindsay muttered. "They're trying to build a whole new one. And we need to stop them."

Ryan and Lindsay glanced at Matt. An unspoken question lingered between them. They were silently asking if he was still a part of this, but more than that. They were looking for a leader.

Matt nodded. "We need to make one stop first."

Jeremy leaned back in his wheelchair, and grinned. Matt thought he was so smart, but he was smarter than all of them combined. He gripped his wheelchair and pushed forward, cursing as the chair almost slid into a pothole. The building didn't have one single inch of stable ground, and it was embarrassing asking the minions for help. For the most part, they left him alone, for which Jeremy was grateful. In the end, he would outsmart them, too.

He heard a retching sound down the hall and paused. In the far corner, a woman was weeping black tears. She hunched to her knees, and black liquid erupted from her lips. As soon as air touched the liquid, it thickened into a foam-like substance. The woman paused, thinking she was done. But of course, she wasn't. She gagged again, and this time a fresh spray of tiny, white eggs impacted against the foam and held on. A few hit the wall instead and smashed. Jeremy estimated that over thirty survived. Still crying, the woman stood and stumbled down the passageway. Even now it wasn't over for her. There was still a little black liquid inside her. Eventually it would turn acidic and melt the woman's insides.

He had seen it happen many times before. His nose wrinkled in distaste.

Jeremy wheeled himself down the passageway, and spotted Father Jacobs and Samantha in a room through an open door. He whispered something in her ear, and she nodded.

"Ah. Jeremy," Father Jacobs said, smiling. "Everything is to your satisfaction?"

"Hardly. I can't believe we're in this warehouse, *Jacobs*," Jeremy replied. "The wiring is pathetic and there's no fucking heat. And, it isn't exactly wheelchair accessible."

The smile never left Father Jacobs' face. "It must be here. This place is perfect. And, it is well fortified." He touched the wall. "The ritual will start tonight. I assume your 'friends' will not be a problem."

"I'll take care of it." Jeremy struggled to move his wheelchair around.

"You know, we never discussed your reward," Father Jacobs said. "When you approached us, the only thing you wanted was revenge. Now that you know what we are, and what we can do, are you sure you don't want anything else?"

Jeremy snorted. "When this is all over, the only thing I need is my shotgun." Without waiting for a response, he rolled away.

Jacobs watched him leave, and the smile faltered from his lips slightly. No matter how much he tried to install hope in Jeremy, it just didn't work. "Samantha, am I doing the right thing?" he asked. For the past few year, he had been patient, slowly building up his army. The warehouse was massive, and now housed forty-five members of the Blue Power Core. A few were crazy, believing that aliens would pick them up and deliver them to a mother ship. Some, like him, were religious. Others were simply decrepit teens, looking for something important because the world had forgotten them. But Samantha...she was special.

Not long after he had joined with Ethan, he had found her on the rooftop of his church one night, about to jump off. He remembered how beautiful she looked…how vulnerable. If there were ever an idea of an angel, she would be it. He had talked her out of suicide, and nurtured her like the rest. Yet there was something about her that made him reveal his innermost plans. Secretly, he hoped that he would be regarded as the next Messiah. It was sinful, and selfish, but after all the years of living at an empty church, he had to believe that he was meant for something greater.

"Of course," Samantha said, surprised. "We're going to open the portal to heaven. We're so close now. Can't you see it?"

Jacobs looked at her, and realized that Samantha was bathed in white light, and there were stars twinkling around her. It occurred to him, and not for the first time, that he might be looking at something not real. Yet, the feeling of comfort still persisted in him. If anything, it felt stronger than ever. "But…your sacrifice."

"Shhhh," Samantha said, touching his lips. "I'm not afraid. What I'm about to do, today, is worth it. I love you."

Smiling, Jacobs gripped her arm. This woman, this miraculous woman was truly sent from God.

"Please," Samantha sobbed, tears running down her eyes. "Please don't hurt me. I swear to God I won't tell anyone, just let me go."

Jacobs gripped her wrist. Drool fell from the corner of his lips and he was grinning like an idiot. His grip, however, was strong as steel. "You swear to God?" he echoed. "You have strayed, child. When I rescued you from your own self-imposed sin, I thought you wanted something greater. Why are you lying to me?"

"Not like this," Samantha blubbered, tears falling from her eyes. "I just want to go home. You said…you said it would hurt—"

Smack! Blood sprayed along the wall as he slapped her across the face. She fell out of his grip and landed on the cold concrete.

"Look at that," Jacobs chided. "Get up, my daughter. You'll ruin your dress."

He walked toward her, and with a startled gasp she was lifted her upwards. Jacobs gripped her by her throat with his elbow, to a point where she couldn't breathe. "Everything worth doing hurts in this world, child. Did Abraham think bringing his child to the altar would be a leisurely stroll? Yes, it will hurt—perhaps quite a bit. But I thought you were my pure angel. I thought you were strong. Was I wrong?"

Choking Samantha didn't—*couldn't*—reply.

He gently lowered her to the ground and kissed away her tears. "Don't worry. There will be a bit of pain, but then the gates of heaven will open. Then, if you want to, you can go home. But if you can't do it—" He clawed into her shoulders, earning another gasp from the woman. "If you can't be faithful, then I will be very disappointed in you."

"I love you…"

Jacobs frowned as everything changed around him. At first, Samantha had been kissing him, encouraging him. Then, she stood in front of him, her lips bloody and her dress dirty. Tears were welling in her blue eyes. He stared at her in outrage. Who had done this to her? "Samantha—"

Whimpering, Samantha ran out of the passageway.

"*Pay no attention to her,*" Ethan mentally reassured him. "*She is just overwhelmed. When the time is right, she will fulfill her part.*"

The feeling of fuzziness was stronger than ever. He closed his eyes, unable to think.

"*Tonight, you will see the gates of heaven open,*" Ethan continued. "*My power will become part of you forever. Your followers will look at you forever as…dare I say, Jesus reincarnated.*"

In the safe house, Lindsay shuddered near the toilet. That… thing had touched her, infected her. She wanted to throw up, but at the same time, she felt something in the back of her throat. A lump. Her tongue lightly touched the roof of her mouth. A sac that wasn't there before. Throwing up felt like a bad idea.

"God," Lindsay whispered. It had forced its way down her throat in the warehouse. She tried to fire back, but it moved fast... way too fast. She was surprised it didn't rip her to shreds.

Any sane person would tell Matt or Jeff. Or go to the nearest hospital. Or just run as far away from D.R.E.X as possible.

But she didn't. Why?

"The mission," Lindsay whispered. There was no time to worry about this now.

At least, so she told herself.

Years ago, she could still see herself curled up in a fetal position near the wall, as her husband loomed closer. *"You are just a useless cunt, aren't you? You can't even pour a glass of water without needing someone's help!"* he had screamed.

A coldness swept over her. Who could she really tell, anyway? She couldn't even reach Jeff. Matt had seen to that. Ryan, her dear brother...was a fucking mess. She could still picture meeting him for the first time. He had almost been too drunk to stay upright.

He's changed.

Maybe...maybe not.

And Matt? Well, he nearly had a spaz attack a few hours ago, didn't he? Ready and willing to shoot them all.

Lindsay's eyes narrowed. No, she was stronger than this. Stronger than all of them. She would wait until the mission was over, and then she would take care of this. And if things escalated past the point of no return...she would take care of that too.

She heard a knock on the door. "Lindsay? Are you ready?"

Lindsay lifted herself up. "Yeah. Sure."

CHAPTER 12

Jalisco, Mexico

La Fiesta Cafe was a small but cheerful restaurant with several white open archways permitting the sunlight to shine through the glass windows. Inside were five small tables, a bar, and a patio outside. As Ryan entered, he could see two men smoking at one table, but no one else. A waiter looked up from his guest book and approached. "Puedo ayudarlo, senor?"

Ryan waved a dismissing hand. "Estoy con alguien fuera de."

The man nodded, and Ryan headed to the outside patio. Catherine was sitting at a table by herself, heavily engrossed in a meal. Ryan couldn't help but notice how beautiful she looked. She wore a white summer dress and sandals.

Ryan walked up to her. "Mind if I join you?" he asked politely.

Catherine's face held no surprise. "Of course not," she said.

Ryan sat down in a wooden chair. For a moment, they didn't say anything to each other. Finally, he grabbed a menu. "So what's good on here?"

"I recommend the veggie quesadilla. How did you find me?"

"I'm part of a spy network, Catherine," Ryan replied. "I have resources."

"Hm, I suppose so," Catherine said, smiling. She took a cigarette from her purse and leaned back. "And where are your other friends? Let me guess, they're covering the back? Maybe one of them has a sniper's view on my head in case I cause any trouble?"

"Something like that," Ryan said, smiling a little as he ordered a drink. "But this doesn't have to be confrontational."

Catherine took a drag and looked away, her expression thoughtful. "Yes, it does," she said. "In the end, it will be."

Ryan shrugged. "Not today. Today...I just want to talk."

"Why? Nothing you've told me so far has been honest," Catherine replied.

Ryan studied her. Matt thought it would be a good idea if he spoke to her alone. For whatever reason, they had some kind of a connection. He couldn't figure out why. "Ryan Kelsler Martin. That's my full name. I've only told a handful of people that."

Catherine considered, then bowed her head slightly. "What do you want to talk about, Ryan?"

"I need information on a group of people. The Blue Power Core."

Catherine leaned back in her chair, giving Ryan a full display of her long, tanned legs. "Surely your D.R.E.X database is capable of that?"

Ryan lowered his head. "D.R.E.X and I...are not on good terms right now. Besides, I have a feeling that the database wouldn't hold a candle compared to what you know."

She raised an eyebrow. "The Blue Power Core isn't real. It's a front."

"Yeah, we know that. Who are they, really?"

Catherine regarded him for a moment, then stabbed her cigarette into the ashtray. "Nothing is ever free, Ryan. I'll tell you what I know, but I want something in return."

"What?"

"Immunity from D.R.E.X. I don't want to be hunted by you people, ever." She gave him a smirk as she played with her glass of water.

Ryan shook his head. "You're a monster."

"And D.R.E.X has killed its own people multiple times. Some of whom I doubt were guilty. Let's not use broad generalizations on each other, shall we? Do we have a deal or not?"

Ryan leaned back at his chair, indecisive. "What are you after, Catherine? Why did you choose to help me back at Vermon?"

Catherine looked at the rest of the people in the restaurant. "I like going to this place, every Saturday morning. Sometimes I go on Tuesday because they have Taco Tuesday. I genuinely like the food here, Ryan. I love cell phones. I like to touch people, and I like people to touch me." She leaned over and touched his hand. "You couldn't find any of those things where I used to come from. Does it bother you that D.R.E.X killed creatures who are capable of rational thought?"

Ryan didn't reply. Her grip on his hand was warm. Trouble was, he didn't know exactly if she was male or female…or even really what she was. He tried to pull away.

But Catherine gripped him tighter. "Do we have a deal or not?"

"Yeah, we have a deal," Ryan said impatiently, breaking free. "What do you know?"

Catherine looked away. "Where I come from there is a dominating force, one who made the world more miserable for the rest of us…if such a thing could be possible. They are called the Brache, and they will murder your race without discrimination. The rest will be turned into slaves, carrying out deeds, which frankly will not be tasteful for me to describe. But they too will die, eventually, and your entire race will be destroyed. And then they'll come after me, and any other race left standing." She released a sigh. "They don't create anything. They will simply burn away whatever is alive. So it is in my best interest to stop them, with your help."

"How can they be stopped?" Ryan asked.

Catherine picked at her food. "I don't know. No one does. I have heard that they first appear as a non-corporeal form, and then they bond with a member of your species. Afterwards, this one person is unstoppable, and capable of anything. They first pretend to be your friend, to have you join in their little crusade. The Blue Power Core believes in this Brache unquestionably. But there will come a time when the Brache will crush them, and never look back."

"And the host is just…okay with this?"

Catherine was thoughtful. "You know, I don't think the host even knows what's going on most of the time. I think the Brache shows him, or her, whatever they want to."

Ryan took a sip of his beer. "Come on, there's got to be a way, right? I mean, what does he want?"

"To open the portal again. To let others in."

Ryan frowned. "Why? I mean, it seems like he's got a pretty good set-up here by himself."

Catherine chuckled and shook her head. "Ryan, you'll never fully understand unless your species becomes extinct too."

He waited for her to say something further, but she didn't offer anything else. He stood. "Enjoy your meal," he said. "Thanks for the tip."

"I didn't do it to help D.R.E.X," Catherine said before he could leave. "I did it to help you. Are you going to try and stop them?"

"Yes," Ryan said.

"Do you believe you have a chance?"

"Yes," Ryan said, but with less conviction.

Catherine bit into her food, then looked at him. "Maybe I'll see you again, Ryan."

As soon as they arrived at the airport, Matt knew they were in trouble. They were supposed to land at a private airport where they wouldn't have to pass through many security checks. However, bad weather forced them to land at Lambart-St.Louis terminal.

"Ah, shit," Ryan said, looking out the window. Matt followed his gaze, and saw several police officers running toward the plane.

"We're D.R.E.X," Lindsay muttered. "We don't answer to them."

"Yeah, well, they seem to think differently," Ryan said. He glanced at Matt. "I say we take them. We can do it with minimal casualties."

Still sitting in his seat, Matt shook his head. There was a time, and not so long again, when he was going to be locked away for at least thirty years. He was never going back to prison ever again.

But at the same time, these weren't bad people. "I'm not going to have a shoot-out on the runway, Ryan."

"Well, what do you propose we do?" Ryan snapped nervously as the cops entered the plane.

"Don't do anything," Matt said.

They were forcibly removed from the plane, handcuffed, and separated once they reached the airport. After being searched and having all his gear removed, Matt was placed in an empty, small interrogation room with an obvious two-way mirror. For almost an hour, no one entered.

Finally, the door opened, and a small woman wearing an FBI jacket stepped toward him. She was quite beautiful, with long, light brown hair, green eyes, and pale skin with a dash of freckles. She dropped a bag on the table and unzipped it. Inside were guns, grenades, and a couple of flashing devices Ryan must have built in his spare time. She raised her eyebrow. "Cute toys." She sat down in the opposite chair. "Are you planning to start a war?"

"Who are you?" Matt asked.

"Jasmine Kelly, FBI," the woman responded. "The question is, who are you? I know you're D.R.E.X, but we've checked your fingerprints, your dental records, hell even your DNA. No record whatsoever."

Matt didn't respond as the thought sunk in. Of course, D.R.E.X erased all of his records. Now he officially had no identity. Not now, or ever again. Surprisingly, the thought didn't bother him. What did he have left?

"Hm? Excuse me?" Jasmine snapped her fingers, interrupting his thoughts. "What is your name?"

Matt leaned forward. "If you know I'm from D.R.E.X, you must also know that you have no authority over me. I don't have to answer any of your questions."

"I know." Jasmine folded her arms and leaned back in her chair. "Scary thought, isn't it? You and your friends can do anything you want, and I can't do a damn thing, from orders of the president himself. Well, nothing legal, that is. But rest assured, the

FBI has been watching D.R.E.X's activity very closely. Since your reinstatement, there have been missile strikes in Paris, disguised as a fire. A town in Vermon has had several unexplainable deaths, and those still alive need counseling for reasons that don't make any sense. And an explosion in Winnipeg—at least that building was empty. Over the past few weeks, you've caused dozens of casualties. Families are demanding explanations that we can't provide." She blinked. "Does that mean anything to you, agent? What do you suggest I tell them?"

Matt looked down. Lisa's death flashed vividly in his mind. "I have a phone number where you can direct your inquiries."

Jasmine smirked. "A phone number." She looked away. "Let me give you a friendly warning. Get back on the plane. St. Louis is my home, and I am not in the mood for any of your shit." She leaned back and looked smug. "You know, the FBI has some influence with the president, too. D.R.E.X's operations and your boss will be thoroughly investigated. In the meantime, Missouri is a no-fly zone for any D.R.E.X aircraft. Anything spotted will be shot down. I don't have enough to put you away, but if you or your friends cause any disturbance, I will be coming after you. With or without my badge."

Matt waited for her to say anything else, but she didn't. "So am I free to go?"

"Yeah," Jasmine said, her voice filled with disgust. "You're free to go."

Matt stood from his chair and headed for the door.

"Hey," Jasmine said, gesturing to the bag. "Don't forget these."

There weren't any safe houses in St. Louis, but finding a hotel wasn't a problem. Ryan hacked a nearby ATM, and they found a quiet, out of the way building where the manager wouldn't ask any questions.

Ryan studied a floor plan of the warehouse on a laptop he purchased at a pawn store. "Okay, the most likely place the portal will be is in the main lobby. It's the biggest room. Lindsay and I will make our delivery, and divert as many of them as we can away from you to block B." He pointed to the left side of the map.

"At the same time, I will enter through lock C," Matt said.

"Hopefully there won't be too many left for you to worry about," Ryan said. "Lindsay and I will be sure to make some noise."

"Plant the charges there and there," Matt pointed.

"That leaves you...what, fifteen minutes to get there and back?"

"About that," Matt said, and glanced at the screen. "Lots of people are going to die tonight."

"That's nothing new for Lindsay and me," Ryan said. "Are you cool with that?"

Matt didn't reply, suddenly remembering a time when he did nothing more than give out fliers. Most people slammed the door in his face. "Yeah."

"Maybe we should call Jeff," Lindsay spoke up, sitting on the couch.

Hearing his name, Matt felt a surge of anger. "We can't. The coms are being monitored. We can't let Jeremy know we're here."

He hoped they wouldn't notice his reaction, but was quickly disappointed.

"And?" Lindsay prompted.

"Jeff believes in shooting first, asking questions later," Matt said. "If he knew they were here, he could nuke the city. With us in it, along with a million people."

"Jesus," Ryan said, closing the laptop. "Matt, are you sure? That seems like overkill. Not to mention a serious lack of faith in our abilities."

Matt didn't reply. "What about security?"

"Please. It's an old security system. I'll have it eating out of my hand. You'll be invisible," Ryan said.

"When do we do this?" Lindsay asked.

"Tonight," Matt said.

There was a knock on the door.

Matt glanced at Ryan, who looked equally alarmed. Matt narrowed his eyes and covered the door. Lindsay grabbed her assault rifle, and very slowly slid open the balcony door.

"Who is it?" Ryan asked when Matt nodded.

"Delivery for three very conspicuous spies. Look, I am too old for this bullshit. Just open the door," a cranky voice replied, one he recognized.

Matt couldn't fault the guy for his honesty. He nodded at Ryan, and raised his gun as he opened the door.

Louise stood in their doorway with a briefcase "Well? Aren't you going to invite me in?"

"How did you find us?" Matt asked. "Jeff doesn't even know we're here."

"Yeah, that's cute, Matt." He brushed past him and placed his briefcase on the bed. "Your clothes are bugged. Your car is bugged. Your bugs have bugs. Just because you threw out your radio doesn't mean that Jeff can't hear every word you have said over the past few days. This hotel is lit up like a Christmas tree. If Jeff truly wanted to stop your little operation, you would not be leaving this room tonight. Might want to think this through next time you want to do things your way."

Matt's eyes widened.

Louis gave them a small smile. "Don't worry about it," he said. "You're new at this, but you're good. It was nice that you avoided an international incident at the airport. Stick around for a couple of years, and you'll be a master."

The man had an edge of sarcasm in his voice. "You're just saying that, aren't you?"

"Yeah, maybe." He opened up the briefcase.

Lindsay rubbed the back of her head. "So why are you here?"

"Because Jeff thinks there might be Blinkers there, and they will probably tear you apart the moment you enter that warehouse. We need to even the odds." He took out cans of what appeared to be spray paint.

"What is that?"

"Pheromones." Louise said. "It'll mask your scent, but it has to everywhere—back of your neck, arms, legs, feet, clothes—everywhere. If your hair has any product in it, wash it out and spray this instead. If you have any scratches, they need to be cleaned and covered. Trust me, if you have a single drop of blood, they will know something is wrong. Their sense is that acute."

Lindsay suddenly gripped her stomach.

Louise glanced at her. "Are you all right?"

"Yeah," she said. "Just something I ate."

"So basically, don't get hurt in the slightest while we're hanging out at the monster den," Ryan said.

"Comforting," Matt mumbled. "Anything else?"

Louise stared at him, and handed him three radios. "The FBI is meddling in our affairs. We can't give you air support, otherwise Jeff would have already ordered a missile strike by now. But we can give you intel, in case you feel like talking again. This time the channel has been scrubbed, I promise you. They've been modified to block out the Kat-su's interference, if you come across it. Look Matt, Jeff sent a squad to Jeremy's house. No one was there. You were right about him. Jeff wants to help you."

"I don't need his help," Matt said.

"Son, I have worked in this business for a very long time. Jeff is honest to you roughly half the time, which makes him one of the better ones." He shook his head. "Don't be an idiot." He grabbed his briefcase and turned for the door.

"You're leaving?" Ryan asked sarcastically. "Hey, don't let your age hold you back. I'm sure we can find a spare Uzi for you."

Louise paused at the door. "You're a funny man," he said. "You know what I've noticed, Agent Martin? They're the ones who usually die first."

Without waiting for a response, he left.

CHAPTER 13

A few hours later, Matt approached a white truck a block from the warehouse. They purchased it as a rental. Lindsay was doing one final sweep of the building's perimeter. Ryan, meanwhile, was working on his laptop in the passenger seat. "I'm getting some kind of weird readings from the prison."

"What kind of readings?" Matt asked.

"Geothermic. It's raining out here, and below freezing. Yet according to satellite footage, the lobby is cooking over eighty degrees Fahrenheit. The Kat-su is definitely in there." Ryan said. "I have full control over the security system. I can loop it so they won't notice you going in."

"And Jeremy? Where would he be?"

"Best guess? I think he would be in the security office. Second floor. It seems to be the only place that is wheelchair accessible. There's both an elevator and a stairwell in factory section A, which leads right to it."

"Are you sure?"

Ryan snorted. "Take it from one hacker to another, this is the area where he would feel the most in control. Until we take it away from him, that is," he added.

"Good job," Matt said, and brushed away the water from his jacket. God, he hated the rain. Worse, it would probably take away their scent. They would have to spray themselves again once they got inside.

"Yeah, whatever."

He frowned at Ryan, who was typing on the keyboard. "Let me ask you something."

"Sure. Shoot."

"Did you kill that man? Simon Jones? Just to clear my name?"

Ryan paused, his face unreadable. "Yeah. I did," he finally said, and shrugged. "Jeff's orders. Took me most of the night to get him in the trunk of the car. That guy was a heavy son of a bitch."

"And you have no problem with doing that?"

Ryan flashed him an irritated look. "Oh come on, Matt. I'm guilty of a lot of things. Why should murder come as a complete surprise to you? I've killed already several times already, courtesy of D.R.E.X, and the guy was hardly innocent. It didn't bother me."

Matt heard his tone shift in the last sentence. "I don't believe you," he finally said.

Ryan shook his head. "You asked me why I did it. Stole money from people."

"Yeah?"

"I've done a lot of things that I'm not proud of. Seven years ago, I was pretty messed up. Drugs, theft, you name it, I did it. Then I met this woman—Lindsay's sister—and we had a daughter." Ryan sighed. "Probably my worst mistake was the way I treated them. To cut a long story short, our marriage didn't last long. But then, when my daughter was only five years old, some asshole kidnapped her at a park, right under my nose." He looked up, his face expressionless. "Whoever it was knew what I could do, and wanted me to give them thirty thousand dollars on a monthly basis. Why they wanted so much money, I have no idea."

Matt studied him for a moment, fascinated. "What did you do?"

Ryan snorted. "What any panicking parent would do. I called the cops. They couldn't find shit. Neither could I. Think about that for a second. I thought I was the best hacker in the world, but I couldn't hold a candle to these guys. And every time I tried, they made it very clear to me that Kacie would be punished. So, I did what they told me to. For six months." He wouldn't look at him. "The really sick, ironic thing was that my daughter being kidnapped forced me to clean up my life. I kicked my drug habits and focused everything to finding and saving her. But after all this time, I still couldn't find her. Neither could Lindsay, for that matter. Even though she found me."

"Does Jeff—"

Ryan swore under his breath. "Yeah, of course he knows. How do you think he was able to rope me into working for him? Commit murder even? Jeff is making those payments on my behalf. So long as I keep working for him, that is. It also prevents my ass from spending twenty years in prison."

Matt said nothing, regarding him.

"So yeah, I've done things that I'm not proud of," Ryan snapped angrily, turning to face him. "But you know what, Matt? I fucking envy you. You've lost your family, and I'm sorry, that is a tragedy. But at least...at least you know." His eyes filled with pain. "You're not stuck in this terrible limbo all the time, wondering if your daughter is actually alive or dead. And knowing you're powerless to do anything about it." He faced the computer. "So there you go. My one 'terrible' secret. No grand government conspiracies going on, I'm just doing what I can to find her." He shrugged. "Lindsay might despise me, but she keeps my ass alive, so I can pay the ransom every month. I don't expect her to be here for any other reason."

Matt said nothing for a moment. Then, he touched Ryan's shoulder. "We'll find her, Ryan. I promise."

Ryan snorted as he resumed typing. "Yeah. You and what army, right? I'm not an idiot. No one stays missing this long and survives. I already know she's dead."

The door to the van opened before Matt could reply. "Got anything?" Lindsay asked, shaking the water out of her hair. She sat in the driver's seat.

Ryan shrugged. "Nothing that I can see. Infrared's dark. Of course that doesn't mean anything."

"What about you?" Matt asked.

"Three guys patrolling the building. They're amateurs. Stay low in the bushes and you should be able to avoid detection," Lindsay said.

"All right," Matt said, and opened the door. "If everything goes according to plan we should be back here in half an hour. Just get in, blow up the portal, and get out."

"And if things don't go according to plan?" Ryan asked.

"Well, I'm sure Jeff can always blow up the building," Matt said, and closed the van door.

Ryan drove the van to the side of the building, near the receiving dock. Seconds later, a man rapped at the window. Lindsay noticed that he had a blue sun tattooed on his right cheek. Must be a hardcore member.

"Who are you?" the man demanded. "What are you doing here?"

Lindsay leaned forward. "We have a delivery for this address. Is your receiving open?"

"It better be open," Ryan chipped in. "We came all this way without a power gate, and we have about eight skids of copper and obsidian in there. I'm not loading this truck again."

The man looked momentarily suspicious. "Show me."

Lindsay glanced at Ryan, and they both got out of the truck. Ryan opened the back door, revealing eight skids of crated boxes. "We're already behind schedule, so if you could find a couple of guys to help us that would be sweet."

"Shut up," the first kid snapped, raising his gun. "Show us."

Lindsay nodded, then whirled around, her knife flashing. She sliced his throat as Ryan stabbed the second guard in the head. The two stabbed them in the chest, finishing them off.

They both got out of the truck. Once they were a suitable distance away, Lindsay pressed a detonator, and the truck exploded.

In the lobby, the worshipers cried out as the walls trembled. For a second the lights went out, and a cloud of dust landed on the floor. Jacobs stared at this intrusion with a slight annoyance. The daemons were trying to storm the building. The very thought. "Have no fear, my friends. There are bugs scuttling in the walls, trying to stop our ascent to glory. But can you not feel it all around us?" He laughed. "They couldn't stop us tonight, even if they launched a dozen nuclear missiles."

Everyone relaxed. He could feel the air vibrate around him as he spoke, and his worshipers sighed with content. The lights flickered back, revealing a dozen people sitting on crude benches, staring at a portal made of Obsidian. They were his inner circle, the ones who would pave the way to heaven. Jacobs took in a deep breath. He had never felt so exulted in his entire life. Years ago, he had become a priest because it was expected of him, but God had been silent. Now his words were loud and clear. He would open the portal to heaven, and set thousands of angels free.

Samantha stood in front of the stage, dressed in a white gown with gold trim. She looked up at Father. He gave her a loving smile, and gestured for her to begin. She bowed her head and opened the book. A loud, cracking noise echoed around the lobby.

Jacobs stared at her. "This is going to kill her," he whispered to himself, as though in a dream. "Her body and soul will be ripped to shreds."

"Sometimes sacrifices have to be made for better things," Ethan replied. *"Sometimes, more than one."*

As they had predicted, the resulting noise from the explosion brought a lot of attention as Lindsay and Ryan entered the building. Ryan opened the door slightly, and Lindsay threw a flash grenade at several men waiting for them with guns. As the flash blinded the cultists, Lindsay and Ryan shot them down.

They reached the left wing cafeteria. Lindsay fired at the open hallway, pinning down ten or so members that were trying to advance. She glanced in irritation at her brother. "Ryan! I can't hold them off forever!"

"Almost there," Ryan said, setting up charges on the pillar. "There. I think—oof!"

Lindsay whirled around as someone jumped from the second floor walkway and slammed right down on Ryan. *Crazy fucker,* she thought. As Ryan struggled to his feet, the man attacked him with garrote wire and pulled him backward, almost off his feet. Ryan struggled for purchase as the man pulled harder. Lindsay took out her pistol and blew the man's head off as soon as she had a clear shot.

Blood and bits of brain splashed on Ryan, but it didn't seem to bother him. "Thanks."

More people fired from the second walkway. They fled into the opposite hallway, then to the right and into a storage room. "Give it a couple of seconds," Ryan said.

Lindsay stared at the detonator, and a cold chill ran down her back. They were murdering innocent people who might be being brainwashed. If there was a hell, she was definitely going there.

Before she could press the button, Ryan clasped his hand over hers, and pressed down on the detonator. Lindsay closed her eyes as both the entrance and exit to the cafeteria exploded, trapping whoever was still inside. Lindsay knew the structural supports would give away, burying the worshipers alive. They looked up as the roof trembled, then became still. It was a controlled explosion, and they should be safe. Should. Lindsay was suddenly aware of how silent everything became and released a deep breath.

A man ran screaming toward them. "You killed my wife, you fucking—"

Ryan gripped her hand tighter, and casually shot him. Lindsay jumped slightly at the noise. "It was me, Lindsay," he said. "Don't worry about it." He turned away.

"Does it ever bother you?" Lindsay asked.

Ryan waved a dismissive hand, but didn't look at her. "Oh please, Lindsay. I already killed five people by the time you first found me in D.R.E.X. This is nothing new."

Lindsay walked forward and gave him a hug, surprising them both. The first time she had killed someone, it had not been a clean sniper kill. Instead, she found her victim covered in blood and screaming, and there weren't any other D.R.E.X members around to help her finish the job. For some reason she didn't imagine it being any better for him. "I wish I could have been there for you."

She expected Ryan to push her away. Instead, he squeezed her back. "Come on. We've got to finish this."

Fearfully, Samantha opened the bleeding Kat-su. She wanted to drop it and run screaming from the room. She had been foolish enough to communicate that to Jacobs, who made it clear to her he would catch up to her and do unspeakable things if she tried. She gulped, realizing how much now she hated the man. Hopefully, she could just read the stupid verse and go home.

She began from the page marked out for her. To a typical human, she spoke in a garbled language akin to snarling and retching. The words terrified her, but the rest of the crowd including Jacobs collectively sighed.

"Ow," Samantha gasped as she doubled over. She touched her midsection, and her hand came away red. It felt as though something had slashed her chest.

Jacobs raised his hands. "Don't be afraid, my people. We are being tested. Our holy sister will triumph."

Samantha continued chanting, then doubled over again. She clutched her side, and a pool of blood spilled to the floor. With a shaky cough, she looked behind her. The air was sparkling, and a small black cloud was drifting from the worshipers toward the portal. Most of them were turning pale and had nosebleeds, but they didn't appear to notice.

"Come on, sister," Jacobs said.

Samantha began the next sentence. Suddenly, she was slammed to the floor, her mouth exploding in red. Most of her teeth appeared broken. She gave a choking gasp and rolled to her side. Then, her lips started to move again, and she continued the chant.

Someone moved to help her, and all of their collective energy was abruptly yanked forward, toward the portal. Everyone's noses and ears exploded in red. The worshipers collapsed.

The unseen force pounded Samantha, again and again, until she was black and blue. Despite this, she struggled to her feet. She was beyond rational thought now. All that mattered was completing the verse so it could stop! "Gala mack plu'noth—" She stumbled forward, her entire body a bleeding, unrecognized mess. Next to her bare feet, several people lay dead. Her eyes shined brightly as she approached the portal. 'Bal Gomez—'

Suddenly, a gunshot rang out, and exploded through her head. She twitched once, then became still. The light from the portal sputtered, then went out. The Kat-su gave an inhuman shriek.

Jacobs stared at all of this in shock. One moment his followers were swimming, bathing in a sea of golden light. The next they were all lying on the ground, dead. His plans…gone just like that. He stared at the intruder, a man with short brown hair wearing a black uniform. Matthew Burke. Did he kill them? "Heathen," he whispered, more out of a childlike wonder than anything else. Why? Why would someone do this?

He felt himself starting to black out as Ethan took over. His rage could not—*would* not be denied.

Closing his eyes, Jacobs disappeared.

Matt watched as Jacobs disappeared into black smoke. He entered the lobby, staring at the bodies of the dead followers. No survivors. "Ryan, I stopped the ritual. Double-back to my position."

"*Matty…*" a voice sang over the intercom. Jeremy. "*You want me, you fucker? Come and find me.*"

"*Great. Plant some C-4 on that thing. We'll call it a day. I'll buy the first round of beers,*" Ryan said over the radio.

"Negative on that. One of them disappeared. I'm going to track him down. And I need to find Jeremy." He kicked the Kat-su over. Even without touching it, He could tell it was burning with energy, and fury. A ticking time bomb.

"*What? No! We have to destroy the portal and get the hell out of here!*"

"And ten years from now, that creature will attempt this again," Matt snapped. "The portal's dormant. Take care of it."

"*You dumb fuck—*"

Matt switched off the radio. He didn't have time to argue. He ran down the passageway.

In the hallway, Lindsay watched as Ryan sighed as he tried the radio again. They had taken refuge in the storage room, which provided some cover against the occasional worshiper. There was supposed to be an easy escape route from there. Lindsay frowned. An escape route they would not see for a little while, apparently.

"All right. Let's deal with the mythical portal of doom," Ryan said, switching off the radio.

"That's not in the plan," Lindsay said. "You know how far away we are from the lobby?"

"Yeah, well, orders are orders."

"And you're following them?" Lindsay raised her eyebrow. "Gee Ryan, you sound whipped."

"Shut up," Ryan replied with a grin, exiting the room. "You're whipped—"

The door suddenly slammed shut between them.

"Lindsay!" Ryan cried out, trying to open the door. "Fuck, not now."

"What's happening?" Lindsay asked. All of a sudden, she felt like she was being watched. She whirled around, but only saw a black wall.

"Some kind of electronic lock," Ryan said behind her. "Don't worry, I've got this. A two-year-old can get through this."

"I do hope I'm not interrupting," a voice said behind her. Lindsay whirled around, and saw a man dressed in jeans and a black t-shirt. She took out her two guns and fired. They connected against some kind of invisible wall. Grinning, the man stepped forward, grabbed her by her hair, and thrust her against the wall. She felt his body pressed against hers and screamed in terror.

"Hm, it's been a while since I've had a good fuck," the man murmured, pressed against her. "Would you like that, Lindsay? Would you like to fuck a king?"

My name, Lindsay thought incoherently. *How does he know my name?* She mentally kicked herself. Of course, he must have gotten it from the file. But it was more than that, his words didn't even sound normal. Every syllable dripped into her mind. Despite the sheer horror of the situation, part of her wanted to make love to him.

Ryan fired at the handle and yanked the door open. The man sighed, and suddenly Lindsay felt the pressure release from her. She whirled around, and saw that he had lifted Ryan up by the throat.

"You know, I was content to ignore you," the man said. "Even when you stormed my fortress. But you just had to shake my fucking tree and piss me off, didn't you? You brought this down upon yourself."

Ryan choked and punched the man's arm three times. It had the effect of a wet paper bag.

Lindsay backed away. "What are—"

"My name is Ethan, missy. By now you should both be aware that my power is absolute. Nothing you can do will hurt me." He snorted. "You two are also very low on my radar tonight in the wake of other things, so I will not repeat myself." He released his hand. Ryan clutched his neck and lunged at him. Jacobs threw him against the wall with ridiculous ease. "I am only using a little of my strength on you, *boy*. Try that again and I will smash your face against the concrete. Even if you could peel your face away, nothing would be recognizable."

His words must have had an effect on Ryan, because he didn't try anything further.

Jacobs studied both of them, and ran a hand through his hair. "You are both children, dabbling in things you can't even begin to understand. This is my kingdom now. If you thought you had a defense before, I am here to tell you otherwise. I can do anything. Even this." He raised his hand casually.

Suddenly, Lindsay felt her body twist in pain and cried out. Her skin was bubbling, and black tears dribbled down her eyes.

"Lindsay?" Ryan whispered "What?"

Jacobs, or rather, Ethan, lowered his hand, and suddenly the pain vanished. Lindsay felt normal. She fell to her knees on the cold concrete.

"Oh dear, has your sister been keeping things from you?" Jacobs smiled, but there was no warmth in it. He stepped forward and touched her cheek. "The 'Blinkers' as you call them are my creation. I can control the black bile in her blood, to a point where she never has anything to worry about it ever again. She can meet somebody nice one day, have children, and live till she's eighty. But at any point in her life, I can just wag my finger, and she would explode in a pile of black gore and bone."

"Don't touch me," Lindsay whispered as tears ran down her face. She was relieved to find that they were real tears.

"Leave her alone," Ryan demanded.

Ethan grinned and gripped her closer by the waist. "And why should I? Perhaps you and I can reach...a compromise. I—fuck!"

Lindsay bit his ear, as hard as she could. At the same time, her talon-like hands gripped his balls. *Shouldn't have gotten close to me, you fucker*, she thought in satisfaction. A second later, her lips tasted blood as he smacked her, and she hit the opposite wall. He walked toward her, murder in his eyes.

Catherine watched in amusement as Matt ran out of the lobby. Once he was out of hearing distance, she stepped out of the shadows. Seeing Father Jacobs made her cringe, but thankfully he and everyone else had been too preoccupied on the ritual to notice her. She had silently watched everything that happened, from start to finish. Toward the end of the ritual, as Samantha spoke the end verse, she had genuinely feared that the portal would be opened. Now, it seemed, her moment had come.

She grinned and stepped leisurely toward the Kat-su, her sandals soaking in blood. The Kat-su lay discarded on the ground, burning with power. A power that didn't affect her in the slightest.

As she stepped past a young boy, he suddenly opened his eyes and drew in a startled breath. Blood covered him. Whether it was his, or a combination from the rest of the group, she didn't know. "Please," he whispered. "Please, call 911."

Catherine bent down, and her mouth stretched wider than anything humanly possible. As the boy gave a startled gasp, she engulfed his head. Her neck had teeth and digestive fluids. It was a simple matter to bite his head clean off. She chewed, and wiped her mouth. Tasty. She would chow on the rest later, if she had time.

"Now," she spoke, to seemingly no one in particular. "To business."

Jacobs advanced toward the woman, absolution on his side. Ethan had shown him the way, and he only needed to look at the truth with his own eyes. Both of these people were glowing with hellfire. They hadn't murdered Samantha—he would be dealing with that one soon enough—but they needed to be dealt with all the same. At first, Jacobs had been content to try to save their wayward souls, but after what that female she-devil had done, he was determined to make an example out of her. Perhaps she would be begging for salvation once he dangled her intestines out of her stomach.

"You're a liar, Father Jacobs," Ryan suddenly said.

Jacobs stopped and frowned. Up until now, he had been content to let Ethan direct him, show him the way. He whirled around in front of the boy. "What?" he demanded. "What did you say?"

The boy was glowing with hellfire, but he spoke with a firm voice. "That's your name, isn't it? Father Jacobs. Not Ethan. He sounds like a bastard, and he's not you. I read your file. A little preacher in the middle of nowhere, but still a preacher nevertheless.

Or, at least I thought so. I presumed to think you were a man of God. What would He think of you now?"

Suddenly, Jacobs' hands shot out, grabbing the man and pushing him back against the wall. He honestly didn't mean to do that, but Ethan was still in control. Didn't Ethan know best? As Jacobs looked around, he could see the paint peeling from the walls, and the stench of Satan not far behind. He was the avenging angel who would save them all.

"I will flay you alive, boy," Ethan's words tumbled out of his mouth. He had no control over them. "Your child is dead. You will never find her!"

Ryan gripped his arms. His eyes were red and his entire body was on fire. Jacobs could literally feel the heat radiating from his body. "Listen to me!" he shouted. "You're being controlled! Whatever you're seeing isn't real. You're a good man. Wake up and help us!"

Jacobs blinked. For a split-second, he could see the man for what he truly was...pushed against the wall, exhausted and covered in dirt and blood, but there wasn't a sign of any hellfire. If anything, the man looked desperate to help him. "What—"

"We need to talk," Ethan suddenly said, his words dripping into his mind. *"Now."*

Jacobs blinked as Ethan teleported him away.

"Are you sure?"

"Take it from one hacker to another, this is the area where he would feel the most in control. Until we take it away from him, that is."

Matt ran through the double-doors into factory A, not without an overwhelming sense of anticipation. This was it! The man who had been responsible for the death of his wife, just right above him.

"Sometimes I don't know why you married me," Lisa whispered. At the time, she was laying in his arms in a hammock.

"Because you're beautiful, you're talented, and you always put a smile on my face when I come home from work," Matt had replied.

"Please...don't ever leave me."

"That will never happen. Face it, Lisa, you're stuck with me."

Only years of training in the army had saved him from what happened next. In the dark room, he could see a long table with benches on both side, and three pressing machines set up on the table. To the left was a stairwell. He heard a dry click, and he moved back against the doorway as bullets spat out from the turret gun. Jeremy must have planted that.

"You should have walked away, Matty," Jeremy said. The gunfire exploded against the crate nearby. *"You were a victim in this, just like me. This isn't your fight."*

"You made this my fight." Matt peered out from around the corner. It could be a while before the turret ran out of bullets.

It fired again, and Matt turned around as a bullet flew past his ear. *"The best and brightest at D.R.E.X. That's what Jeff secretly called your team. And I defeated all of you. Me! A fucking cripple!"*

Matt peered out from the doorway. Could he make it to the tables? "I wasn't responsible for what happened at Owphiyr. None of us were!"

"No, but you're part of D.R.E.X. You dishonor the memories of those victims every day you wear that uniform! I lost my body..." A high-pitch giggled ended the sentence, which abruptly ended in a sob. *"But they didn't need to die. And we...we...oh fuck."*

Suddenly, the turret died, and the radio switched off. Puzzled, Matt peered out from the doorway. He waited, but the turret didn't move again. Gun in hand, he moved up the crackled concrete staircase. He listened at the door, but heard nothing. Puzzled, he slowly opened it.

Anna stood over Jeremy, her gun pointed at his forehead. A shotgun lay on his lap. He didn't try to reach for it, and stared at her in amusement. "Go ahead, Anna. We're the last two that need to answer for our crimes. Can you really bear all that guilt by yourself?"

"Anna?" Matt called out. "How did you get here?"

"Followed you. It doesn't matter. Not anymore," Anna replied. "All that matters...is this. I have never felt guilty. Everything that happened at Owphiyr was out of my control."

"Do you really think so? I spoke up, and Jeff took everything away from me....except my conscience. I did everything I could to give those people justice. But you...you kept your mouth shut when I needed you the most. Together, we could have shut down D.R.E.X. Like a team." He laughed hysterically. "Even though I did everything right, I can still hear their screams at night. So don't you dare tell me that you only hear your cows when you go to sleep."

"Does that still excuse what you did?" Anna asked.

He stared at her, almost with love. "The road to hell ends with my death. I know that. But if you have any shred of honor left, dear Anna, you will pull the trigger on your own head."

Anna bit her lip.

"Anna, stop this," Matt said, stepping forward.

"Why?" Anna asked. "Jeremy is right. This needs to end. I've done worse." Her voice became a whisper. "So much worse."

"You're right," Matt said. "But one person still needs closure. Me. Anna, I need justice."

Anna glanced at him, frowning. Her red hair fell in front of her eyes as she considered. Finally, she raised her gun and walked toward the door. "Don't worry about the shotgun. I took the bullets out. Make it quick. Or don't. I'm not sure I even care anymore."

Jeremy watched her leave, and stared at Matt with profound hatred. "Fuck you," he whispered. He snatched up the shotgun and fired. Matt automatically tensed, but a dry click answered back. "Fuck...fuck..."

Matt moved forward. He hesitated, than reached for the weapon.

"Fuck..." Jeremy closed his eyes, tears running down his pale cheeks.

Matt snatched the shotgun from his lap, and tossed it behind his shoulder.

Jeremy glared at him. "Well, you beat me, big man. You want to kill me? Take your best shot."

Matt stared at him as Anna left and closed the door.

Chapter 14

For a long time Lindsay and Ryan sat in the storage room, gripping each other tightly. Ryan lifted his gun every now and then, expecting someone to appear, but no one did.

"How did you know he would disappear like that?" Lindsay finally asked.

"I didn't," Ryan admitted. "I guess running my mouth finally worked for once." He looked down. "Why didn't you tell me?"

Lindsay closed her eyes in pain. "I couldn't," she admitted. "I was too afraid. I didn't want to think this was real."

"Jeff can help you," Ryan said. He stood, about to help her up. "Come on. We need to get you back to D.R.E.X."

"It'll be too late, and we both know it," Lindsay said, as tears ran down her face. She wasn't ashamed of them. "I'm not going to leave this place."

Ryan folded his arms. "Stop talking like that. You're getting out of here," he said. "I'm not leaving a good tracker behind."

Even in her despair, Lindsay had to laugh at him. "I see. So you're doing this for selfish reasons. As usual."

Ryan sighed and raised his arms in an *'I give up'* gesture. "Why do we always have to argue, Lindsay? I know you hate my guts. But you came looking for me, going through God knows what. That's gotta count for something, right?"

"Really? You really want to do this now?"

"Come on. Tell me."

Lindsay shrugged, looking at her dirty knuckles. "We both know I found you for my own reasons, which have nothing to do with you. I did it for Kacie. I wanted her to see her dad."

Ryan was silent for a while. "We've been arguing for years, even before D.R.E.X. What started that?"

"Hm, let me think," Lindsay said sarcastically. "Maybe it was when my sister introduced you to my family for the first time, and you were too drunk to even stand up, and apparently that was one of your 'good days'."

"Yeah, I was pretty messed up," Ryan admitted, then turned to face her. "But that was a long time ago. I haven't touched a drug in years. I've changed."

Lindsay laughed in his face. The idea of tormenting her brother was instantly more appealing than thinking about her own reality. "You only changed because Kacie was kidnapped. The minute you find her, you'll go back to the drugs. I know you, Ryan. You're all talk, and we both know you're weak. Louise was right. When the chips are down, you're going to be the first to fall."

"Maybe," Ryan admitted, sitting back. "But until that happens, can we at least pretend that I'm a changed man? Is that too much to ask?" When Lindsay didn't reply for a long time he sat down and sighed. "I'm not going to ever find her, am I? I'm just kidding myself."

Lindsay studied him, then wrapped her arms around him. "Don't say that," she whispered. "You'll find her. I know that."

Both of them jumped as someone kicked open the door. A cult member.

"There you are," he whispered, insanity in his eyes. He aimed his gun.

Ryan shot him in the head as Lindsay turned around. "Goddamit! I'm not going to leave you," he said. "We can beat this. I know we can!"

Lindsay gripped his hand, terrified. "Ryan, I—"

Suddenly, the cult member's radio crackled to life. "*Unit eight, come in. We're headed to your position. Make sure the gates are open with us. We're going to get these fuckers. We've got more than enough people. Over and out."*

"Backup," Ryan whispered.

The fuckers had backup.

Jacobs appeared on the rooftop, studying the cloudy sky. Below, he could see a dark green field. Only a short time ago, the very possibility of teleporting from one place to another seemed like a blur. Now, it came as naturally as breathing. Whatever he wanted, Ethan would provide.

He studied the peaceful-looking dark grass, wishing it could soothe his soul. Lately everything had become a jumbled blur. He had fought those two D.R.E.X officers, thinking they were possessed by daemons. Ethan had assured him that he was trying to save their souls. But for a split-second, that man had called him by his name. And he had actually seen…

"They are nothing," Ethan said, standing in front of him. "Just appetizers for the main course. That is, assuming you're strong enough."

Jacobs lifted a hand to his head, fighting off another dizzy spell. Before, he had been so sure he was doing the right thing. The portal to heaven was supposed to open. But now…

"Minor details," Ethan said. "We will find someone else, and force them to read from the Kat-su. Our new bible. And then the gates to heaven will finally be open."

'What you're seeing isn't real. Wake up and help us!'

Jacobs shook his head. "I…I need time to think-"

"Think about what?" Ethan challenged, stepping forward. He spread his arms. "You want to end this now, Father? Shall I send you back to Toronto? I am sure the little old ladies are missing your sermons." He chuckled. "Your words barely kept them awake. Remember when you walked on the water? People certainly paid attention to you then."

"This isn't about me, God damn you!" Jacobs snapped.

"Of course it is. And why shouldn't it be? We are both royalty, you and I. The blood of kings runs through my veins, but you—you are Jesus reincarnated."

Jacobs said nothing, and shook his head. "Vanity is a sin," he muttered.

"It is not vanity to state the truth, Father. The truth you have suspected all this time." Ethan stepped forward. "I named you prophet, but I could see you were so much more when I found you. I never gave you the ability to walk on water, or see the hellspawn. That was your ability." He lifted his head at the cloudy sky. "Can't you hear them?"

Jacobs lifted his head. If he could focus hard enough, he could indeed here an angelic choir, and the voice of his Father, reaching out to him...but they were muffled.

"They are calling out for you, but we need to get that gateway open. Only then can Earth and Heaven be the same, and you can finally embrace your destiny and lead these people to Heaven," Ethan said. "And I can go home."

"How?" Jacobs closed his eyes, marveling at the noise above his head.

"We need to confront the spawn of Satan."

Once Jacobs accepted his role as the son of God and the savior of Earth, his power grew immensely. Before, he was very much mortal, shackled to this world, letting Ethan guide him along the way. Now, he could reach out and touch the minds of everyone in the warehouse, perhaps the entire world if he tried hard enough. How could he believe that Ethan was responsible for all this power? The so-called 'King' couldn't even find his way back home. No, it was him. Before, his own fear held him back—fear of offending God with his ambitious, wicked thoughts. But as Ethan had so eloquently stated, he was the chosen one. The Son reincarnated. Nothing would stop him now.

It was child's play to find the spawn of Satan, who was running down the hallway with a female—Anna. They were heading back to the lobby. As Jacobs watched, unseen, Matt turned on his radio.

"Ryan, come in. Did you guys destroy the portal?"

"*Um…about that…*" Ryan began.

"What happened?"

"*We were intercepted by Jacobs. We couldn't take him down, Matt. We didn't have a chance.*"

"Are you guys all right?" Anna asked.

"*No,*" Ryan said flatly. "*Matt, we need to get out of here now. More cultists are coming. We have to clear the warehouse, and somehow convince the FBI to let Jeff call in an aerial strike. It's our best chance to survive.*"

"Negative on that, we're almost at the lobby now and haven't met any resistance. Stay put. We'll find you after we're done," Matt said, turning off the radio. He glanced at Anna. "This guy has got to have a weakness."

Jacobs grinned. The very thought. Both of them were caked in their own filth and wickedness. It was time for them to see the light. He teleported behind Anna. "Hello, Matt," he said, politely. "It's wonderful to see you again."

Anna whirled around, raising her gun. Before she could shoot, Jacobs grabbed Anna's arm, and with a twist broke it. She screamed. Some lessons were harder to learn than others. Matt fired his gun, and the bullets bounced right through him. Jacobs sighed. At the moment, the woman was nothing, and he wanted her out of the way. He hurled Anna against the wall, and heard a terrible *crack*. Anna slid to the ground and didn't get up again.

"My power is absolute, and the weapons designed by this world can never touch me," Jacobs said. "But if it makes you feel better, Matthew, then by all means try."

Matt lifted his assault rifle. "Glad to," he said, and fired a full clip into him, with no effect. Jacobs closed his eyes in peaceful serenity. It almost…tingled. Matt grabbed his knife and hurled himself at Jacobs, meaning to stab him through the head. Jacobs moved to the left ever so slightly, missing the blade. Not that it could actually do anything. Jacobs reached out to grab him. Matt backed away and kicked Jacobs in the side. The thought of that hurting him was laughable. It was time to end this foolishness. He grabbed Matt's following punch, and broke three of Matt's fingers. Matt grunted in pain and fell to one knee.

"You surprised me once, Matthew," Jacobs said, calmly stepping around him. "But now you are starting to bore me. You should have listened to your friend. I am beyond any of you."

Anna gave out a groan. Matt didn't move. "Listen to me," he said. "You're being controlled by a being called the Brache—"

"That type of tomfoolery might have worked on me once," Jacobs said, raising a dismissive hand. "But now, my faith is absolute. I can see into your soul. Both of yours. If I really wanted to, I could simply take control of your feeble mind and read the words I need to open the gates to heaven." He crouched down and smiled. "But the Son of God is better than mere trickery."

"You think you're the Son of God?" Matt echoed in astonishment. "Father, even *you* can't believe that. If you open that portal, thousands of monsters will pour out, most we can't even comprehend. Billions of people will die!"

That gave Jacobs pause. Ethan whispered in the back of his mind, reassuring him. Another trick, of course. He raised his hand, and Matt automatically flinched. "If that's true, then why does the evil in your soul shudder at the sight of me?" He paused. "I know you, Matthew, better than perhaps you know yourself. You were once a good man, but the pain of your wife's death has led you astray. You know, we met once. A long time ago, in Ottawa. No particular reason. I was just passing through, looking for followers to my cause. When I drove past the prison, I could feel your despair. It burned stronger than anything I had ever felt in a while. So I decided to pay you a visit. I even offered to give you a good book to read." He paused. "The offer still stands."

"What?" Matt asked, not comprehending in the slightest.

"I still need someone to read the Kat-su for me," Jacobs said. "It is, shall we say, primed with power. All it needs is a catalyst, a simple verse to set it free. Once that happens, this can all be over."

Matt stared at him in astonishment. "And you can't? Why can't *you* read from his own bible?"

Jacobs scowled, annoyed. "My words have no effect."

"Still think you're the Son of God?" Matthew laughed.

Surprisingly, Jacobs echoed his laugh. "Don't think that tiny revelation will change anything, Matthew. You will do this for me."

"Why?" Matt stared at him defiantly.

"Well, I could tell you that I have your wicked friends in my power, and their only hope in survival lies with you. I could free them. I could give you anything you want in this world." Jacobs grinned. This man was a minion of Satan, and he could read his soul inside and out. He would drag him, kicking and screaming, into the light. "But none of that really *matters* to you, does it?" He pointed. "Look."

Matt followed his gaze, and Jacobs could feel him radiate with fear, and horror. Lisa was standing behind him. Her arms and legs were shackled with chains, and she was covered in blood.

"Matt!" Lisa sobbed.

Matt stepped forward. "Lisa—"

Jacobs snapped his fingers, and her body surged with fire. They both could smell the sickening scent of burning flesh as her body exploded.

"No!" Matt shrieked, grabbing his gun and firing. "That wasn't real!"

Jacobs smiled patiently. "Exactly how many times do you have to fire before you realize that has no effect?"

"*Matt, are you there?*" Ryan called over the radio.

"My wife is not in hell," Matt snapped.

"Oh yes she is, and you know why," Jacobs said. "She should have reported what D.R.E.X had done from the start. She could have helped victims like Jeremy. But she kept her wicked mouth shut, and now she is burning for that mistake." He shrugged. "But,

I am a forgiving God. After all, I have made plenty of mistakes in my time. Help me, and I will bring her back to life. A chance for both of you to start over. Refuse and Satan will keep torturing her for his own amusement."

"I don't believe you," Matt said.

Jacobs snickered. He knew different. "If any part of you does believe, you will help me," he said simply. "But let's say you're right, unbelievable as it may be. Look around you, Matthew. Do you not see the world already doomed? Even if you did succeed, you might end up like poor Jeremy one day. A grenade ruining your life. Or perhaps Jeff will set fire to another nation, and their deaths will be on your hands. But if the monsters you fear are released..." He shrugged. "Perhaps exposing them will unite the world, and show them a truth they desperately need." He shook his head. "We both know you don't care for anything here, Matthew, so why not take a chance that I might be right, and save your wife? If I were you, I would—"

He paused in mid-speech as he realized something. "That bitch," he said abruptly, and disappeared.

Lindsay watched as Ryan paced back and forth, trying his radio.

"Matt, come in!"

Static answered back.

"Fuck, fuck, *fuck*!" Ryan screamed. He tried again. "Can anyone hear me?"

Nothing.

Lindsay stared at him, not without sympathy. "Ryan," she whispered.

"We're going to be okay, Lindsay. We just need—"

"Ryan, you have to stop them."

Ryan glanced at her. "What?"

"You have to leave me," Lindsay repeated. She felt her body quake with fear, and struggled to keep her voice calm. Ryan looked horrified, and Lindsay soon discovered why. One touch told her that she was crying black droplets.

He stepped toward her. "I am not going to kill my sister! Fuck, do you really think I can do that? I failed my daughter. I'm not going to fail my sister too! I am going to get you out of this," he said firmly.

Lindsay looked away, tears falling in front of her eyes. "Ryan, listen to me. I am not getting of this, but you can. You have to live. To find her. That's why you're here—why we're *both* here. Don't let her die because of me."

Ryan shook his head. "No."

Tears fell from her eyes. "I forgive you, and I know you don't have a choice, okay? Just do it already!"

"*Ryan, come in,*" Jeff said.

Ryan's hand flew to the radio. "Jeff, you have to help us. Lindsay's infected!"

"*I know,*" Jeff said calmly. "*Everything is going to be okay. I know a way we can help Lindsay, but I need you two to focus.*"

"Okay," Ryan said, relieved. "What do we do?"

"*The Blue Power Core has reinforcements on the way. I'm reading about twelve cars headed toward your position. They just passed highway seventeen now. By my calculations, they will be at the compound in ten minutes. You have to stop them from entering the building. If they get past you, then Matt doesn't have a chance to destroy the portal.*"

"How are we supposed to stop them?" Ryan asked.

"*Getting out of this room would be a step in the right direction,*" Jeff said dryly. "*Find a way outside. I'll be in touch when you are in position. Over and out.*"

Matt helped Anna get back on her feet, and they both ran back to the lobby. As soon as they entered, Matt stopped, astonished at what he was seeing.

Catherine was holding the book and chanting. The entire room was trembling with power. Beside him, Anna gripped the doorframe for support. Matt could see different trails of black color dancing around the room, blurring other things it flew past. Matt felt dizzy just from looking at it. Was she trying to open the portal? He didn't think so. She was facing Jacobs, not the portal, and the look on his face was one of unmistakable rage.

"And so Jezebel has come to try and kill me," Jacobs said. "Your wickedness will be defeated, and my dogs will eat upon your carcass, as it is stated in the bible."

Catherine tried to chant a few more words. Jacobs waved his hand, almost dismissively, and she was instantly slammed against the wall with enough force to partially break through the stone. Anne shrieked behind him. Catherine's body hung at an odd angle, eagle-spread, supported only by the uneven rock. She didn't move. Alive? Dead? If she were human, that would be certain.

Jacobs stared at Matt, then smiled. "My son," he said brightly. "It is time. Time for us to open the gates of heaven."

"Father," Anna said calmly. "Think about what you are doi—urk!" Anna gasped as she was suddenly lifted upwards by an unseen force.

"Shhh," Jacobs said. "Your part in this is done. Besides, we both know what Matthew is going to do. Don't we?"

Matthew, the Kat-su sighed. The overwhelming feeling of sheer power was intoxicating. He took the fallen book from where Catherine had dropped it, and as he did so, it felt as though an electric charge ran up and down his arm. His fingers tingled with power. The cover of the Kat-su was soaked in blood, but the lock itself was open. The book was open on the page that Catherine was reading. "Let her go," he said, almost disinterested.

Jacobs gave an almost childlike laugh and dropped Anna back to the ground. He waved his hand, and she disappeared.

Matt glanced up sharply. "Where—"

"Fear not. She is safely out of my temple," Jacobs said. "I do not like killing innocent people...unlike your former D.R.E.X members. No one will ever know the truth, will they? The same thing will happen to you, eventually. Do you really want to feel what she did? Or, you can expose it all right now. God's truth."

Matt said nothing, staring at the words. His vision became spotted, and blurry. The book was screaming at him to speak in a language he didn't understand. Yet, he felt intoxicated with power.

"The back of the book," Jacobs breathed. "The last page, Matt, and the last verse will open the portal. We're almost there."

Matt glanced again at the book. It was primed with power, ready to explode with one word from him. Jacobs was right. By opening the portal, he would expose the ugly truth he tried to hide every day. People would die, but did he still give a damn about the world? Not since Lisa and his daughter Cheryl left it. Revealing all the secrets and bullshit might eventually make the world a better place.

And yet...

What was Catherine so focused on doing that upset Jacobs? His finger was still on the page. A verse to stop him maybe? Doubt nagged his mind. If he was wrong, Jacobs would dismember him within seconds. And Lisa would not come back either way.

"Matthew?" Jacobs asked with a hint of impatience. "The angels are waiting. Heck, the world is waiting. Say the words."

Matthew swallowed as the gravity of what Jacobs said hit him. Whatever he did next would alter the world, forever. But he wasn't a hero. If it hadn't been for D.R.E.X, he might be rotting in jail by now. The world didn't care about him.

He flipped to the end.

Ryan didn't see anyone as he and Lindsay exited the main doors to the outside of the factory. He aimed his pistol, but only saw an empty parking lot...for now. He turned on his radio. "Got any plans, boss?"

"*Yes. Stall them,*" Jeff said. "*Don't let them inside.*"

"Do we know how many of them are coming?" Ryan asked.

"*Hm, heat signatures indicate around fifty tangos,*" Jeff said.

"How can he be so calm about that?" Lindsay asked.

"Because he's not here," Ryan muttered back. "His fat ass is a continent away."

"*Insulting your boss is not going to look good on your performance review, Ryan,*" Jeff said.

Ryan rolled his eyes. "Okay, I would like to respectfully point out that two against fifty is not great odds."

"Three," Anna said, surprising them both. Her head was bleeding, but she didn't act concussed. "Jacobs sent me here, to make sure I stayed out of the way," she explained. "It's all up to Matt now."

"*I don't expect you to win. Just slow them down. Leave the rest to me.*" The radio clicked off.

"Are you okay?" Ryan asked her.

Anna shook her head. Her eyes were sad. "The bastard broke my arm. I just wish I could have done more for him. Matt."

Ryan wiped away his forehead. Even though the air was cold, the heat was getting unbearable. He studied the empty parking lot. "We might not live through this one."

"Hell no," Lindsay agreed. "But maybe we could buy Matt enough time to save the world." She glanced up at the emergency stairwell leading to the roof. "I can get some pretty good shots from there."

"I have some C-4. If I collapsed the main gate, we might be able to slow them down," Anna said. Ryan followed her gaze. There were two pillars in front of the doors, and an empty security office to the left. They could find adequate cover in both.

"I should get ready," Lindsay said, breaking his musing.

Ryan gripped her arm. Hard. "Sis. Be careful."

Lindsay smiled. "Don't worry little brother. I'm not—"

"Hands up!" a female brunette said behind them, aiming her gun.

Shit, Ryan thought. He met Lindsay's gaze, and they were both thinking the same thing—it was the same FBI agent they had met at the airport.

"Ryan?" Lindsay asked. She had a clear shot. Ryan could turn around, and try to shoot her. Even if she fired at him, Lindsay would take her down. Fucking cops. They never arrived when you wanted them to.

Ryan managed a goofy grin. "Good evening, officer. What brings you here?" he asked. "And how did they manage to get past the thermal scan, Jeff?" he muttered to his jacket.

"*Well...I actually called her to make a citizen's arrest,*" Jeff reported, his voice strangely unapologetic.

"Of course you did," Ryan said.

"Get down on your knees! Hands behind your head!" Jasmine snapped.

Ryan complied. "Do what the nice woman said, ladies," he said. "No one here but us law-abiding citizens."

Lindsay complied along with Anna, but her eyes were burning. "What are you doing? We can take them."

"I know," Ryan said. "But we need them. If we play this right..." he didn't finish, as his hands were cuffed behind his back.

Jasmine approached them, her hands on her hips. "Where's your friend?"

"Inside," Ryan said. "But trust me, you won't have time to see him. In about five minutes there are going to be dozens of people arriving that are quite interested in killing us. You too, as a matter of fact."

Jasmine raised her eyebrow. "Oh good. More people for me to arrest. I don't know what you're playing at, but the people in this town know I'm a federal agent. If anyone even tries to do something that stupid, they would spend the next thirty years in a maximum-security prison." She looked up at another officer. "Hoffman, read them their rights."

"What are you talking about?" Anna snapped. "We didn't do anything!"

"*Not according to what I told them,*" Jeff said.

Ryan glanced at the road. Sure enough, fifteen cars were driving toward them. "Look, officer, these people want us dead, and you too, just for being here. And they have the numbers."

"*For now,*" Jeff said over the radio.

Jasmine studied him, no doubt trying to figure out if he was actually being serious or not. She watched as the cars parked. "What is this?" she finally asked.

"The end of the world," Anna stated. "It's what we deal with. You can either help us, or get out of sight. Because in about one minute, there will be a bloodbath."

Jasmine shook her head. "Stay here," she ordered, and took out her badge. "Evening, gentleman, I'm officer—"

Ryan pushed her to the ground as they opened fired. "Get down!" As Lindsay covered them with her assault rifle, they made their way to cover. Jasmine shouted a warning at them, and someone responded by shooting at her. After that, it was clear what their intentions were. The three other police officers took shelter behind the pillars and fired back.

"I cuffed you!" Jasmine said in astonishment, noticing his free hands.

"Yeah, I got over it," Ryan said. Beside him, Anna tossed several smoke pellets at the cultists, creating a cloud of confusion. In the meantime, Lindsay had found a spot on the roof and was aiming her sniper rifle. She squeezed off a shot, and a cultist fell. The FBI was firing more blindly, but with enthusiasm. Between all of them, they were keeping the cultists at bay, cowering behind their car. For now.

"I can call for back up!" Jasmine shouted. "The FBI can be here in an hour."

Ryan reloaded his gun and twisted around. "My back up is faster. But I need you to lift the air support."

Jasmine chewed her lip. "That might take some convincing."

"Do it soon if you want to live." Without waiting for a response, he got up and walked straight into the battlefield. "Hey! Stop, you idiots and listen to me!" he shouted.

"Ryan, what are you doing?" Lindsay demanded.

"What I always do. Running my mouth off," Ryan replied.

They couldn't get a good shot at him in the smoke, but miraculously the gunfire ceased. A young man about twenty years old cautiously peeked his shaved head out. "Trying to surrender?" he sneered.

Ryan smirked. "Trying to save your lives. Because I'm pretty sure I just doomed us all." He lifted his hands. "Come on, I don't bite. Let's take a break. What's your name?"

"Jason," the kid said reluctantly, stepping toward him.

"*Ryan, get to cover!*" Lindsay snapped.

"What do you mean we're all doomed?" Jason demanded.

"A missile strike has been called. Probably in about five minutes a three-mile radius will be completely leveled, and guess what? We're all in it."

"You'll be killed," Jason pointed out.

"I can't help that my boss is an asshole," Ryan said, hoping they would take him seriously. Unlike the people of Vermon, these people weren't crazy, or possessed. Misguided and desperate, maybe. Stupid, definitely. But they were still people. "Come on. Your boss doesn't care about you. You're not even cool enough to be in the inner sanctum. You have a chance. Go home."

For a moment, there was silence, as the cultists looked at each other, uncertain.

"*So that's what you think I'm going to do,*" Jeff stated in his ear.

"*Why not?*" Anna asked.

"*I know you don't agree with some of my methods, and I made some mistakes in the past, Jeremy being one of them. But you're wrong about one thing. I would never leave you, Anna. None of you. Not when there is another way. And I have far more resources than you realize,*" Jeff said.

Jason shook his head. "If I go home, I'll watch my father beat up my sister every day, and there is nothing I can do to stop him. Father Jacobs said that I will see the portal to heaven, and that our faith will be tested before the end." He looked up. "I…am…worthy."

Ryan flicked his gaze back and forth. No one was leaving, and seemed pretty determined. "You'll see it before I will." In one motion, he reached forward and snapped Jason's neck. He brought Jason's body close as the resulting gunfire impacted against his body. With his own gun, he fired at three cultists, but he knew he could be killed anytime. A bullet flew past his arm, scratching it. At least he bought Matt some time.

A light shined down from the sky. "All combatants, drop your weapons and get on the ground, now!" a voice shouted, one he didn't recognize. There were five other choppers in the sky.

The cultists aimed their guns and fired at the helicopter. The distraction gave Ryan all he needed to fall back to his previous position.

"*I'm out of bullets for my rifle. I'll join you in a sec,*" Lindsay said.

"I got the radio support lifted," Jasmine said.

"Well no shit," Ryan said with a laugh. "Who are these guys?"

"We're your friends, mate," a thick, Australian voice said to the right. Ryan glanced to the left, and saw a muscular man with curly brown hair unhooking a harness. More people were zip-lining from the helicopter. He stuck out his hand. "Max Alexis, from the Australian branch. Your handler had us hovering near Missouri until the FBI stopped meddling in our affairs."

Ryan frowned. "Australian branch?"

"Yeah, branches all over are starting up. We have people from Canada, France, Germany, no one from Russia though, the lazy twats." Max grinned. "We're all from D.R.E.X. And we're going to help you clean up this mess."

Nearby Anna smiled. "Sounds good to us!"

Matt opened his mouth, about to speak, but couldn't. Tears burned his eyes. One landed on the book, which instantly sizzled. He wanted to open the portal, and make his pain go away. He thought about his daughter, and all the times he tickled her in the crib.

With a bored look, Jacobs lifted his hand. "Enough delays. Say the last verse, and the doorway opens forever. God will arrive."

Power surged around him, inside him. He flipped through the pages, looking for the correct spell.

"Toward the end," Jacobs encouraged, unable to keep the eagerness from his voice.

Matt raised his eyebrow. "You are right about one thing, Father," he said.

"What's that?"

"This is a really good fucking book," Matt said. He flipped back to the page Catherine had spoken from. The writing burned slightly against his fingers. He began to speak from where he thought she left off.

"What are you doing?" Jacobs demanded. "Stop!"

Matt could feel the book, and by extension his body, tremble with power. It was like being tethered to a circuit. As his mouth formed the alien words, they seemed to take on a life of their own and physically injure Jacobs, who struggled to move.

This is wrong, Matt thought as he spoke, but couldn't stop. He had never felt more sick in his life. His heart raced against his chest, and he wanted to throw up and pass out at the same time. At the same time, the walls to the lobby seemed to move, and the entire room became...thinner. Was that even real? Or just a hallucination?

The final word left his mouth, and Jacobs collapsed to the ground. Matt leaned back against the wall, gasping and covered in sweat. The book dropped from his fingers to the ground. He aimed his gun at Jacobs. The priest glanced at him, and Matt recoiled slightly in fear. Blood was trailing from Jacobs's eyes, nose, and ears, fast enough to stain his clothes and gather in a pool around his body within seconds.

"Help me," he gasped, in a deep, pitiful voice. He opened his mouth, and Matt could see that some of his teeth were missing. Cuts were forming all over Jacobs's face and hands. To Matt's horror, he could see that something black was oozing through the blood.

Even worse, there was something trying to push its way through his flesh. "Help—"

Matt fired his gun before he could finish his sentence, and the priest fell to the ground, dead. He collapsed and released a shaky breath. When he opened his eyes again, he realized the Kat-su was gone.

So was Catherine.

As the night wore on, the D.R.E.X team moved through the smoke to clean up the rest of the cultist force. For a few minutes, Ryan and Lindsay fought back to back. A man ran toward Lindsay, and she shot him in the head. Then, her hands suddenly flew to her face as black tears fell and she collapsed to her knees. "Ryan!" she screamed.

Ryan killed the man advancing toward him and caught Lindsay just before she fell. "Oh my God," he whispered. Black blood gushed from her ears and nose, with no sign of stopping. Within seconds, her entire face was covered.

"Ryan, help me please," Lindsay sobbed, her face barely visible in the mess.

"Hang on, sis!" Ryan said, struggling to keep her on her feet. The chopper couldn't be far. They needed to get her back to D.R.E.X. "Max! I need to—"

Whack! Something clipped behind Ryan's right ear and abruptly everything went black. His legs turned to Jell-O and he fell to the grass.

As he stirred to consciousness, someone was dragging him away from Lindsay. Even though her face was unrecognizable, she screamed at him pleadingly. At the same time, two people in black walked toward her, holding assault rifles.

"No," Ryan whispered. He struggled to get up and help her, but Max held him back. "Get the fuck off me!"

"This has to be done," Max said. "If she explodes her blood will burn away your skin. I'm giving her a merciful end."

Blindly Ryan tried to punch him. Max dodged the blow and twisted Ryan's arm behind his back almost to the point of breaking. At the same time, he calmly shot another cultist running toward them.

Lindsay screamed as the men fired on her.

"No!" Ryan screamed. With his free hand, he grabbed the knife from his belt and swung it behind Max, startling him enough to release him. Lindsay was still moving. Another man carrying a flamethrower advanced toward her. In the distance, he could see Anna, standing by herself and not moving to help Lindsay. Ryan didn't think, he just ran toward his sister.

Max tackled him to the ground. "Sorry, mate, you don't need to see this part."

A second blow connected to his head, and all lights went out.

Pain gradually brought him back to consciousness. Ryan cracked open his eyes, not without some difficulty. It felt like his head was about to explode. Someone had propped him against the wall of the building. His guns were gone. How much time had passed? Lindsay...where was she? In the distance, he could see Max fighting with another member of the cult. "You said you would help her," he accused through dry lips.

"*I did help her,*" Jeff said. "*I helped both of you.*"

Max's gun went flying through the air, and a cultist was forcing a knife toward his face. The two were locked in battle. Ryan spotted a discarded knife on the ground. Swearing, he grabbed the weapon and ran toward them.

"*Ryan, don't!*" Jeff ordered, and Ryan ripped away the radio. He savagely hurled the knife against the skull of the cultist, which connected with a sickening *crunch*. Blood splattered against his uniform, and face. As Max watched in astonishment, Ryan dislodged the knife from the man's head.

"Your men killed my sister. You let it happen," Ryan whispered. "I want you all to myself."

Quick as a flash, Max grabbed his gun from the grass. "Gun beats knife every time, mate. Stand down."

Before Ryan could reply, they both heard a blood-curdling scream. As they watched, Jasmine shuddered once, than disintegrated into a cloud of blood and bone.

"What the..." Max whispered.

"The Blinkers," Ryan whispered, and glanced at his bleeding arm. Their scent had come off! Suddenly Ryan screamed as one of the invisible beasts clamped around his arm, dragging him across the grass.

"Get off him!" Max shouted, shooting once above him, but the bullet was slow, much too slow. Through the corner of his eye, Ryan could see members of the Blue Power Core also being attacked. At least the dogs were dumb enough not to tell friend from foe.

Ryan suddenly felt hot, putrid breath on his throat. Only instinct saved him as his hands lifted, preventing the beast's jaws from clamping down on him. He groaned as he realized how strong the damn thing was. How long could he even last? Knowing what he had seen, the dog would likely chew on his meat and lick up any remaining spots within seconds.

Abruptly the Blinker jumped off him and scurried away, its paws landing on his chest for good measure, knocking the breath off him. Ryan glanced in astonishment as he heard a strange whistle, one that came from Catherine, standing behind them.

"It seems I can't go five minutes without rescuing you, can I?" She smiled at him.

"What?" Ryan asked dumbly. "What?"

"They're from my side of the world," Catherine said, placing her hand in what seemed like mid-air, but was likely the nape of some beast. "They're easy enough to control. If you know how."

Ryan glanced at the rest of the field. He could see the bodies of several D.R.E.X officers, but the Blue Power Core had suffered considerably more loses. A few were trying to fight, but most of the surviving force had either surrendered or were trying to flee. They had won.

Max stepped toward her. "Do you have all of them under your control?" he asked, taking out his gun.

"Yes," Catherine said, a bit uncertain. "I don't want you to hurt them. Jacobs was controlling them. They're not evil."

"Look miss, I am a huge dog lover myself—I have five border collies at home, it drives the wife nuts, but these things have ripped apart my men and done considerable damage in France. They might not be evil, but they have done much harm. They have to be put down. You know that, right? We can't let anything survive from the portal. That is our mandate," Max said gently.

Catherine's eyes narrowed, and Ryan could tell what she was thinking.

"Please, Catherine," Ryan said weakly. "Max is right. They're too dangerous to be allowed to live. Human flesh is their preferred dish."

"It's also mine!" Catherine snapped.

"You have an intelligence. These things don't. The moment they're out of your control, they'll go after us again. Please."

Catherine hesitated, and finally her eyes narrowed. She looked away. "I just...don't want to be alone."

Max took that as acceptance, and moved past her. "I'll make it quick. I promise."

Catherine said nothing. A moment later, they both could hear the unmistakable howls of dogs dying. She lifted a shaking hand to move away a lock of blond hair from her eyes.

Ryan gripped her tightly. "It'll be all right," he said. "I promise."

But even as he spoke, he glanced at a large charred spot in the ground. At least the sun was rising. He swallowed a hard lump in his throat, not believing he would even see another dawn. In the distance, several police cruisers and ambulances were headed their way. He knew he looked like hell, covered from head to toe in dirt surrounded by several bodies, but...he was alive. They had won.

"You've suffered loss," Catherine observed, watching him.

Ryan didn't even bother to deny it as he studied Jasmine's body. It was mangled, almost beyond recognition. All of the FBI that helped them were dead. He knew he should care, but he just felt tired. "How do you know?"

"Your scent," Catherine stated, as though it should be obvious.

"My sister. She died."

"I'm sorry." Suddenly her body tensed. Ryan turned around, confused. Matt and Anna were standing nearby, guns raised.

"Where is it?" Matt asked.

"What?" Ryan asked weakly. "I don't—"

"She took the Kat-su, Ryan," Matt explained. "And we can't let her leave with it. Stay out of this. Or better yet, back away. She's a killer."

"Aren't we all?" Ryan asked, glancing at Catherine. "Catherine?"

Catherine smiled and ran her hands over her skin-tight clothes. "No pockets. Sorry, Matt, but I don't have it."

"There is no other possible explanation," Anna said.

"Hm, well, there's one," Catherine said, running a finger over her pink lips. "Did it ever occur to either of you that the Kat-su itself is a living entity? One that is capable of making its own decisions?"

"What are you saying?" Matt asked.

"Merely that the Kat-su might be a lot like me. One that simply wants to live here, peacefully, without interference from anyone else. Trust me, I know what that feels like more than anyone else here." She gripped Matt's hands. "You used it, didn't you?"

"Yes," Matt admitted.

"I'm shocked you're still alive," she said. "I've heard those who use it…are never the same again."

Matt said nothing for a moment, then jerked his head. "Anna, let's check on survivors." He glanced at Catherine. "I don't want to see you again."

Catherine nodded meekly.

Ryan waited until they were out of earshot. "That is such bullshit. The book didn't grow legs and walk away," he remarked. "You really do have it, don't you?"

Catherine smirked. Her hands reached into her stomach, and with one solid yank took the book out of several layers of flesh. Ryan watched this with an almost morbid curiosity. None of her flesh tore at all. It was almost as though it parted to make way for her hands. "Most men aren't brave enough to tell a woman when she gains weight," she said. "Are you going to arrest me?"

Ryan considered as he studied the book. On some level, he knew that the power had been spent. It would take considerable energy, or several more lives, for it to be priming with power again. Yet, even now, he yearned to touch the book, to read the mythical writing again. It was an addiction. "No, I won't tell," he finally said, gripping her hand. "I think you were right all along. This Kat-su, this thing, isn't safe enough in my hands. Or any human hands. Hell, I'm not even sure it's even safe in *your* hands. But you stand a better chance than I do."

Catherine grinned. "You're learning. Took you long enough," she said, and kissed him. As she did so, the book stealthily went back into her stomach.

"Come back with me," Ryan begged. "I'll protect you."

Catherine paused, a small smile on her lips. "Huh. I think you actually believe that. But once I go back to your base, they'll dissect me. Besides, even if they didn't, I refuse to live in some underground base. Why would I want to be there, when I have a world to explore? Maybe one day you can come with me. I can show you all kinds of things you wouldn't believe," Catherine whispered. She looked up as other D.R.E.X officers approached. "Time for me to go."

Ryan stared at her. "So this is goodbye."

She touched his cheek. "Hardly. Think of me as a free agent. I have your scent now. If you need me, I won't be far behind."

Ryan stared at her, honestly not sure if that was a good thing or a bad thing. Sure, she saved their lives, but he also had a feeling she hadn't told him everything. It was the story of his life. "Just tell me one thing. What are you, really? A man or a woman?"

Catherine laughed. "I am whatever you want me to be." She smiled at him. "Goodbye, Ryan." Without waiting for a response, she turned and ran through the smoke.

"Hey," Matt suddenly said behind him, followed by Anna. "Is she leaving?"

"Yeah," Ryan said, and folded his arms. "We just saved the world, didn't we?"

"Seems like," Matt replied, studying the damage. "Could have gone better, though."

Ryan nodded. "Still...that's pretty badass."

Before Matt could reply, another voice said, "You guys won. With a little help, of course."

They turned to see Max approaching. "If it's all the same to you, we're going to bugger off. We've got another problem happening in Montana. Seems like you yanks can't take care of yourselves."

Ryan shook his head. "What you did...I can't ever forgive you."

"Cry me a river, mate," Max said, his eyes cold. "In case you've forgotten, we're both in D.R.E.X. There's a long list of victims who can't forgive me for my actions. One day we can compare notes, and see whose list is bigger." He shrugged. "Anyway, your boss ordered it, so your gripe is really with him, not me."

"How do you do it?" Matt asked. "How can you live with your actions?"

"By knowing I'm making a difference, you idiot," Max said, and started to walk toward the helicopter. "The lives we save outweigh the ones we ever have to destroy. In case you haven't noticed, we saved the world today. If you can't see that, well, than frankly you're in the wrong business."

Ryan didn't reply as Max boarded the helicopter and left. At the same time, another appeared in the sky. "I think that's our ride."

"Are you going to be okay?"

"Fine. I just wish…I had a body to bring back," Ryan said. He looked for and found the charred mark on the field. "I have nothing left, Matt."

"Yes, you do," Matt stated. "Your daughter."

Ryan closed his eyes in pain. "Come on. She's dead."

"You don't know that," Matt said slowly, emphasizing every word. "If she's alive, then we're going to find her."

"We?" Ryan asked, some of his usual sarcasm returning. "Does this mean you're still around for a while, boss?"

In the distance, Anna watched them closely.

Matt shrugged. "Even if Jeff fires me today, I'm still going to help you find her, Ryan," he stated quietly. "And I won't stop until I do."

Without waiting for a reply from either of them, Matt walked toward the helicopter.

EPILOGUE

The next morning Matt sat in the main command center, fiddling with a pen in his hands. His thoughts were racing.

After a few minutes, Jeff entered the room. He sat down at the opposite end of the table. The two men regarded each other in silence.

"You never did tell me why you were dishonorably discharged," Jeff said. "In the army."

"You never asked," Matt countered.

Jeff flipped open his folder. "Hm, I think it had something to do with a failure to obey orders."

"Maybe. Or maybe making the wrong moral choices has never agreed with me."

"Jeremy wasn't found on the base. Neither was his body. What happened to him?" Jeff pointed out.

"He won't be a problem anymore."

Jeff studied him. "So. It looks like we've reached the end of our agreement."

Matt said nothing.

Jeff shrugged. "You found Lisa's killer, and saved the world. For that, I can't thank you enough. You know a little more about D.R.E.X than I'm comfortable with, but as long as you don't mention it to anyone, I promise you'll never see any of us again." He pushed a folder toward him. "I expect you to keep full confidentiality, of course. Otherwise, you'll be spending the next twenty years in jail. Then, when you are released, you'll find yourself mysteriously unable to hold a job for more than a month. If you're lucky."

Matt stared at the very long non-disclosure form. "So that's it? I can just go?"

"Yep, pretty much."

Matt dropped the form. "What about Ryan? His daughter, I mean? Have you found any trace of her?'

Jeff folded his arms. "So, he told you about her. And no, not yet."

"Why doesn't that surprise me?"

"What do you mean?"

Matt leaned back in his chair. "I just have this feeling that you're not exactly working your ass off trying to help him. Because if Ryan did find his daughter, there's no reason for him to stick around. Right? Jesus Christ Jeff, he just lost his sister. Give him *something*."

Jeff drummed his fingers against the table. "You know, when I first had eyes on Ryan his rap sheet was about four pages long. Doing everything short of murder, although I'm pretty sure he would have reached that point eventually. This was before his daughter was kidnapped, mind you. After that happened, he kicked away a lot of bad habits to save her. I wonder what will happen after he finds her, after that one motivation to do something right is gone."

Matt said nothing.

Jeff shrugged. "I give Ryan a hard time every now and then, but the truth is the kid is a brilliant hacker. That's why I recruited him to begin with. And yet, after all this time, Ryan can't find these people. Neither could the cops, although that's hardly shocking. And neither can we, and I have a dozen hackers at my disposal."

Matt blinked.

"But make no mistake, we know that the people who have his daughter want thousands of dollars per week, and they know what D.R.E.X is. That much I am positive about. This doesn't sound to me like someone who wants to buy a new house. What does that sound like to you, Matt?"

"A terrorist organization," Matt said.

"One that we seem to be funding," Jeff replied. "That really doesn't sit well with me. So you can be sure, Matt, finding these people is first and foremost on my mind." He glanced at his watch. "I'm late for an appointment, so if you can sign the form I would appreciate it."

Matt grabbed the pen, and stared at the form again. He could hear Anna's warning ringing in his head. Lisa wouldn't want him here. And yet, he paused. "Are we absolutely sure that all the creatures from the portal are gone? And that the portal can't be open again?"

Jeff shrugged. "We missed these ones years ago. I honestly can't say for sure. Trust me, right now, my inbox is full of people reporting strange events. Could be nothing. Or it could be something D.R.E.X should investigate."

Matt glared at him. "Who is really in charge of D.R.E.X?"

"I'm sorry, Matt. You know I can't tell you that. If you were caught or compromised, that knowledge alone could cripple our entire network. This way any potential damage is minimal."

Matt slammed his hand on the table. "I've had enough of this spy bullshit, Jeff. If you're not in charge, then what exactly is your job?"

"The one I want, which is making sure my agents are safe. Also making sure they don't do anything stupid," Jeff said, studying him. "Some agents are harder than others."

"And exactly how many agents are you in charge of?"

"Several," Jeff said.

"And you only sent four people to deal with your portal problem?" Matt demanded.

"We're all working on the *same* problem. Just from different angles. Besides, there is usually more than one apocalyptic problem happening at the same time," Jeff replied, and smiled. "D.R.E.X is a little bigger than you thought it was, isn't it?"

"Jesus," Matt said, and thought about the past few days. His hometown, which had abandoned him, a job that was gone, a family that was dead. He could easily spend the next few years wandering, looking for his place in life. Or maybe he had already found it. "This was Lisa's dream," he stated, looking at Jeff.

"Yes," Jeff agreed. "It was." He leaned forward. "What are you trying to say, Matt? You found the answer to why your wife died."

"Or maybe I'm still searching," Matt retorted. "Even after what you did, she didn't expose you. She loved this place too damn much. I want to understand why. And, it's odd...when I'm here, I feel closer to her than I've ever been."

Jeff hesitated. "Matt, you know me pretty well by now. I use emotional leverage to manipulate situations more than anyone, but don't torture yourself by chasing her memories here. If you want to stay, you're more than welcome, but do so because you want to make a difference. And I promise, you will do good here. You will save lives. That's the one thing that keeps me going, and everyone else here."

"I saved the world," Matt pointed out. "That's not impressive enough?"

"Pfft. In my book, no," Jeff said, his eyes glittering with amusement. "That's just the beginning."

The next morning, Matt stood in front of his wife's grave. Weeks ago, before he had sought out D.R.E.X, he had placed lilies in front of the tombstone. Now the flowers were dried up. He replaced them with new ones.

"I understand why you didn't talk about work," Matt said to the grave. "It was the same when I was in the war. Even now, there are days from my tour when I just couldn't..." He trailed off. Would it have changed anything if Lisa did tell him? If nothing else, he would have got around to buying a security system. Or he might have taken Lisa to a mental institution. "I wish you had told me, so we could have talked about D.R.E.X. About everything. I would have been there for you."

He paused as tears threatened to sting his eyes. Angrily he fought them off. "Lisa…I can't forgive you for what happened. You might think that's a terrible thing for me to say, but I cannot let something like D.R.E.X take away my sense of right and wrong. If you're hearing this, maybe that will make you proud. And just because I can't forgive you doesn't mean I will ever stop loving you. Even though some of our time together was based on lies, I know you tried to make it as truthful as you could." He kissed his hand, and touched the tombstone. "I love you, Lisa, more than anything. Goodnight, my sweet dear."

He walked toward the end of the cemetery, and ran into Anna. She was wearing jeans, a leather jacket, and a white scarf. It was a little surprising to see her in casual clothes.

"I didn't want to interrupt," Anna said politely.

Matt walked toward his motorcycle parked on the sidewalk. "A little detour on your way home?" he asked

Anna sighed. "Yes," she stated. "I can't go back to D.R.E.X. I can't face that same pain again."

"It won't be the same," Matt said.

Anna frowned. "Why not?"

"Because I'll be in charge. And unlike certain members of your team, I'm not going to follow D.R.E.X blindly. Jesus Christ, Anna, if any member of your team had asked questions about that creature in Owphiyr, you might have never been in that situation to begin with. For all you know, he might have been trying to live peacefully there."

Anna's frown deepened. "He was our enemy. Anything that exits the portal has the potential to wipe out the human race."

"Was he? What do you call Catherine? Is she our enemy?" Matt started his motorcycle. "There needs to be a better way. Things are going to change around D.R.E.X, Anna. You'll see."

Anna laughed. "You might think that, Matthew. But Jeff will shut you down. He will trick you and withhold vital information, all in the name of 'teaching you a lesson'. He won't stop until you're completely corrupted from your own ideals, and eating out of his hand." She shook her head, still grinning. "Do I even need to tell you that he's listening to this conversation right now?"

"No, and I'm not afraid to say that mistakes will happen. Good thing I know some great people to keep me in line," Matt said. "If you want to make a difference, Anna, I'll see you on Monday. If not, good luck with the farming." He revved up his motorcycle.

Anna blinked, and backed away. "I…I'll see you on Monday," she stammered, and headed toward the cemetery. "Goodbye, Matt."

Matt smiled a little, which quickly faded as she left. He looked down at his hand.

It was glowing a little.

ABOUT THE AUTHOR

Natasha Bennett is a Canadian author who lives in the mild climate of Vancouver Island, BC. In her spare time she likes to watch horror movies and help other authors on the road to publishing. She also loves to spend time with her husband, James, and her two cats.